Jubel's Children

LENARD KAUFMAN

Jubel's Children

RANDOM HOUSE
NEW YORK

for my first reader

Jubel's Children

Autumn had fired the maples and they burned yellow and red. All around the house the bright leaves flew, like little flames and sparks from the blazing trees. They fluttered to the road where the automobile tires smothered them. They drifted down to the porch where the black cat jabbed and cuffed at them and chased them to a standstill.

"Pitch. Pitch, come over here."

The cat raised his eyes and his nose from the trapped yellow leaf. He looked at the old man in the rocking chair. Then he lifted his paw to let the leaf go, stretched himself and strolled over. He sniffed at the old man's foot and turned his head into it, bumping against the ankle with his neat little skull. He rubbed and weaved himself through and around the old man's legs. He looked up at him. His golden eyes and the small cry he made were inflected.

"You miss her, too, don't you, Pitch?" He picked up the cat and placed him across his knees. "Doesn't seem possible, does it? Here one minute, gone the next. Here a whole lifetime . . ."

The cat percolated a melancholy purr. The old man looked out over the small patch of lawn in front of the house to the fence around it and the sign just above bearing his name: "Jubel Watson—Antiques." The word "Antiques" was newer than the rest of it—it was painted over the blocked out "Cabi-netmaker"—but somehow Jubel never saw it. Whenever he looked at it, it was "Jubel Watson—Cabinetmaker" just as it had been for forty of its forty-five years. And no matter what the sign said, he was still a cabinetmaker even though the years had taken his trade away from him. He had minded it at first, it had bothered him, but better to have no craft than to do poorly at one. When a man's hands couldn't guide a groove plane any more, it was time for him to give up his work and go into a business. Besides, Amy had wanted it that way. She used to say, after the children had all grown up and left home, "You ought to give it up, Jubel. A man like you, a handsome man, who can meet and talk with people, shouldn't spend the whole of his life fussing around with sticks and tools, being a carpenter." She liked to tease him that way, calling him a "carpenter" when she knew better. Poor Amy. Poor Amy. Poor him without her.

Jubel leaned over in his chair to look down the highway. It was the main street of the little Pennsylvania town and the cars speeding through it were like migrating birds, moving by in dark flocks. From where he sat, straining his eyes through his glasses, he could just make out Staley's Funeral Home at the far end of town. It was the nicest house around, all white with green awnings; Amy always said there wasn't another house she'd rather live in. Now she was in it, but not the way she had hoped for; just waiting for the children to come home before she was buried.

Jubel brushed his lapels. Whenever he thought of Amy, he gave himself some personal attention: fingered his tie, flattened his hair with the palm of his hand, flicked at the specks on his black suits. Everyone who knew Amy Watson knew that her husband and her children were neat as pins. "They may not amount to much," she always told Jubel, "but they'll be clean while they're home with us." And Jubel was clean, too; so clean it was hard to tell he was a man who had worked most of his life with his hands, so clean that now his face and hands

4

and hair seemed scrubbed white, instead of aged white, and where there was color under the skin, it seemed that the blood had risen there by friction.

Pitch stretched his chin against Jubel's hand, asking to be scratched. Even the cat was part of Amy's pride in Jubel's appearance. They had always had black cats; black because Jubel always wore black suits and the shedding hair didn't show. She considered everything, he thought, everything. She was a good woman, a woman who loved him, a woman who had built a home and a family around him and every bit of her living—her dress, her cooking, her housekeeping, her homemaking, her raising of the children—was done for him. She wasn't like most women who became mothers and stopped being wives after the children were born; Jubel was first, always first. Even in the naming of the children it was all his way. The first one, Bertram, was for his father. She would have preferred to have it Jubel, Jr. but he had wanted it like that. When Amy Helen came, it would have been just "Helen" for his mother if he hadn't insisted and raised such a fuss. In the end though she had her way because she raised the child as Helen. The third one was a girl, too, and Jubel gave in without a struggle. It was "Eve" for his sister. After Eve there was a five-year gap and he and Amy had thought there would be no more, so the fourth child was a surprise and the happiest part of it for Amy was that it was a boy and she could name it Jubel, Jr.

He wondered how the children would take it when they read the telegrams and found out their mother was gone. The wires must be on their way now; if not on their way, then just about because Agnew left for the telegraph office more than fifteen minutes ago. Agnew was a good neighbor, a good friend. He had taken everything out of his hands as soon as he had walked into the house; after Jubel had opened the window and called to him. He had phoned the doctor—just to make sure—and Staley's Funeral Home after the doctor left, and then he had his oldest daughter come in to keep house the rest of the day for Jubel; to finish all the little chores that Amy hadn't had a chance to do. And, finally, now he was down at the telegraph office sending wires off to the children.

It would be a shock for them, all of them, especially the girls and young Jubel, too. He didn't have to worry about Bertram so much; he would be stronger than the rest. And maybe Amy Helen might stand it better. But Evie and young Jubel, those were the ones it would really hurt. Those were the babies, those were the ones who were all heart. He could see Evie with one of her own little ones over her shoulder, tearing open the yellow envelope, the fears showing on her face even before she knew what it was. And he could see the clutch of it as it gripped her, the stark shock of it scratching her pretty face, bringing the tears to her eyes. . . . With young Jubel it wasn't that clear. He couldn't see him at all but he could hear his voice just as though he were standing right next to him now: "Did she suffer, Pop?"

"No, son. It was a beautiful day and it was a beautiful way to die."

It was the truth, too. He didn't know that death could come so quietly, so sweetly and be welcomed with a smile. It was early in the morning, only this morning. They rose at six, and just after breakfast Amy had put the cake in the oven, double chocolate layer, Jubel's favorite. She turned from the stove with an odd, tired look on her face.

"What is it, Amy? What's the matter?"

For a moment she stood there, her eyes closed, her body swaying a little. He helped her to the chair at the kitchen table.

"I'm all right, Jubel. Just tired, that's all. Don't worry."

He brought her a glass of water. "Didn't you sleep last night?"

"Course, I slept. I always sleep. Now go over there and sit down and stop worrying about me."

"Think, maybe, I ought to get the doctor?"

She shook her head.

"Maybe it's the heat; furnace and the stove both going to-

6

gether." He lifted the window and let the sparkling air pour into the house.

Amy took a long, deep breath. "It's a beautiful day, Jubel," her voice began to fade, "and you're going to have a beautiful cake, a beautiful cake."

She smiled, her head dropped to her chest, and that was the way she had died. He was glad it had happened that way because he could tell it to young Jubel and the rest. He could say "heart attack" the way the doctor had but that wouldn't do it; it wouldn't describe the gentleness of her passing, her almost breathing in of death as though it were part of the fresh bright air coming in through the window. He must try to make young Jubel and Evie see it that way because they would mind it more and death to them would be a terrible personal experience. Funny that he should be so sure of them, especially of young Jubel who had gone through a war and seen death all around him and maybe killed a few men on his own—he wasn't sure of that because they never talked about it but it was likely—but even a war can't change a man, make him really different from what he is inside. It might bring the insides out but they were there all the time anyway. And no matter how often young Jubel might have seen death, he was sure he had never gotten used to it because for him, and for Evie too, everything always happened and would always happen for the first time.

The cat stiffened in his lap. Jubel looked up. It was Agnew on his way back from the telegraph office and somewhere along the way he had picked up his dog. Pitch leaped to the steps, landing with his back up, and began a slow, catercornered, bristling advance to the gate.

"Watch out for your dog, Agnew."

"Got him. Got him." Agnew blocked open the gate just enough to let himself through. "Go on home, Lady." He latched it behind him. "It's not my fault. Pitch just won't have any part of you."

Pitch stood there waiting, spitting a dare at the dog. They

7

all knew, even Lady, that the fence itself meant nothing. Pitch could vault it without trying if he had really wanted to fight; it was just that he didn't want Lady on his property. The dog stood for a minute, covering them with his hurt brown eyes; then he turned and padded off, his tail waving like a melancholy plume.

"Never will understand that cat of yours, Jubel." Agnew lumbered up the porch. He was a big man and he settled himself heavily on the top step. In spite of the season and the breeze, he wiped his brow and opened his coat. His stomach was so large and overflowing, it sat in his lap. "He comes over to our place and plays with Lady and they get along fine but he just won't let my dog in here."

"No use trying to understand cats, Agnew. They're too much like people; everyone's just a little bit different."

"I guess that's so." He called to Pitch but the cat ignored him.

"He doesn't always come when I call him. It depends on his mood. But he's a good pet. He loves us and he's jealous." He said "us" without even thinking. Now, there was only one left; one for Pitch to love and one for him to be jealous over.

"I got the wires off, Jubel." He took a yellow blank out of his pocket. "I didn't know what to say. I guess I should have asked you. Anyhow, it was the best I could do." He read to him: "Mother died this morning. Funeral Monday. Come home."

"That's fine, Agnew, fine." They'd know he hadn't sent it. He never called Amy "Mother," but it was fine.

"I didn't know how else to say it. I tried it a couple of other ways but this seemed the best."

"It's the best. Don't worry about it."

"Mr. Peters was on at the telegraph office, Jubel. He said he was sorry. Everybody I've talked to is sorry."

"Thank you, Agnew."

"They'll be around to pay their respects."

8

He wished that they wouldn't. But it was the civilized thing to do and people always did it. He himself had done it, more and more as he had grown older, and the people he knew began to drop off one by one, but condolence calling was a bit of civilized torture. What was there to be said? What was there to be done? How could anyone help helplessness? "That's fine, Agnew. I'll be glad to see them all."

"Mr. Peters said the wires would get everywhere by tonight the latest. The ones to New York and Boston, to young Jubel and Amy Helen, in a couple of hours. Just about the same for Bertram's too, out in Columbus, Ohio."

"What about Evie?"

"Well, Mr. Peters wasn't so sure about that. I told him Bellford, Georgia was somewhere near Atlanta."

Jubel nodded. "Thirty miles south."

"Just what I told him but he didn't know if it had a wire office or where the closest one might be. Said he'd check into it. On the outside, though, he thought it'd get to her before midnight."

Before midnight. It might wake her out of her sleep, her and the children, too; Evie and the two little ones in her arms, crying and scared.

"Think Evie will bring along the children with her?"

"I don't know."

"Never did get to see them. How old are they now—the little ones, I mean?"

"The oldest one's five. That's the girl: Jinny. The boy's about a year, I think."

"Just two grandchildren; eh, Jubel?"

"Just two."

"Two from four."

"Two from four."

"Bertram never did have any, did he?"

"No."

"Families are getting smaller and smaller, it seems to me. You have four children and all the four have are two."

9

"Helen and young Jubel haven't had a chance yet, you know."

"That's so. Young Jubel might just come through, at that. Might get himself married off and have six little ones running around."

"And Helen's not too old; she's still under forty." He felt he had to say something for Helen, not write her off completely even though Amy and he had decided long ago not to expect it. A girl with an important job who had made good in a big city like Boston. . . . Well, you couldn't hope that marriage and children would mean the same; especially after they passed thirty and thirty-five.

"Still and all, families are getting smaller, Jubel. You've got two from four. I've got one from three so far and you take Mr. Peters down at the telegraph office. He and his wife never did have any at all."

"That's true enough, Agnew, but I keep reading and hearing the country's growing—the population's getting bigger."

"I do, too, and the only reason I can figure out is that people are just living longer these days." He looked as though he could have bitten off his tongue. "I'm sorry, Jubel."

"That's all right, Agnew. I was lucky to have her with me as long as I did. People are living longer, maybe not long enough but longer, anyhow."

Agnew looked away. His eyes went over the house behind him. "I don't suppose you've thought much about what you're going to do, Jubel."

"Do?"

"Yes. You're not going to stay on here alone, are you?"

"Well, I don't know. I hadn't even thought about it." He hadn't. He hadn't given anything or anyone a thought but the children and Amy. But he could see what Agnew meant. Life couldn't be as it was any more; even if he did nothing, even if he stayed where he was, it couldn't be.

"I guess it is a little early to think along those lines yet but you've got to look ahead, Jubel. You've got to go on living."

10

Jubel laughed a little. "That's something I'll have to start doing for myself again, thinking. Amy always used to do it for me. And it isn't too early at all, Agnew. Have you any suggestions?"

Agnew moved around, shifting his stomach from one thigh to the other. "Well, there's the children. Any one of them would be glad to have you, I'm sure."

"No, no. The children all have problems of their own." He said it without even thinking. And when he did think of it, of living with Bertram and Bertram's wife, or of living with Helen up there in Boston, he just couldn't fit himself into it. He could imagine staying with Evie but Evie had the two children to take care of and her husband, too. And young Jubel had troubles enough of his own trying to make his way as an actor.

"You'd do it for them, Jubel, any one or all of them."

"That's what being a father means, Agnew, doing things for your children until they're old enough to do for themselves. Amy always said, 'Give everything and expect nothing and if anything does come out of them, it's like finding an extra ten dollars in the sugar bowl.' I don't want to saddle any of them with their old father."

"That's plain foolishness, Jubel."

"Maybe."

"If they want you, you'll go."

"We'll see."

"And another thing. What about your business?"

"I guess I wouldn't miss that too much if I got rid of it. I'm not really an antique man, Agnew. Oh, I like them and I appreciate them but I'm still a cabinetmaker. Of all the stuff I've got," here he stopped and pointed into the house and saw for a minute all the rooms and the attic and cellar, too, overwhelmed by the extravagant left-overs of the colonial, early American, Federal and pre-Federal periods, "of all the stuff I've got," he went on, "there's one, maybe two things I care enough about to own, myself. The rest of it—oh, they're genu-

11

ine enough antiques—but all they've got to recommend them is a little crust of age." He smiled. "Maybe that's being better off than we are, Agnew, but a good workman wouldn't own up to most of them."

Agnew looked back at the house. "You wouldn't want to sell out, would you?"

The cat came back to Jubel now, his fur calm and sleek again. He rubbed against the old man's legs until Jubel leaned over and scratched his head.

"I don't know, Agnew. I might. Would you want to buy?"

Agnew gave the other end of the cat a thoughtful petting. "I don't know, Jubel, I might . . . Funny thing about cats and dogs, you even have to pet them differently." He looked out at the road to watch a car speed by. He followed it until it was out of eye's reach. "That was a Massachusetts car, Jubel. Might even have been from Boston. Think Amy Helen will be coming down by car?"

"No, Helen doesn't drive. Bertram will drive and maybe Evie, too."

"What about young Jubel?"

"Actors, young ones, don't have cars, Agnew."

"I suppose not. He's working, isn't he?"

"I'm sure he is. I don't exactly know which play he might be in but I'm sure he's doing something."

"I guess they're all pretty busy, Bertram and Helen, too. Helen's got a pretty big job, hasn't she?"

"Yes, Helen has a fine job and Bertram does well."

"You think they'll all be able to get away and be here by Monday, Jubel?"

Funny that Agnew should ask that when he had been thinking about it himself; remembering it had been a long time since all the children had been home together. Even for their fiftieth wedding anniversary, young Jubel was at war, Bertram couldn't make it and Helen was out west, someplace, traveling for her firm. So even then, it was only Evie and Bertram's wife who came home, and Amy always talked about a day when all the

12

children might be home at the same time and be together again; some Christmas or Thanksgiving, but it had never happened, not since they had grown up and gone away. There was one or the other, every once in a while, but not all together.

"You do think they'll come, don't you, Jubel?"

Jubel picked up the cat and spread him over his lap. He looked out at the road. "They'll be here, Agnew. I don't know how they'll manage it, but they'll be here. You'll see."

ii

He drove with almost reckless speed. Not that he was in a hurry but he wanted to get where he was going and have it over with. He thought to himself: Four hundred and eighty miles and I'll have to do it all over again. Back the same way, over the same road, four hundred and eighty times two is nine hundred and sixty, nine hundred and sixty miles of gas and oil and tires, nine hundred and sixty miles of wear and tear and depreciation. Well, it would still be cheaper, after it was all over, than going by train or flying; especially with two of them.

At both ends of the horizon two sliding doors of gray clouds were closing off the day. In forty minutes, maybe a half hour, with the days getting shorter, it would be dark and they'd have to do the rest of it night driving. He hunched himself over the wheel, swallowing it with his big body and arms, and leaned heavily on the gas.

"Bertram, aren't you driving too fast?"

He looked at her sitting beside him in her black cloth coat, her black dress and shoes and he became aware of his own oxford grayness; he was even wearing his dark overcoat and he didn't like to wear it for driving because the wool was soft and wore easily.

"We still have a hundred and seventy-five miles to go, you know."

She smiled at him and it made her face seem smaller and daintier than it was. "You're not going to try to make it all in one day, are you? Not all four hundred and eighty miles."

"Why not?" He bit on his lip, covering all of his mouth with his thick black mustache. "If you had been up on time this morning we could have made it all in daylight."

"You know I was too upset to sleep after the wire came. I just about dozed off at six o'clock this morning."

She was upset! What did she think he was, calling him at the office and when she couldn't get him there tracking him all over town until she found him in Mr. Weston's office right in the middle of things. What difference would an hour or two have made? What could you do about death? She could have waited. She could have shown some consideration. Of course, he wanted to know about his mother. Of course, of course, of course, but to have to hunt him down in Mr. Weston's office, trailing him over telephone wires so that everyone in town knew she wanted him, even Mr. Weston when he picked up the phone.

"It's for you, Bertram."

He had taken the phone wondering who it could be. No one knew he was there, no one; the whole business with Weston was supposed to be a secret. You didn't talk about a deal like that, spread around a proposition that might mean really big money at last.

"Hello," he had said finally.

"Bertram, this is Ella. I've been looking all over town for you. Your mother died this morning. Pop sent a wire."

"Bad news?" Mr. Weston asked, and he supposed it had shown on his face.

"Yes." No use denying it. "My mother died this morning."

"Oh, I'm sorry to hear that." He waited a respectful moment. "In that case, Bertram, we won't discuss business any more. You'll be going home?"

"Yes, but I don't know when; Ella didn't say . . . Mr. Weston, we could settle this today, couldn't we?"

15

"There's not that much of a hurry, Bertram. I have to see several other people; I promised to. Besides, there's the money. You haven't been able to raise it."

"I will raise it . . . somehow."

It had to stand there. You couldn't go on talking business with your mother's death still ringing in your ears. Mr. Weston's attitude made that plain. And it wasn't at all necessary. If Ella had only waited until he came home to tell him, then he could have had it practically settled with Weston. True, he didn't have the money yet but there'd be some way of getting hold of it; if everything else failed, he was going to call on Pop again. The important thing was to have Weston sold on him as the man who would be right for this deal. And he was selling him until Ella had called and loused it up for him. She was always maneuvering him into a position like that; always making things hard for him.

Ella's head turned with the road sign going by. "Missed that one, too. Are we near any towns, Bertram? It'll be dark in half an hour."

"About forty miles out of Allentown."

"That won't be too bad. We certainly ought to find a hotel in Allentown."

"I'm not staying at any hotels," he grumped. "I'm making the house tonight."

Of course, you are, she thought; that's why you wanted me up at six in the morning. You want to make these four hundred and eighty miles in one day so that you won't have to spend the price of a hotel room. God, how could a man be so cheap, and how could she keep asking herself that question after seventeen years of him? By now, she should be able to accept anything, accept it and not be surprised, but he always managed to come up with something new that caught her breath. He was like a zealot looking for new ways to worship his golden calf. She wouldn't care if he had money, if he had ever had it, but to stand on your head and crawl on your knees for it and still have none of it in your hands, that was too much.

16

When he came home yesterday afternoon from that man's office where she had finally been able to find him, there wasn't any sadness in him; there wasn't any heartbreak. He was just mad.

"Why did you do it! Why did you do it!" he had shouted at her before he had both his feet inside the house.

"Do what?" She didn't know, she honestly didn't know. She was waiting for him, shaken herself by the news, wondering what to say to him, how to comfort him.

He threw down his hat and coat. "Do what you did, of course; call me at Weston's office right in the middle of everything."

She had followed him into the dining room, watching him while he poured and gulped a straight drink. "Bertram, didn't you understand me? Didn't you hear what I told you over the phone? Didn't I say that Pop had sent a wire?"

"Yes, you said it." He turned around and faced her. "All right . . . my mother's dead. You told me, I know it. You chased me all over town to tell me. But what can I do about it? I can't raise the dead, can I!"

"Bertram!"

"If she were dying, I could understand it. If she needed blood, I'd run to her and give her mine. But she's dead and you had to chase me to tell me; just when everything was working out fine with Weston, too."

She remembered how he had stood there, the glass shaking in his hands, and the little box-like room in their little box-like rented house seemed to tremble with his frustration. She had left him then and gone into the kitchen to make dinner. It was too early for that but she didn't know what else to do to get away from him.

"Where is that wire?" He had followed her; he wouldn't let her alone.

"Monday, Monday." He walked around the room with it, crowding her to the kitchen table where she had to sit and look at him. "What's the old man's hurry? Married more than fifty

17

years and buried in two days. It's indecent, I tell you, indecent."

"It's not two days, Bertram. You're hysterical. Today is Friday; the funeral's Monday."

He slumped down at the table. His eyes watered. "I can't go, Ella. I can't go. It'll ruin everything, everything." He wasn't sobbing but he might just as well have laid his head on the table and wept.

That's right, she had thought, go to pieces; go to pieces but don't go to your mother's funeral. She had seen him do it so many times; so many times in so many crises. If he were a little man and he cried, it might not matter, or if he cried real tears, but to see the dry frustration eating away at him until he crumbled before her, that undid her. She felt, whenever it happened, that she should put her hands over her eyes or leave the room. But she never did and so she had always given in. This time, though, there was nothing he wanted from her, there was nothing she could do for him, give him.

"Bertram, it's your own mother. How can you not go?"

"That's it. How can I not go and how can I go when this whole thing with Weston has come to a head? Why does everything have to happen at once and at the same time? It's always like that."

It had just been a problem of timing to him, that's all; not a tragedy, not a great loss, just a conflict of arrangements; his mother's death against a business deal. This time she was almost tempted to encourage him in his way. His mother would be better off with no son at her funeral than one who didn't want to be there. She might even prefer it that way. But it was the living you had to consider and old Jubel would never get over it. She remembered the fiftieth anniversary and how Bertram had begged off from that, too, at the last minute; it had something to do with business, another one of his deals or some other kind of obligation, but he didn't go. She went alone and bought gifts for Jubel and Amy with her own money and said Bertram had sent them. But it was money thrown away because she never saw such empty eyes. And that was the year

18

Helen didn't come home either and young Jubel was in the army.

"Bertram, listen to me. It won't do you any good not to go."

His eyes were fogged. "What do you mean? In three days there'll be six, maybe a dozen, men trying to cut me out. Don't you understand?"

"Of course, I understand. But Mr. Weston knows what's happened, doesn't he? You had to tell him why I called."

"Sure, I had to tell him. No one was supposed to know I was there."

"Then no excuse is going to stand up. He must expect you to go to your own mother's funeral."

"Sure he does, but you fixed that up for me. You put me in that pretty little spot with your fool phone call. Jesus, couldn't you wait until I got home!"

"You don't have the money for Mr. Weston, anyhow."

"Don't change the subject. I'd get the money. The point is, you had to call me there. You had to chase me all over town until you found me and put me on a spot I can't get off. It's your fault, Ella. It's your damn fault if I don't make the money I should be making."

He had raved at her for the rest of the evening but she didn't care because what he said was true: she had put him on a spot, even if she didn't know it when she did it, and in spite of himself he was going to have to go home now.

The cars in front of them and behind them began to light up, and the road seemed darker for it. What's their hurry, he thought to himself. Everyone was a smart guy: turn on the lights before it gets dark, take out the winter coat before the first snow, put money in the bank against the rainy day. Security. Everyone was looking for it; everyone was busy piling it up like little beavers; everyone but him. Forty-two years and nothing to show for it; not a nickel in the bank, just a wife, a rented house, a few pieces of clothes, a five-year-old car and a sales job, and all of them costing more money than they were worth, all of them making you spend more money: for front, for convenience, for upkeep.

19

"Can you see all right without your lights, Bertram?"

"I can see fine." She didn't care whether he could see all right. It was just her way of needling him into admitting it was getting dark and that it'd be a good idea to stop for the night in Allentown when they got there. Well, he wasn't going to stop. He wasn't going to pay ten or twelve dollars for a dumpy hotel room, maybe pay for a garage too and meals—dinner and breakfast—and then tips all around to bellboys, to waiters, to everybody with the open hands, all of them making more money than he was, monkey suits or no.

Why did all this have to happen to him? It wasn't right. It was a conspiracy. If he had only had a couple of more days with Weston, he would have had that proposition sewed up. Sure, there was the money but he would have raised it somehow. There were fifty places he hadn't tried even though the banks had turned him down. They wanted security, too. People were so short-sighted. Couldn't they see this was more than just buying into a wild scheme? This was buying a piece of a business. He'd be a partner. He would have raised that money, someone would have seen it his way if he had been given half a chance. He hadn't even gotten down to the family yet. Pop would have been good for something, even a couple of thousand more. And there was Helen; with all the money she had been making for years up in Boston, she was bound to have some put away. About Evie and young Jubel, he didn't know. Things weren't supposed to be so good with Evie and her husband and the auto-court business. But then you couldn't be sure; it might just be that southern poor-mouth talk. They owned the cabins, they owned the land. They might be doing better than they let on. If they weren't, it was their own fault. Evie could have done much better than marry that Georgia hillbilly. She was a good-looking girl. It was a shame. She could have married real money. He didn't have to think much about young Jubel. What kind of money could an actor have? Of course, he might have come out of the army with a couple of thousand. You heard all kinds of stories about back pay and

20

bonuses and crap games on troop ships; even black market deals. Why, he heard some of those men came out with thousands and thousands of dollars, even jewels and paintings; enough to take care of themselves for life. But young Jubel wasn't that smart. Chances are, he got out with only the shirt on his back and a discharge paper in his hand. All in all, it wasn't much of a family to look to for any real help. And on top of everything, poor Mom was gone. He had a great feeling of loneliness and despair as he rushed the car to meet the coming darkness. He switched on his headlights.

"I don't think we ought to go beyond Allentown, Bertram."

"Why not?"

"Because it's dangerous and you don't know these roads."

"They're all good Pennsylvania state highways." She'd have to do better than that.

"We might get lost and drive around all night."

"Not a chance; the markers are good." Better than that, too.

She let it rest there. There was time. Besides, she was sure they'd be putting up in Allentown for the night; she'd talk him into it. It wasn't that she was so clever but she knew his weaknesses. A little issue like this was nothing. He was a man who had given up everything for something he didn't have.

It was that way right from the first; two years of college behind him, a chance to study medicine and he had tossed it away.

"It's such a long pull, Ella," he had told her. Then he didn't have his mustache. He was much thinner, too, and he had a lovable, awkward kind of charm. She guessed she had been different, and she wondered how he thought she had changed.

"But it'll be so worthwhile, Bertram, every year of it."

"Eight, ten years? It's a lifetime and suppose I flunk out along the way?"

"You won't."

"I might. Besides, even if I do make it, what guarantees have I got that I'll make money at it? I might end up in some

21

one-horse town with a shingle on my house and a cellarful of unpaid bills. Heal the sick, all right, but who's going to heel me? No, Ella, it's not for me. I want money. I want it now, while I'm young enough to enjoy it."

She remembered how his talk of money had bothered her; there was an unnatural hunger in it. "But it's a career, Bertram, a wonderful work."

"Romantic garbage. There's nothing wonderful about work unless it pays off. A starving doctor is no better off than a starving bricklayer."

"There are no guarantees in anything, Bertram."

Then he had taken her by the arms and lifted her high in the air. "I have something with a guarantee, sweetie; a big, fat hundred dollar a week guarantee. More money than delivering babies, and we can get married right away; no waiting."

"No waiting." She supposed, in her own way, she had given in as easily as he. But she loved him and whatever he had wanted would do. The only thing, it wasn't more money than delivering babies for long because the job didn't last a year. It took them out to Ohio and dumped them there. After that, he had found something else but it wasn't as good and he went from one selling job to another; passing up the steady, long-range ones for the flashy bonanzas that never panned out. He had tried, she couldn't say he hadn't, but they were the desperate, naïve tries of a schoolboy spitting in the face of experience and common sense. Hang a scheme in front of his nose and he was off like a goof chasing rainbows with a butterfly net. For a man who had wanted guarantees, he had certainly managed to get along on promises. All of them were wonderful, sure-fire deals that couldn't miss; like that button thing he tried to sell after the war started, the simulated pearl pasted on a blue button with the word "Remember" above it and "Harbor" beneath it, or that concoction he was working on with the corner druggist, the anesthetized salve women were supposed to apply before they plucked their eyebrows to make it painless, or that radio program idea that used only sound effects to tell stories. All of them were sure-fire, all of them would make more money than delivering babies. There were more, many more that she couldn't remember, and here was Mr. Weston with his proposition, his editorial service that would be all things to all editors who published weekly papers all over the country. Mr. Weston was going to revolutionize the newspaper business, offer editors twelve tailor-made editorials on six subjects, one pro and one con for each subject at a nominal fee. They would take their choice, depending on which side of the fence they sat. Of course, it would take money—there was a large amount of direct-mail advertising to be done and a staff would have to be hired to write the editorials and maintain the service—and so Bertram would have to produce ten thousand dollars to get things going. This, too, was sure-fire. It, too, would make more money than delivering babies.

Everything was better than delivering babies—even their own. You'd think she would have forgotten that by now but she hadn't; it still rankled in her after all these years. What she had wanted most when she married him was his child. She loved him so much, it was as though one of him weren't enough. She tried to tell him that, she tried to make him understand it but he wouldn't listen.

"No, Ella, not yet. It's too much of a responsibility. We haven't been married a year. We'll wait a while; we're both young. I've got to see how things go first."

She guessed he was right then and she had let it go. But time didn't matter and with him there were only two kinds of times: good times and bad ones. In the good ones he was always waiting to see how things went first. And in the bad ones: "How can you ever think about a family when we don't know where our next dollar is coming from?"

"Oh, Bertram, people have babies with or without dollars. We'll get along. It's only one more mouth to feed, and a little mouth. Besides, you will make money."

"I don't want to discuss it any more."

23

"Bertram, you've got to discuss it. I want a baby. I want it now when I'm young enough to have it and want it both."

"It seems to me I ought to have something to say about it, too. I don't want a baby. That's all there is to it." And he'd walk out on the conversation.

After talks like that, and they had them regularly, he'd watch her carefully for several weeks to make sure she didn't "pull any tricks" on him. But in the end, she did have to resort to a trick. She had reached the point, after six years, where even she had gotten sick and tired of talking and fighting for a baby. She decided to have one, whether he wanted it or not. She really believed it was the thought of responsibility that frightened him more than anything else. Once it became a fact instead of a fear, once he realized he was to be a father, then pride and love would take over and he would be as happy as she was.

Nevertheless, it was a trick and the thinking and planning of it made her feel a little like a criminal; not a criminal whose crime is one of commission but of omission. The details bothered her but not enough to stop her. After all, it was only a matter of letting nature take its course.

That's all there was to it. Nature, beautiful nature, working in the dark places of her body, would do the rest. It did. When she was sure, she had the wonderful feeling of belonging to the world, of being a part of it and adding to it. She knew she had been right and it had seemed to her that she bloomed and glowed, even when it was too soon to bloom and glow, and she wondered how he could not notice the difference in her. But he didn't and she didn't tell him. She had decided to put off telling him because, when he finally did know, there would be fewer months for him to wait.

In the end, though, she didn't have to tell him. He discovered it for himself and the way he discovered it made it seem a shoddy business of deceit with all her first criminal feelings coming back to her. She had gone shopping into town. At one of the department stores they were showing Indian infant

24

moccasins. They were soft, snow-white buckskin, fringed and trimmed with tiny beads of blue and amber and red. They were so incredibly small and lovely; she decided if a baby could be born with shoes, it would be those. She brought them home and forgot about them; how or why she never knew. But that evening, after dinner, when she was unwrapping her packages in front of Bertram, the little white Indian shoes tumbled out on the table.

"What are these?" He scooped them up in his fist.

She had been so horrified by her own stupidity and forgetfulness, she couldn't answer him.

"Ella, what is this nonsense?" He had squeezed them into a deformed ball.

She made a grab for them. "Give me those!" Now, she didn't have to tell him. It was all over her face.

He stood up, holding the lost little white shoes above his head. "Why, you cheat. You're nothing but a tricky little cheat." The veins stood out in his neck, like purple snakes choking him with their anger.

"I'm not a cheat. It's your baby."

He flung the shoes across the room and against the wall. They dropped softly to the floor. "It's not my baby. It's not going to be my baby." He sat down. He was controlling himself. The snakes began to slide down into his collar.

"Ella, how long have you been this way?"

"Two months."

"Are you sure? Did you go to a doctor?"

"Yes, I went to a doctor. I'm sure."

"Was it an accident or did you do it deliberately?"

She walked over to where the shoes were, picked them up and began straightening them out.

"Well, it doesn't matter because you've got to get rid of it, Ella."

She remembered how he had sounded: as though he were talking about something dirty, as though they were a pair of criminals with a piece of stolen merchandise on their hands.

25

"Why should I get rid of it? We're married. It's legitimate. It's about time you became a father. It's more than time for me." She went over to him. "Bertram, doesn't having a baby mean anything to you? Don't you want to leave anything after you in this world? Haven't you any instinct for anything but money?"

"You don't understand, Ella." He was talking with clenched teeth. "We can't afford it."

"You've been saying that for years. You'd keep on saying it if we were millionaires."

"We're not millionaires. We'll never be millionaires if we have a family hanging around our necks. Don't you know what it costs to have a baby these days? Doctors and hospitals and diets and clothes. I'm not going to be saddled with kids for the rest of my life. I've seen too many men who were afraid to take a chance because they had so many mouths to feed and so many bodies to clothe . . . No, Ella, we're not having this baby."

"It's too late, Bertram. We are having our baby. In seven months you're going to be a father whether you like it or not."

He didn't let her sleep that night; his words, his arguments, his pleas pecked her awake when she drowsed. She left the bed for the chair at the window but it didn't stop him. She went down to the couch in the living room. He followed her. She locked herself in the bathroom. He talked through the door. Once, she threw a shoe at him but he caught it and tossed back words. She couldn't get away from him in the house, so she wrapped herself in her coat and stood out on the porch. He didn't follow her; he let the cold work for him. She shivered there in her slippered feet until she felt blue and numb and she began to worry about catching pneumonia. She wondered if that was what he wanted, if that was the way he hoped to "get rid of it." She went back into the house. Let him talk, let him argue, let him plead; she could be as stubborn as he was.

But that was only the beginning. The next two weeks were

26

trials: scenes and sulks, threats and pleas. His strategy changed with the wind. There were two times, in the first week, when he came home with flowers and candy and promises, and she thought how ironic that she should have perhaps the one husband in the world who was trying to bribe his wife into *not* having a baby. But those were only two times; for the rest of the week he was nasty and mean, fighting with her at every turn, trying to wear her down. He never let her sleep. There were nights when she was so tired, she would fall off with his voice in her ears. When she did, he would start shouting her awake and when that didn't work, he'd nudge her back to listen to him. "You've got to listen to me, Ella. You can't let this happen. Do you want to ruin my whole life, every chance I have in the future?" She didn't have to listen to him. She knew it all by heart, but he wouldn't let her sleep. So she had to change her habits and sleep during the day after he would leave the house. But that lasted only until he guessed it and started calling her every half hour. She would have taken the phone off the hook but they were on a party line, so there was no real rest for her and she had spent those days and nights sick and swollen with tiredness. She didn't know how he had managed to keep going unless he was so keyed up, he was walking around on the tips of his nerves.

All of it—the battling, the constant pounding, the sleeplessness, the ugliness of the whole situation—was something she could take. In spite of it, she was determined to be as stubborn about it as he was because she knew she was right and because she loved him and wanted his baby and because she believed this would pass; that once he realized he was getting nowhere, he would give it up and in the end, when it was all over and they had had their child, he would be just as happy about it as she was and ashamed of this harrowing time and try to forget about it. But she hadn't figured him right. Suddenly, it all changed. The fighting stopped. There were no more scenes, no arguments, not even words. He became a silent, tragic lump of a man who barely touched food, who sat without talking,

27

without reading, who breathed in sighs and stared at walls and floors. After a few days, he stopped going in to work; he let his job go.

At first, she didn't know what to make of it. She thought he was sick.

"No, I'm all right, Ella."

He wasn't surly about it. There was no anger in him.

"Then what is the matter with you?"

"I don't know. I'm just tired, I guess."

"Is that why you gave up your job?"

"I suppose so. I don't seem to have any ambition left."

She remembered how boneless he seemed; how he looked slumped over and weeping while he sat dry-eyed and straight.

"Has it got anything to do with the baby?"

"I don't know."

Of course it had and it made more noise for her than all the shouting and hounding he had done. He wasn't faking, she could tell. The man had collapsed inside and that was something she couldn't take. She let him go for a few days, standing it as long as she could, even leaving the house just to get away from him, but it was only a matter of time because she couldn't see him go to pieces.

"All right, Bertram," she had said, finally, "you win. We won't have our baby. What am I supposed to do now?"

It seemed to her that the whole experience had borne the stamp of acquiescence. She had *let* everything happen: let the baby get started, let Bertram scheme her out of it, let them take it away from her. But that didn't make the guilt less, it didn't make the frustration easier to bear. She wondered how many nameless, unheard of crimes were *omitted* by people. And how many of those same people, like her, carried around their guilt with them all their lives? Was their guilt as great or greater or less great than the guilt of people who committed crimes? How did Bertram feel? Here he was riding beside her, years after it had happened. Was he thinking about it? Did he ever think about it?

28

"Bertram."

What was it now, another argument for stopping in Allentown? "What is it?"

"Bertram, how long have we been married?"

He gave her a quick look. "Seventeen-eighteen years. Why?"

"Do you ever stop to think that we might have had a child of ten by now; a boy who'd be riding along with us to give your father some joy and comfort?"

This was the sort of thing that made women difficult to live with. From somewhere, from nowhere, from out of the blue they dug things up. "No, I never give it a thought." The only thought he ever gave it was that he was glad it never happened. That's all he needed, a boy; things weren't tough enough. And that would have been only the start. No woman ever had one child if she could help it. It wasn't supposed to be good for her or for him or for some damn foolishness they called the family unit.

"Have you ever been sorry, Bertram, that we never did have our child?"

"No, I've never been sorry and let's not go into it."

He concentrated on the road again. Sorry; he could be sorry about a lot of things but that wasn't one of them. For one, he was sorry that he hadn't been surer of his ground when he married her. But how sure could he be unless he had had a look at her old man's bank account? It wasn't that he wasn't fond of Ella; he liked her better than any of the girls in her crowd and they were all supposed to have money. But Ella had something special about her, she was so comfortably little beside him. And she loved him. He guessed that was important too; a man had to be loved, had to be loved a lot. It had all looked so good, though. It took money to keep a girl in college and to keep her in the clothes that Ella wore. Her father was a builder. She said he built "rows of houses." What more could you ask? Why should he go on knocking himself out, working his way through school? All he wanted was money, anyway. Sure, his mother wanted him to be a doctor and his

29

father would have been proud, too, but why do it the hard way?

It had looked so good; looked, *looked*. But it wasn't. Those were the days when every builder wasn't a millionaire, when there wasn't a housing shortage and when he learned that "rows of houses" could be empty rows of houses and that when no one bought them, the banks moved in. Well, it was water over the dam and no use drinking the same old brackish dreams. The thing to do was look ahead, not back, think of the future, try to figure a way to raise that money for Weston and really make a big go of it this time. He didn't like to think about the past anyway; a sign of old age and decay. It was just that Ella brought things up, every once in a while; just like she did with this baby thing. What a life. It wasn't bad enough you had to keep worrying about the future, did you have to keep picking at the past? And it could have been so simple, so easy all around. It wasn't that he had married Ella for the money he thought she had but it wouldn't have hurt; it wouldn't have hurt at all. A man had a right to want a little out of life.

"Bertram, we are going to stop in Allentown, aren't we?"

"No, we're not stopping in Allentown."

"I don't think that's wise at all, just for the sake of a few dollars."

"A few dollars, huh? A few dollars here, a few dollars there, and where are you going to get a few dollars when you really need it? Can you go back to the places where you spent it?"

"That's nonsense, Bertram. The point is you've been driving all day. You're tired . . ."

"I'm not tired."

"All right, but other people are and you can't be responsible for the way other people drive. Do you know what an accident would cost you?"

He knew. He didn't have to ask her. She didn't have to bring it up, either. Just one fool driver—a kid or a drunk—and you could add up the bill in the hundreds. Chances are, they

30

wouldn't be insured either; they never were. Or it might not be their car; it might even be stolen. Those things happened and if they did, they were sure to happen to him.

He eased up on the gas pedal and began to give more room to the passing cars. When the first outpost streetlights of the Allentown suburbs appeared, he was glad to see them. Why, he asked himself, couldn't Evie have her cabins up here instead of down there in that cracker country of Georgia where he'd never have a chance to use them? A fine family he had; even when they had something that could be used, it wasn't where he could use it.

"There's another reason why I think we ought to stay in Allentown, Bertram."

"What's that?" This time there wasn't much fight in his voice.

"Your father."

"What's he got to do with it?"

"Well, you haven't given him much thought. You might want to spend a night thinking of what's to become of him."

"What do you mean?"

"Suppose he doesn't want to live alone. You couldn't blame him."

"Huh! What did you say?"

"It's only natural, dear. He's an old man, over seventy. He has four children. You're the oldest one. I think you ought to think about that."

He looked at her several times. She wasn't fooling. Jesus, that would never do; never, never do. Why, it'd be just the same as having that baby after all. It would be another mouth to feed and a body to clothe. It'd be responsibility; old or young, it didn't matter. But why did it have to be him? There were three other children. He thought of each of them—Evie with her own two kids probably living on turnip greens, young Jubel filling himself on hamburgers on Broadway and Helen alone up in Boston, even if she did have money—and then he began to scan the skyline to see if he could find the electric sign of a hotel in the distance.

31

iii

The auto court stood on the top of a sharp rise on the road to and from Atlanta. It presented itself so suddenly to the motorist that before one could be fully aware of it, it was gone. Unless the traveler were a native or a regular commuter, he went by with only the knowledge that he had just passed "Neal's Auto Court." On a return trip, if he remembered to look quickly, he would see a group of white cement-block houses, each with a red door and blue shutters. These, along with a larger house closer to the road that was fronted by two gas pumps and repetitious signs advertising Barbecue and Hush Puppies, made up the entire establishment. Women travelers, if they saw it, said it was "cute." Men travelers said, "What a helluva place for an auto court!"

Evie said it too when she saw it but that was after Neal had bought it and she had a right to say it. "Neal, you fool, how could you do it? You'll have to build roadblocks to make people stop here."

He had laughed when she said that. But that's the way it always was: she could never make people mad at her, no matter how she screamed or what she called them.

"It's the way you say it, honey," Neal would say, "and the way you look when you say it. You just get prettier and lighter looking no matter how dark-ugly the words are."

Her father had said it too, years ago; not the same way but it amounted to the same thing. She had come crying to him after a child's fight with Helen.

"Pa, I hate her. I hate her. I never want to see her again."

He held her against his chest and said it into her ear. "Now, Evie, you don't hate anybody. You couldn't. There's no hate in you, only light."

She remembered how that made her stop crying and run to the mirror. She looked hard for the light but it was only in her hair and in her blue eyes and her rosy skin. She wondered if her blondness was the light her father meant and she wondered, too, if only dark people could hate, the ones with black and brown hair and black and brown eyes like Bertram and Helen. She ran to young Jubel, who was as light as she was, and asked him.

"Aw, you're crazy," he said. "Look at me. I got light hair and light eyes and I hate everybody." And he proceeded to throw stones at the squirrels and pull at her braids to prove his point.

"We won't have to build any roadblocks, honey. We're thirty miles out of Atlanta. Folks are going to want to bed down instead of driving into a big city at night. Besides, we'll get some signs spread out along the road just as soon as we make some money."

They had never made enough for the road signs—just enough for themselves and the two children—or for any of the other things that needed money, like Neal's drinking, she thought bitterly. Of the six cabins only two were good enough to show to people and expect them to pay their money for a night's rest. The others had bad plumbing and cracked walls or needed new floors and new beds and furniture that didn't sag as though it were always in the middle of a big wind. If the two good cabins rented for a night, and fortune sent them another weary traveler, they would hope he would be weary enough not to care or, if he did, too nice to want to make a fuss about it and ask for his money back. She had to resort

33

to little tricks, too, to hide the glaring defects: a piece of furniture or a rug over the large cracks and holes, an arrangement of lights to soften the tears and rents, a juggling of furnishings and cabins with the better going to the worst and the worst to the better.

Those were the problems when they had the business but the big problem was to have it at all. Most nights just the two good cabins were rented, many nights just one of them and some nights none at all. Neal had said it was a good proposition: six cabins meant thirty dollars a night and thirty dollars a night meant two hundred and ten dollars a week because it was a seven-day business with people traveling all the time and people needing to sleep all the time. Besides, there were the extras to be made from the roadstand, the barbecues and soft drinks. All of it added up to a good proposition except that none of it ever happened. In the first six months they averaged one and a half customers a night. It climbed to two and a half after the first year because, between the two of them, they had been able to make enough cover-up repairs and painting to keep a few of the customers from saying, "Five dollars for a dump like this! I'd rather ride all night."

The best nights were the nights it rained suddenly and without too much warning as it did sometimes in Georgia. Then the travelers would drive slowly enough through the downpour so that they could give the auto court a second look and be able to stop and back up to it. Or, if the sallow lights didn't seem inviting enough at first and they drove on looking for something better, they knew where they would come back to after driving five or six miles without any luck. The people didn't complain on the rainy nights. They had a roof over their heads and the roof didn't leak.

There were other nights, too, when business was brisk. Occasionally, the local Klan would round up its members and start a night ride through the countryside. There would be a double line of forty or fifty cars, lights blazing, horns blaring, pushing up the road, forcing every bit of traffic off the highway. The natives, knowing what it was, laughed or good-naturedly cursed the Klan for its foolishness. But the travelers, especially the northern travelers, spilled off the road in a panic and stampeded for the nearest retreat. The motorists from Jersey and New York and Massachusetts didn't complain about the beds or the walls or the plumbing on those nights. It was Evie who greeted them and took care of them. Neal said it was better that way; they'd all be so happy to hear a northern, Pennsylvania accent.

"But I don't like it, Neal, I don't like it one bit. It's a cheap, shoddy way to have business."

Neal would put on his amused patient look when she talked like that and lean against something handy. He always leaned when he talked, just like the cowboys in Western movies. She often supposed she never would have fallen in love with him if she hadn't been such a tomboy when she was a kid and gone to all those Saturday matinees with young Jubel.

"There ain't nothing cheap or shoddy about it, honey. We're here and they come running to us, just like they come running in out of the rain. You might almost say it's an act of God."

"Act of God! Why, that's blasphemy, Neal, and you know it. How can you even say such a thing!"

"Now, honey," he'd soothe her, "I'm only trying to make it easier for you. What's the use of getting yourself all riled up over something you can't help? You wouldn't turn those folks away no matter what brought them here; now, would you? Besides, it boils down to food for the kids and for us, too."

That would take the sparks out of her. "I just wish we didn't have to make a living out of people's misfortunes."

She didn't say that she thought he was quietly pleased with the Klan's rides or that she sometimes suspected he might even have encouraged them by spreading the word among his friends in town of what he caught in their backwash. What was the use of talking ethics and attitudes when the argument was meat on the table for your own children? She often thought that it

35

was one hell of a note the way necessity could beat down your principles.

On one score, though, her principles did stand up. She wouldn't, just wouldn't, open the cabins to itinerant lovers; the sex-hungry kids who went tramping up and down the highways looking for a place to mix their bodies for a few hours. It wasn't that she was intolerant of passion or, now that she was married, that she had the licensed smugness that went with legitimate sex.

"I don't care how much money it means. I won't let you do it, Neal."

"It ain't a matter of *doing* anything, honey. We don't *do* anything when anybody wants a cabin. We just take their money and let them stay. We don't ask to see anybody's marriage license."

He was arguing in his usual smooth fashion and she had felt herself being pushed into a corner. Neal could make black seem like gray with a little talking—with a lot, he could make it seem white. She used to think, before she married him and for a little while after, that he was clever, that any man who could make something seem different from what it was was a clever man. But, later on, she realized it wasn't really cleverness. It was a sort of simple stupid kind of optimism, a seeing of things not as they really were but as he would like them to be. And even though he could make things sound gray or white for a while, they were still black in the end. That's the way it had been with the auto court—he had made it sound like a good proposition—that's the way it would always be with Neal. But it wasn't going to be that way with the minors.

"Of course, we don't ask to see marriage licenses; married people don't carry them. Don't you see, Neal, it isn't that I care if people are married when they drive in here to rent a cabin for a night. I just want to be sure they're old enough *not* to be married if they don't want to be."

"And what are you going to do, dole out sex on the basis of age? Seems to me you're forgetting you were young once, too, and you had your share of urges."

36

"I'm not forgetting anything, Neal. I'm not forgetting that you bought this miserable auto court because you thought you could make two hundred and ten dollars a week on it. You can't. You never will unless you turn it into a whore house. Then you can make more. In a week, you'll be cutting the nights in half and you'll be making four hundred and twenty dollars a week. In a month, you'll be changing the sheets on the hour and you'll be lousy with money. Lousy," she had shouted. "Do you hear me? Lousy with money."

He had taken her by the arms and shaken her until she was still. "Let's forget it," he said and he walked away.

But she couldn't forget it and she was so afraid he might do it in spite of her, or just to spite her, that she brought it up again.

"Neal, I just want to say two things. You can't expect us to bring up decent children in an atmosphere like that."

"What's the other?"

"The other is that if you open the cabin to minors, sooner or later something is going to happen. You'll find yourself in a mess of trouble. They might even close the auto court on you altogether."

"Is that all?"

"That's all . . . except, don't do it, Neal. Please don't do it."

She never knew whether it had resolved itself by a yes or no on his part; he never told her. It didn't happen. Whether she had talked him out of it, scared him out of it or insulted him out of it, she never found out. Maybe it had been all three of them or a little of each or none of them. Maybe it had nothing to do with her or with him at all. Maybe he had wanted to let the minors in but they didn't come. It would be Neal's kind of luck to have it happen that way.

Whatever it was, though, she had both the satisfaction and guilt that went with running a legitimate auto court. And she couldn't, after that, throw it up to him or even look as though she was thinking there wasn't enough meat on the table or

37

enough milk for the children because he could always say, "Don't bitch to me about it. Go eat your principles."

But the funny thing about it was that you really could eat your principles; or, at least, season your food with them and enjoy what little there was of it. It wasn't the ideal kind of life but it had its compensations. Because the auto court was stupidly built on top of the sharpest rise in the neighborhood, it was the first spot the sun hit in the morning. The view was lovely, too, and the air was spiced by the flowers and green things it touched before it reached them. It was a good place to raise young children. It might not be so good when they would be old enough to go to school—then you'd have to worry about getting them there, driving them to and back or fretting about the school bus and if it were safe enough to let them use it—but there was a good year before Jinny would have to go and more than four before Tommy would be ready. Time enough then to worry about the business of getting them to a school, even a southern country school whose shortcomings she'd have to worry about, too.

All that was future and it was silly to bother your head about future because you always caught up to it if you lived long enough. For now, for the present, in spite of the scrimpings, life was good enough. It was hard work and no new clothes and God forbid sickness or any other emergency that might call for solid cash but it was living and growing with your children and loving your husband as much as you could, knowing him as well as you did, and hoping, always hoping: hoping for Jinny and Tommy and hoping for Neal and hoping, especially, for the horrible auto court and that it would make enough money for all of them so that she wouldn't have to hope too much for anyone or anything else. The wire from home stopped all that dead.

It had come in the middle of the night, reaching out a thousand miles to jolt her out of sleep. It wasn't that sleep for her made unbroken company with night. Many times the night bell would clang uproariously at one or two o'clock in the

38

morning—this after waiting through the end of the day and the evening for customers who didn't come—and some traveler who had pushed himself as far as he could with his eyes still open stood miraculously at their door. But that was always like the sound of an alarm clock and she rose automatically to it; it didn't even wake the children. With the wire it was different. Mr. Ed Gault who brought it in from Bellford wasn't a customer. So he came right to the house door and pounded on it.

It was like being waked by personal violence. Tommy opened his eyes and began to cry. Jinny, who was old enough not to, was scared into tears. Neal turned over in his liquid stupor and mumbled, "Someone's at the door." She threw on her robe and let in Mr. Gault.

"Mighty sorry to disturb you this way, Mrs. Sabin, but this is mighty important . . . I'm afraid." He left with a quick respect which she wasn't aware of until the next morning when she remembered it all.

Then Tommy began to scream and Jinny stumbled out into the light. She took them both into the kitchen and, with Tommy over her shoulder and Jinny clinging to her knees, she tore open the yellow envelope and read the paid-for phrases: "Mother died this morning. Funeral Monday. Come home."

"What's the matter, Mommy? What does it say? You're crying."

"It's nothing, Jinny, nothing. It's from Grandpa Jubel. He wants us to visit him; that's all."

"Then why are you crying?"

"I'm not crying." She pulled the girl away from her knees. "And you're going to bed."

After she dropped the baby in his crib and tucked Jinny in, she stood for a moment shivering in the dark cold house. She didn't know what to do. It was two o'clock in the morning. Daylight was four hours away. She didn't want to turn on a light or start the heater; it would bring the children out again. She crawled back into bed beside Neal. There was the

39

smell and warmth of sleep there but she shook as though the sheets and blankets were cold-wet.

"What's the matter? What's all the commotion?" He tossed himself around but he sounded as though he was sleep talking; his voice was fuzzy and mumbly.

"Mama died this morning." She remembered the telegram and how it was worded and she knew her father hadn't written it. It might have been Agnew, who lived next door, or the man at the telegraph office. She thought of him all alone now, sitting and waiting for them to come home. She thought of poor Mama; gone now, gone, and she choked, "She died this morning."

Neal's hand went around her shoulders and held her.

Mama died this morning and how many times had she laughed since this morning? How many things had she done without knowing? How many times had she breathed the air and felt the sun, played with the children, ate food, worked, smiled while Mama lay stiff and cold? And not one thought of her today, not one thought of her or of Pa. Some days she could think of nothing but them, but not today. She couldn't remember once, today.

Neal pressed her to him. He didn't speak, he didn't ask questions. He just gave her the comfort of his flesh and, somehow, that was her need: to feel the blood and life of another in her, filling the void.

Somehow morning came. She had breakfast ready before the sun, and the few changes the children needed she had picked out and packed up. There was Tommy's milk to worry about but she could take a bottle along and manage somehow along the way. They could drive it in two days. She'd let the children sleep until the very last minute.

Neal sat down at the table. His hair was freshly damped and combed. He watched her as he sipped his coffee.

"What are you doing?" He caught her in between rooms.

"I want to leave right after breakfast, Neal. It's a long drive."

She was in and out of the kitchen half a dozen times, bringing things, folding them, putting them away, before he talked to her again.

"What are you doing?" he asked again.

"You'll have to lock all the cabins—the windows, too—and turn off the water. You'd better not waste too much time. There's so much to be done before we go."

He put down his cup. "I'm not going any place."

She stopped and looked at him. "Neal, don't you remember? Last night? My mother died yesterday. The funeral's Monday. We're going home."

He shook his head. "I'm not closing this court for anyone, especially for anyone who's dead."

"Neal!"

"Don't 'Neal' me. This court's my living. Can't afford to close it."

"We didn't have one customer last night. We may not have any for the rest of the week."

"Weekend's coming along. Customers will, too."

She stood there for a moment, furiously silent.

"What's the use of going home now? What good is it going to do?"

"You can't bear to leave Luther and your other drunken cronies in Bellford, can you?"

He got up, went to the stove and poured himself another cup of coffee. "Christ, everyone runs to the dead. Why don't they run to the living instead?"

"Because you have to have money to run and I haven't had it for two years."

"You don't have it now, either."

She didn't want an argument. She went in to the children, woke them, washed them, dressed them.

He was still in the kitchen, waiting, when she came back.

"What good is it going to do? Just tell me that. What good is it going to do?"

"Neal, I don't want to talk about it. I'm going; that's all."

41

She fed the baby while she coaxed Jinny into eating her breakfast.

"How are you going?"

"I'm taking the car."

"Mama, isn't Daddy coming with us to Grandpa Jubel's?"

"What am I supposed to do?"

"I don't care what you do. Just leave me alone."

He put on his hat and went out of the house. She didn't see him again until she was in the car and rolling down the driveway to the road. There she had to stop to *listen* for traffic—the way the court was built, you couldn't see it—and Neal stood there, about fifty yards away; as though he wanted to see them off but not too closely. He shouted something to her as she waited but the motor was noisy and Jinny was talking, so she wasn't sure she heard. It sounded like, "And don't bring your old man home with you, either." She was so mad, she jerked the car into the road and sped down the hill.

"Mama, Daddy's waving."

But she didn't turn to look. Could he wave after saying a thing like that? She decided he could do anything after speaking the way he had this morning. It was indecent, that's all; just damned stinking indecent. She didn't know what could have happened to him, what had been happening to him in the past four years. It had been a mistake to move down here. There was something about this sweet, lovely, lonely land—where things grew without encouragement, where the earth and the sun were red and vengeful—that colored the blood. She hadn't wanted to come down here. She told him that before they were married but he had been only six months out of the army and he spoke of Georgia with an almost aching tenderness, as though this state were molded of special clay with a sun and a sky of pink and blue flesh. He was a nice boy then and even his longing for it was nice.

"You'll love it, Evie. There's something about the air and earth that makes you part of it. Maybe the sky isn't bluer but it seems bluer. Let's just try it for a little while. If you don't like it, we can always come back. But you'll love it, Evie, you'll see. It's different, once you've lived there."

He even talked differently then. He didn't say "ain't" and he didn't slur and he didn't swallow his talk. But it wasn't only his speech; it was ideas and attitudes. When they first came and they lived in Atlanta, it wasn't so bad. It was big-city life and whether you liked big city or not, you couldn't ignore the civilization of it. But Atlanta wasn't close enough to the land for Neal and he had to buy the auto court, the only one in the state, maybe the only one in the world, that perched like a bird on the top of a hill. After that, he became part of it: the peanuts and the peaches and the people.

She drove for about ten minutes with the baby lying quietly on the front seat beside her and Jinny occupying herself in the back with a doll. Suddenly, she saw the road in front of her—a long, flat, endless stretch of it—and she realized she was alone with two children and the miles were all ahead of her. The morning died in her eyes. She felt gloom, then fright, then panic. She pulled to the side of the road and stopped the car.

"What's the matter, Mama? Do we have a flat tire?"

Oh, God, she thought, don't say it; don't even think it. She sat, gripping the wheel, looking over the dashboard. There was half a tankful of gas—if you could trust the gauge—the battery was charging and she couldn't tell about oil and water. She listened to the tick of the motor as though it could tell her something. But what could an eight-year-old car tell you when you pick it up, without even as much as a pat on its hood, and tell it it's got to go? It should have been greased and examined and tuned up and had done to it whatever you're supposed to do to old cars before you expect them to carry you for a thousand miles.

She scurried into her bag to see how much money she had. With change, there was a little over eleven dollars. Eleven dollars and she would have to live two days and a night on the road with that, supporting two children, herself and an aging car.

"Keep your eye on the baby, Jinny. I'm going out to look at the tires."

She literally looked at them; she didn't know what else to do. She had seen Neal and other men in her lifetime kick at a tire, so she gingerly put the toe of her high-heeled shoe to one of them but it didn't prove anything; not that it would go a mile or ten or blow in the next twenty yards. But she did touch each of them with her toe—noting the smoothness that meant age in inanimate objects—as though she were blessing them for the journey.

"Are they all right, Mama?"

"Yes, they're just fine, dear, just fine."

Should she go back to Neal, ask him for more money? A pitiful eleven dollars, it would never do. But she'd be damned, damned, damned before she'd go back and ask him for anything. She jumped into the car and started off again. Somehow, it would get her there. Somehow, with God's help, it would hold together until she got home, and young Jubel or Bertram would tell her what to do with it. She had to laugh to herself when she thought of young Jubel lifting an eyebrow over the car, saying, "You know what you can do with that, Evie," and slapping her over the backside. She had a happy few minutes thinking about him but only a few because she realized how far away he was, how far away home and Pop and Bertram and Helen were, too. And Mom was farthest away of all. Neal was right in a way about everyone running to the dead. Chances are, they'd all be home this time; not for the golden anniversary, not for Christmas or Thanksgiving, not for just going home for a visit and seeing them alive. Death made life look so funny, so stupid . . .

The children were good and the miles went quickly. They stopped once for lunch and once for gas. She had milk, too. She wasn't hungry anyhow and, besides, you never knew how far an extra dollar might go in an emergency. She took the well-traveled routes going through towns, cuddling close to the service stations because she was scared of the nowhere stretches.

She finished with Georgia in mid-afternoon and went into the Carolinas. The country was hilly there and she could save gas by switching off the motor and coasting. She wished the whole trip could be a hill going down. She hated to think of tonight and the drive tomorrow and the money they would cost. She played with the idea of driving all night but she didn't know the roads too well and she might get lost or run into some trouble, God knows where. Besides, she couldn't do that to the children; they needed a night's rest; they had to be cleaned up. She was pretty exhausted, herself.

She began to pay attention to the auto courts. Most of them were attractive, in good condition. All of them stood level and inviting on the road. Leave it to Neal to try to balance an auto court on the top of a hill. That man! That aggravating, stubborn, thoughtless man. But maybe it wasn't all his fault. Life was doing something to him; she could be a little more tolerant this far away. Funny, how unreasonably she had loved him at first. She guessed she still did—she was missing him now—but not like she used to. She wondered if all marriages were like hers: like . . . almost like a set of tires, rugged and tough and full of interesting grooves in the beginning and then wearing thin and smooth as they rolled through time until they blew out or seemed ready to blow out. From rapture to rupture. Maybe the institution wasn't made for poor human beings or for rich ones, either, if they were human. She must have a good talk with young Jubel. He must be careful. No, he mustn't. He must do what he wants and enjoy the privilege of making his own mistakes.

She turned into an auto court just before dark. It was the first one after a long empty stretch and she didn't know what lay ahead. The cabins looked bright and cheerful and there was a tree and a bench in front of each one.

"Are we going to stop here, Mama?"

"Yes, dear. It's almost dark and I'm tired."

"I'm tired, too, Mama, and hungry."

"Of course you are, Jinny. You've been a very good girl."

45

She parked in front of the office. "Now, you just wait here until I register. Watch the baby."

The man behind the desk told her she was lucky; there were only two cabins left. He held the book for her while she signed her name and put down the address. She had to go out to the car to get her license plate number; she could never remember it. By that time, another car drove in and she thought how nice it would be if she and Neal could fill up their place like this. The traveler followed her into the office.

"Be right with you, sir," the man behind the desk said while Evie put down the number. "That'll be eight dollars, ma'am."

"Eight dollars!" She felt herself turn sick at the figure. "Why, I thought all auto courts charged five, no more than five."

"Not in this part of the country, ma'am."

The robbers, she thought, the highway thieves, holding you up, taking advantage of you. She turned to the traveler.

"Isn't this outrageous!" she cried.

He was a tall man, gray, with rimless glasses.

"Why, for eight dollars you can go to a hotel!"

The traveler looked at her as though he were trying to figure her out. He was more than middle aged and there should have been sympathy in his face but there wasn't; just a kind of curiosity with a callous on it.

The man behind the desk pulled the book away. "No one's forcing you to stay, ma'am."

"Oh, I'll stay. I'll stay. What else can I do with two children on my hands?" She unsnapped her pocketbook. She didn't have to count the bills. There were seven; the rest she had to make in change.

"Thank you, ma'am. Your cabin's number ten."

She picked up the key and went out without looking at either of them. She was trembling and she could have cried but she controlled herself; she didn't want to get Jinny upset. She hung on, she had to, for quite a while after until she had the children fed—milk for Tommy and milk and a horrible frankfurter for Jinny—and bathed and put into the twin beds. After

46

they were asleep, she fell apart. She sat in a big chair by the window and sobbed. A fine refuge for the night. A trap, that's what it was. Sixty cents left and half the trip to go. What was she going to do? How was she going to make it?

She got up and went outside. She didn't want to wake them. It was dark and she sat on the bench under a tree. She must be hungry but she couldn't feel it. She was so tired, so alone, so far from any place, just lost in between. All she could think of was tomorrow and how she could go on. But she couldn't really think because she was so miserable. All she could do was cry.

She heard one of the cabins open and someone coming down the court. The footsteps stopped when they came to her walk and waited. She looked up. It was the traveler; she could tell from the size of him and the way the cabin lights touched his glasses. He turned in and came up to her.

"What's the matter with you?"

She didn't feel anything in him: no sympathy, no annoyance, not even a real curiosity now. She guessed he knew.

"Nothing. I'm all right."

He stood there, looking down at her. "Broke?"

"Sort of."

He sat down. "If it'll make you feel better, all the cabins along this road charge eight dollars. I know, I've traveled it."

She blew her nose. "That's comforting, I guess, but it doesn't do me much good."

He seemed to measure her for a silent moment. "Ten dollars do you?"

"Oh, no. I couldn't."

"Couldn't what?"

"I couldn't take money from a stranger."

"We wouldn't be strangers." He laughed; just a short bubble. "Want to come over to my cabin for a drink?"

47

The wind was sharp with a slap to it. He faced it as it came from the east on the turnpike, blowing along the early morning traffic. He had been standing there an hour without any luck. He guessed he was out of practice; either that or he should have put on his old army uniform. A car whizzed by, ignoring his elegant thumb. He turned, following it with his eyes, and caught the laugh on the driver's face.

"Very funny," he said aloud. "I'm rolling them in the highways."

He jaunted his homburg hat, pulled at his Chesterfield coat. Okay, so he didn't look like a hitchhiker. What was he supposed to do, lift his pants over his knees? The world was coming to a fine state when a hitchhiker had to look like a hitchhiker. He dug out a cigarette and lighted it. The flame felt good in his cupped hands. The first breath of smoke warmed his lungs and filled his empty stomach. Not even a lousy cup of coffee, but no complaints; he was lucky to have had enough for bus fare after last night. That was another thing; to have to take a bus so that you could get to a place where you could even hope for a ride. He looked over the Jersey flats. New York seemed a long way off but it wasn't much more than across the river. He had a long way to go.

He watched another car go by and he decided that the army

48

had had it all over this. Patriotism, sooner or later, was sure
to grab someone by their big heart and make them pick up
a poor soldier. You had to hand it to the army, it knew how
to handle a situation. If a man lost his mother, the tragedy became a government project. You were shot through the eche-
lons like a dose of salts: through the squad and platoon leaders
to the first sergeant, to the commanding officer, to the chap-
lain, to the Red Cross and back again. All they needed was a
verification of the death and you had an emergency furlough
in your hand, money in your pocket and you were off. The
army recognized the importance of mothers, its source of sup-
ply.

But this wasn't army. This was four years after and no one
gave a damn. You could tell one of these fine motorists your
mother had just died, and that you were trying to get home
for her funeral and that you didn't have train fare to your
name, and they'd look you up and down.

"You're six foot one, fellow," they'd say, "strong looking,
good looking, wavy hair, blue eyes. You ought to be able to
get along."

Sure, he could get along. He had gotten along. There wasn't
another hitchhiker in the world who ever stood on the road,
almost flat broke and waiting for a ride, while his wife slept
in a satin bed in her father's money-stuffed East Side house surrounded by a staff of servants and five telephones, including
one in the bathroom. That one in the bathroom he could never
understand. How busy can a man be, he'd ask her, that he can't
take time out for the necessities of life without a telephone at
his elbow.

"You just don't understand, Jubel, and besides you resent it.
Why, Father can lose thousands of dollars if he happens to
be taking a bath and misses a call from his broker. You have
no idea how the market works."

Sometimes he thought he had no idea how anything worked
with the Sheffield family, not only with Alton Sheffield, his
father-in-law, but with Toby herself. Why had she married him

49

in the first place? He had asked her that last night when he took her home.

"Because I loved you and because I still love you."

"Then why do you insist on keeping it a secret? We've been married six months. Aren't you ever going to let your father know?"

She had shushed him because she thought he was talking too loud and someone might hear: her father or one of the servants, maybe that creep of a butler who walked through the house as though the rugs were made of six-ply dollar bills.

"Let's walk around the block. We can talk better outside."

"Suits me."

They went out into East 74th Street and walked the square bounded by Madison and Park. She came up to his shoulder as they moved along the quiet streets like two silhouettes. When they came under a streetlight, he'd look down at the sharply delicate little face with the high forehead and the hair drawn tightly back and he'd say to himself, she looks like a schoolgirl; she's my wife but she looks like a schoolgirl. I can see why her father never even guesses.

"Jubel, if we must do serious talking, why do you always wait until you get me inside the house?"

"I wasn't going to, Toby, honestly, but that place brings out the worst in me."

"It's about time you got used to it. You're going to be living that way someday, yourself."

"Not me. If I had all the money in the world, I wouldn't live that way."

She laughed. "It's very nice living, Jubel."

"You married an actor, remember? If I got the biggest break in the world, a good part in a hit show, I couldn't even hope for more than five hundred a week."

"That would be enough to move you out of your basement apartment, wouldn't it?"

He could remember when she thought his one-room basement apartment was *charming, delightful*. And he could remember the first time he had brought her there and she had cooked a spaghetti dinner for them. It had been a lot of fun watching her putter around in his two-by-four kitchenette, wearing his spotted kitchen apron over her seventy-five dollar blouse. The funny part of it was, she actually produced a meal: veal scallopini, spaghetti with tomato sauce, a green salad, wine and coffee.

"I didn't know you could cook, too, Sweetie."

"You've been listening to too many of those stories about the idle rich. You don't know it, but someday I'm going to make a wonderful wife for some lucky man."

"I know." He had leaned across their candlelit table to kiss her. "I wish it could be for me, Toby."

By that time, they had known each other long enough to know about love. It was like getting on the same step of a department store escalator: a short ride but you went through all the stages, feeling all the exciting promise as you went up together, choosing your floor or just going on and on to the top.

"Why couldn't you be, Jubel?"

"Because I can't afford a wife, any kind of a wife. Most times, I can't even afford myself."

"You will, Jubel. You'll get a break. You've got too much talent to be ignored."

He certainly agreed with her but sometimes he couldn't help wondering. That night, though, with just the two of them alone in his little apartment, anything seemed possible, especially with a girl like Toby encouraging you. And it wasn't that she didn't know what she was talking about. She had had a taste of the theatre. She had spent a summer in stock, even though she had gone as an apprentice and her father had paid her way. And she had seen what he could do the night they met. Everybody was everybody's friend at those experimental productions down in the Village. Toby had come with a friend of one of the kids who played a heavy and they all ended up backstage congratulating one another. That's the way it was with those productions: all congratulations and no money and no notices.

51

But it was good theatre and you had a chance to act. You acted like hell because you loved it and it was what you wanted to do if someone would give you half a chance. But that was neither here nor there as far as Toby was concerned.

"I could never afford a wife like you, Toby."

"You don't have to afford me. I have money."

"That's just it; too much of it. Besides, I know what your father thinks of struggling young actors."

"Father doesn't have to know."

"Now, look, Toby. Let's not get into one of those."

"Why not? We love each other, don't we?"

"I hear love is only a minor ingredient these days."

"Don't you believe it. It's everything. It is for me. Let's get married, Jubel. Tomorrow!"

"Wait a minute. We're losing our heads. This is no life for you."

"That's just it, Jubel. We'll have separate lives—you yours and mine mine—but we'll have a togetherness, too."

She was like an uncontrollable child. He knew she was twenty-four but she was almost jumping up and down with excitement.

"Then what's the point in getting married?"

"Because that's what we want to do. Because, if we don't, we'll regret it for the rest of our lives." The lines were corny but you couldn't look in her face and doubt them.

"And what about your father?" He hadn't met Mr. Sheffield but he had heard enough about him.

"We won't tell Father. We won't tell anybody."

"He's going to have to know sometime."

"Let sometime take care of itself. This is *now* for us, Jubel."

"You really want to?"

"Yes, more than anything else."

They had flown down to Baltimore the next day. He had an old army buddy, Patrick Paul Johnson, who was now a Maryland politician. Back in the ETO, he was P.P. Johnson and he was a good Joe. P.P. was still all right. He pulled strings and

52

tied a waiver on the details: they were married in an hour and *then* they took their blood tests.

"I'll send you the results by mail, Jubel."

They drank champagne—P.P.'s champagne—and P.P. drove them to the airport for the trip back.

"Just name the first one after me; P.P. Watson."

It was six hours from the time they left New York to the time they came back, not even long enough for anyone to ask questions. They had dinner and then they spent their wedding night in his basement apartment. At three o'clock in the morning he took his wife home to her father's house.

Since then he had been taking her home regularly. Toby was having her two little lives—the daughter of a rich man and the wife of a poor one—and enjoying both immensely. There wasn't a practical reason why he shouldn't have felt the same way but it wasn't working out for him. For one thing, he didn't like the secrecy, the feeling that he was smuggling her in and out of his apartment and his life. And he didn't like leaving her at two or three in the morning when he really wanted her to be there beside him when he opened his eyes, to have breakfast with him and be there waiting for him when he came home, either to cheer him or celebrate with him. Most of all, he wanted to be able to introduce her as "Mrs. Watson" instead of "Miss Sheffield" and to be able to take her home to his father and mother. Maybe those were silly intangibles; Toby certainly made them sound that way when he brought them up, but he couldn't help feeling the lack of them.

There was more to it, too. He didn't like the idea of being hidden. He wasn't ashamed of himself or of his career. He was proud to be an actor, and it was just too damn bad if Toby's father didn't think actors were good enough. Suppose he didn't like wealthy Wall Street operators? He didn't but that didn't stop him from marrying Toby. Why should fathers be so particular? If all the prospective sons-in-law in the world started being choosy about their prospective fathers-in-law, there'd be darned few marriages. In most cases, it was just a matter of

53

money: "Can you support my daughter in the manner to which she is accustomed?" If he could it wouldn't matter. He would still be an actor, supporting her with cheap theatrical money. Actors were déclassé to the Sheffields. If he were a seventy-five dollar a week clerk with an investment company or a young hopeful in a bank, he'd be acceptable. But an actor? Horrors! He wondered what went with Alton Sheffield. Did the old man have a bad time in his flaming youth with a chorus girl? It could be something as stupid as that. Or maybe not that reasonable; it might be just plain snobbery. Whatever it was, it put him beyond the pale.

If he didn't love Toby so much, he'd be inclined to think their marriage took place to satisfy the whim of a very immature girl. In a way, she was immature. Twenty-four, but what could you learn in two dozen years if you spent them in boarding schools and colleges along with a couple of years of sheltered travel? Shelter was shelter, here or abroad, luxurious or otherwise. She might even have married him as a protest against her father's domination. But what kind of protest was it if he didn't know? She had made speeches on the plane down to Baltimore.

"I know how to handle Father. You never tell him you're going to do anything. You go ahead and do it. Then you confront him with the *fait accompli*. He can't give you advice then. He can't tell you *not* to do it. It's already done. Don't you see?"

He saw it, all right, but he was still waiting to see Toby confront her father with that *fait accompli*. He hadn't wanted to make an issue of it, so he had let it ride for more than a month. When he finally did bring it up, she pushed it aside.

"But what difference does it make, dear? We're all happy the way things stand: I'm happy, Father's happy and you're happy."

"I'm *not* happy, Toby."

"Poor dear. Would it make you happy if Father were unhappy?"

54

"I'm not interested in your father's happiness or unhappiness. All I want to do is tell him that we're married."

"Why?"

"Because it's the honest thing to do. Because you can't keep a secret forever. It'll come out, somehow. And it would be a lot more decent if we were the ones who told him."

She went over to the windows and drew the shades. Then she came back to sit in his lap.

"See, that's exactly what I mean. If all this wasn't such a big secret, you wouldn't have to draw the shades before you can sit in your husband's lap."

He wished he could be angry with her, at least for a little while. But when she put her arms around his neck and her nose against his cheek, he felt too many other things to feel anger.

"Jubel, I don't want the world to intrude on us. This is our secret life. As soon as we tell anyone, our love becomes public property."

"Silly cat. You're just scared of your father."

"A little. But how can I tell him I married the most wonderful, beautiful, penniless actor in the world?"

That was true enough, so he had let it drop. You were always hoping, anyway, that something would happen tomorrow to take you out of the penniless class. Besides, he was a little sensitive about his father-in-law's money. He didn't want Toby ever to have the idea that he wanted to get in on the Sheffield fortune in any shape or form. Sometimes, after he'd taken her home, he'd lie in his bed and worry about what would have happened to her if she had married some heel who might have moved right in. Other nights, he'd go through imaginary conversations with Mr. Sheffield in which he broke the news to him.

"Alton, old man," he'd say, "shake hands with your son-in-law."

"And who are you?" Mr. Sheffield would look up at him, over his pince-nez. He was almost as little as Toby.

55

"Me! Don't you remember me?" And he'd rub Alton's freckled bald head affectionately. "I'm Jubel Watson."

"Oh, yes, Mr. Watson. You're the young man in merchandising."

"No, no, Alton. That was one of Toby's little jokes. She didn't want you to know what I really do. I'm an actor."

Here, the conversation would take one of two turns. Mr. Sheffield would run screaming to the fireplace for a red-hot poker to chase him out of the house, or he would say, "Oh," and fall weakly into his winged chair.

"What kind of an actor are you, Mr. Watson?" he'd ask in the latter version.

"Serious actor."

"And where do you act?"

"Well, as a matter of fact, Dad, I'm not acting in anything at the moment. Doing a little radio here and there. Looking for a good part in a good play. You might say I'm freelancing."

"Doesn't that mean you're unemployed?"

From there on, it would get a little uncomfortable and he'd put it out of his mind. But he couldn't always put it out of his mind; last night was a perfect example. They had been married six months, half a year, and he had tied himself in knots to make it a celebration.

There was a pickup in traffic and he stepped into the road to make his thumb and his presence more obvious. The cars veered enough to give him a wide berth and passed on. They didn't even slow down. He wondered if it would do any good to take off his hat. Maybe, if he looked a little less formal, he'd stand a better chance. He might be scaring people; no one wanted to help anyone who looked as though he might be better dressed than they were. Nuts! If he was going to get a ride, he'd get one; hat or no hat.

Why did he have to spend all that money last night? If he hadn't been such a big time Charlie, such a fast man with a dollar, he might have had enough left over to pay his way home. He might be walking into the house right now if he had had the price of a plane ticket. But you never know about those things. Emergencies always come at the wrong time; that's what makes them emergencies. Besides, he didn't really regret the extravagance even though it had meant scrimping for a month, giving himself what amounted to a salary slash on his two small sustaining local radio jobs so that he could save something, going to Philadelphia to cut a couple of transcriptions at under-scale rates and making one shameful television appearance on a show which would have ruined him if anyone had seen it. It had been a very nice evening: dinner out, a show and then a club afterwards. It was his own fault it had ended in a wrangle. He didn't have to display the old wound on their anniversary night. If he had waited, he'd still be on speaking terms with his wife and he might have borrowed his traveling fare from her. But taking her home again and into that house was too much for him and he started in again on the business of telling her father. Now that he knew how she felt about things, it was just as well because he wasn't sure that he'd want to borrow anything from her.

It was that crack she had made about making enough money so that he could move out of his basement apartment.

"I can remember when you thought my basement apartment was *delightful* and *charming*."

He had mimicked her and he remembered the look of annoyance on her face as they made the turn into Park Avenue.

"It *was* charming. It *was* delightful."

"No more, huh?"

"It isn't where I'd choose to live."

"Would you choose to live with me *anywhere?*"

"Certainly not the way you're acting."

"What did I do? All I did was ask when you're going to get around to telling your father we're married."

"When I can be proud to tell him."

"You're not proud now."

She stopped. They were halfway between the street lights

57

and he couldn't see her eyes but her voice made him remember something her father had told him once in a very brief conversation: "Toby was born with clenched fists, Mr. Watson. They were clenched so tight, they cut into the palms of her hands. Her poor mother, rest her soul, cried at the sight of them."

"Jubel, I won't tell my father we're married if I have to make excuses for you. I refuse to be ashamed of my marriage. I won't admit to anyone, especially my father, that my husband is an unemployed actor. I love him too much for that."

"You knew I was an unemployed actor when you married me."

"I had hoped that you'd be some place by now. Father wouldn't have been happy about it even then but, at least, he couldn't say you can't support me."

"You knew all these things, Toby."

"Of course, I knew."

She started to walk again, slowly. After a few steps, he followed her.

"Jubel, I do love you. I'd wake Father and tell him tonight but I can't, not the way things are."

"What do you want me to do?"

"I think you ought to give up acting, get a job somewhere, something solid, respectable. Father would help us."

This was the girl who told him he had too much talent to be ignored. He didn't talk, he couldn't, until they were in front of her house.

"Good night, Toby."

"You will think about it, Jubel, won't you?"

"I'll think of nothing else but. I'll think of what a fine little snob I've married, and I'll think of her wonderful father who couldn't stand the shock of being told that his son-in-law was a legitimate actor. Good night, Toby!"

He had walked home mad through. She'd whistle loud and long before she saw or heard from him again. He wished she was as mad as he was and that she'd wake her father now and tell him and that they'd do something about getting the whole

58

thing annulled. He was through. He had taken all he was going to take. He had become less of a man in the past six months: stealing around corners with her, hiding, lying. And for what? So that she could tell him to give up his work? A man was no man without his work. She had no right to say that. What if he wasn't born a howling success? He wasn't the flop she made him out to be. He had had a couple of parts. He had understudied a lead role in a play that ran for three months. Was it his fault that the star didn't break a leg or come down with a strep throat? And he had a couple of strong parts in the last few plays that didn't click. Was it his fault that the plays were lousy? He had done almost a year in stock; he knew where he was going. And he was able to keep himself afloat on the radio jobs that came along. Of course, he never made the big network money in radio because he didn't have the stomach to join the circle of hungry sycophants who bootlicked their way up to the top. She had no right to talk to him like that.

And then he was home. He banged open his door, switched on the lights and stared at the telegram on the floor. He picked it up, turned it over and knew immediately it was from home; no one else used the jr. after his name. He read it. He read it again. He read it a dozen times, not believing the words. He let it drop to the floor and then he picked it up. He read it through a tumblerful of whiskey with his hat and coat still on. He lighted a cigarette and sat for a few minutes, trying to absorb the shock of his mother's death. Poor Mom, he thought, she didn't even know I was married.

After a while, he had stood up, buttoned his coat and left the apartment. He knew he didn't have enough money for train fare but that didn't bother him. He'd get a bus over to Jersey and hitch a ride home. What did bother him was the feeling that he had left his mother dead on the floor while he had spent the night celebrating.

That had been hours ago and he was still in Jersey waiting for that ride.

"Come on. Come on," he said to the cars as they went by,

slapping the air in his face. He watched them coming at him from a distance—the headlight eyes, the radiator snouts, the low-slung bodies looking as though they were running along on their knees—and he wondered why man had to make his machines in his own image. Maybe it was the God in him but all of them, the airplanes, the automobiles, the steam shovels, even the telephone poles carried the resemblance. Man-like machines and machine-like men and not a heart in a roadful.

A big, stupid looking truck with a "No Riders" sticker, sucked on its air brakes and pulled up in front of him. He looked at it without moving.

"You want a ride, don't you?" The driver shouted at him.

He climbed in. "Thanks." He nodded at the sticker. "I guess I believe in signs."

The driver muscled the truck into gear and they took off. He was bare-armed, a man about forty, much smaller and slighter than a truck driver was expected to be. Sitting there, behind his big wheel, he had the look of a worried elephant keeper.

"I'm not supposed to pick up anybody but you looked so damn funny, standing there in that getup, I just couldn't help myself." He said it without laughing. Then he looked at him and began to tickle all over. "What's the idea of the outfit?"

He might have known. Wait a year for a ride and when you finally do get one, it has to be with a character.

"No idea in particular. It's a hat and coat, that's all." He took off his homburg and unbuttoned his Chesterfield. It was hot in the cab.

"Well, I thought I seen everything. Did someone drop you off the social register?"

Jubel laughed politely. "No, I never had it that good. To tell you the truth, Mac, it's very simple. This is the only coat I own and this is my only hat. I can't afford a larger wardrobe."

"Don't tell me you work."

"Of course, I work. I'm an actor."

60

"An actor!" The man came to life. "Burlesque?"

He hated to let him down but he had to. "No. I do what they call 'legitimate theatre.' You know, plays."

"Oh, that talking stuff . . . I thought maybe you were in burlesque. Those guys get all the stuff in the world, I bet."

"Stuff?"

"Heads. Tail. Women."

"Oh, I see what you mean."

"I hear all those dames walk around naked back of the stage."

"That should be interesting."

The man was obviously disappointed in him. It didn't promise a very sociable trip. He was undoubtedly a great conversationalist in his own field but sex on an empty stomach was a little raw. Besides, he wasn't sure he appreciated this popular conception of the drama.

"Where you headed for?"

"Home."

"Giving up the acting business?"

He wanted to say, "Yeah, I'm going to start driving a truck," but he said, "Mother died. I'm going home for the funeral."

"You got the right clothes for it."

Some people could have the weirdest sense of humor.

"Old man still alive?"

"Yes."

"Any other kids?"

"Three."

"Who's going to take care of your old man?"

"I don't know." He answered automatically. He didn't know. He never gave it a thought. Maybe Bertram, Helen, Evie. *He* couldn't take care of himself. "Oh, I guess Pop'll manage all right."

"How long you been out of work?"

"I'm not out of work. I've got a couple of jobs."

"Sure. But when you got a couple, it means they don't add up to one living."

61

The guy had something there but only in a limited way. "Oh, I'll get something in a little while."

"Sure. If you're any good, you will."

He let it ride. What was he going to do, tell him about the theatre and what a tough nut it was to crack? And just suppose he told him he was married to a million dollars if he'd give up acting? He could just hear him saying, "A million dollars? And you hitching a ride! You must be soft in the head." Maybe he was. He didn't know.

"Nice truck you got here. What's your run?"

"Boston to New York to Harrisburg."

"That's most of my ride. I go only about twenty miles beyond Harrisburg."

He didn't seem overjoyed.

"Guess you get to see lots of the country, driving around like this."

"Enough."

"Well, they say travel is broadening."

"Broadening, hell. It's narrowing."

"What do you mean?"

"I mean I pushed trucks all over this country: Maine to Louisiana, one coast to the other. All you ever see is something that reminds you of something else. A street in Boston looks like a street in New Orleans. Cape Cod, Laguna Beach, it's all the same. And if you live in New York what do you have to go to Frisco for?"

"Yes, but the scenery . . ."

"Scenery!" He spit without spitting. "Hell, I got scenery up to my eyeballs. Good scenery looks phony. If it's too good, you don't even believe your eyes. I'd rather stay home and look at picture postcards."

He eased up on the gas and bounced them off the road to a diner.

"Here's where we eat."

They jumped down from the cab and walked over the gravel. When they were inside at the counter, looking over the menus, he said, "You better fill up. It's a long drive and it's on me."

Jubel looked at him. He guessed he'd never understand people.

"Thanks, Mac, I can buy my breakfast."

v

She had called Raymond and said, "I'm flying home. My mother died yesterday."

"Oh, my dear, I'm sorry."

He was in his office and she knew he couldn't talk. She could just see him sitting at his mahogany acre of desk, leaning intensely over to the telephone, his crisp, studded cuffs inching out of his dark blue sleeves.

"When does your plane leave?"

"In an hour."

"Damn!"

She knew he was running a nervous hand through his sun-bleached hair. A summer of Cape Cod sun stayed with him a long time; especially when he helped it along with a lamp.

"Helen, I want to see you. Can't you take a later plane?"

"No."

"It's just that I'm tied up solid. I've got two authors waiting for me." His voice smiled. "You know how they are."

She did know. "I didn't expect you to meet me, Raymond. I just wanted you to know."

"Of course. Will you call me when you get back?"

"I'll call you."

"All right, then. Take care of yourself, dear. And . . . God bless you."

God bless me, indeed, she had thought all the way to the airport and until they took off. God bless me for being a fool and an idiot and a little white mouse on a treadmill; white because she was turning gray fast. God had better bless her— He had stood between them long enough. She was glad she was on this plane. You had to draw the line somewhere. You had to stand up and say, "No!" sometime. Not that it really mattered; a few hours' difference, that's all, and she'd still be home that day. It wasn't as though she were giving him up, either. She'd call him and see him when she got back and then, all over again, there'd be no saying "No" to him. If she only had the strength not to call him, not to see him.

He was the only one she thought of when she came home last night and saw the wire. She had to talk to him, she had to have his shoulder. Even though it was late, she had called his office.

"No, Mr. Oliver is gone for the day."

"Do you know where I can reach him?"

"At home, Miss Watson."

That snippy little smart-aleck secretary of his: "At home, Miss Watson." Well, she had every right to recognize her voice; she had called him often enough. But the girl didn't have to be so blatant about it. The indignities you had to endure sometimes. She had toyed with the idea of calling him at home; just toyed because she knew she wouldn't do it. There were laws governing illicit relationships, too; one was that you never, never called your married lover at home. Even though his wife knew about you, even though she had known about you for years, you just didn't do it. Once he entered the sacred precincts, he was departed from you until the next day or the next week and no matter what happened—whether your mother died or you almost died—you didn't call him.

Why did she keep thinking about him? It was almost indecent, going home to her dead mother. She looked out of her window. Boston was fading down and away from her. A world full of people, a world full of things, a world, and all she could

65

think about was Raymond Oliver. There must be something the matter with her. No one in their right minds permitted anyone to eat their lives. She wished she had someone sitting in the seat beside her; someone to make conversation with, someone to make her stop thinking about him.

Had she forgotten to pack anything? She had taken one dress and the dark suit she had on. She couldn't remember packing. It wouldn't surprise her, when she got home, to find she had forgotten half her things: handkerchiefs or stockings or her eye cream. She thought bitterly about the eye cream. When you realized you were racing into forty, you bought items like eye creams and the other hopefuls. You knew in your heart they didn't do any good but you used them as amulets to fight off the wrinkles and hold on to what you had left. It wasn't bad enough being in love with a married man, you had to worry about holding him, too. Of course, you liked to think you were the only other woman in a man's life but even one other led to another. Why did men have to stay so damned young at forty? Why did they have to keep looking so annoyingly fit and ready for anyone else who might come along?

That building there, off to the right, was that Symphony Hall? It did look like it but she couldn't tell. She wasn't an experienced air traveler and from up here so many of the buildings looked alike. Flying wasn't her favorite way of getting places. It never gave her the sensation of traveling; just being delivered. She guessed the concerts would be starting soon. The long wintersful of comforting Saturday nights came back to her now. Those were the early days of it when the hardest thing in the world was to get through a weekend without him. A man was home with his wife and children weekends and you had to find something to do. So she would sit there in the balcony and the music would lose her in time and space. It was like watching and listening to the sea. The stage teemed for her with schools of fish: stringed sardines, lungfish brass and the bassists who rode their sea horses over the wave of a page. Around them the cymbals crashed wild spray and the lone seagull flapped his wings above them. She could forget then for a little while the physical ache she had for him except for the times in the music when the flute and clarinet mated for a duet.

She was patient in those early days. Love was a fever; it burned but it could wait until Monday. It was funny how everyone in the world struggled through their work week, with the heydays of Saturday and Sunday under their noses, while she wallowed in her labors, wishing there were something she could do to bring back the six-day week. It was a labor of love with her and because she was young she could become properly incensed at the jokes people sometimes made about bosses and their secretaries. It had lasted for two wonderful years and then, one night, in a hotel room, it had ended abruptly.

They were smoking, wishing they had something to eat but not wanting to go out and leave each other, even together. And the telephone rang. It screamed at them, took a breath and screamed at them again.

She said, "Good Lord! Who's that?"

Raymond flushed. "Does anyone know you're here?"

"No, of course not."

They listened to it while it went on.

He dashed out his cigarette. "Maybe it's a mistake. Maybe they're ringing the wrong number."

"It might be just the desk calling about something."

They both sounded silly.

"What shall I do, Raymond?"

He thought for a moment while it jangled them. "I guess you'd better answer it."

She lifted the receiver.

"Yes?"

"Miss Watson?"

"Yes."

"This is *Mrs.* Oliver. Would you be good enough to tell my husband I'm waiting for him downstairs?"

She put down the phone without answering.

"Who was it, Helen? . . . Helen!"

If she had only called her something: a tramp, a slut, anything.

"It's your wife, Raymond."

"Marjorie!" His face was shattered. "Oh, God!"

"She's waiting for you downstairs."

He stopped just long enough to absorb the blow. "How did she know? She must have followed us . . . or had someone follow us." He choked under his necktie. "And I have to face her down there."

"Darling, I'm so sorry. . . . Would it do any good if I went down or went down with you?"

"Don't be ridiculous." He took a deep breath. "Well, good night, Helen. I'll see you in the morning."

She had left the job with him the next morning. She went to work for another lecture agency, a bigger one than Raymond's where the authors were better known and more in demand because they wrote books that had more four-letter words in them and used them more often. Here she became a minor executive and handled some of the clients herself. There was more money, more glamour—she even had to travel a little—but no Raymond Oliver; not enough of him, anyway. She still saw him but it was only once or twice a week or, sometimes, not at all in a week. She stopped going to the concerts; they didn't do her any good any more. They were fine when she had only a Saturday and Sunday to do away with but when you didn't know how many days, and their affair settled down to fitful meetings in her apartment where they could only snatch at each other for a few hours, the concerts failed her.

She went out with other men but she wasn't much good to anyone else. She was quiet, moody, unappreciative, unresponsive. She had no patience for people. She stopped going out. She stayed at home, waiting, waiting for Raymond to call her. Then she entered a period of sleeplessness and began taking pills to cure it but they left her so groggy she couldn't work the next day. So she saved the pills for the weekends and took enough to sleep through most of the forty-eight hours. He found her that way one Sunday when he managed to get away from the house.

"Helen, for God's sake, what are you doing to yourself?"

He got her out of bed and took her out for coffee.

She came to after a while but she was still drugged enough not to care too much what she said.

"Didn't you know, Raymond? This is how I go away over weekends."

He was plainly upset. "You've got to stop it, Helen. You can't go on this way."

"I can, too. I've been doing it for a long time." She took out her mirror. "Excuse me, darling, for looking like hell. What are you doing out on a Sunday? Did she give you a pass?"

"She's out visiting with the children." He took her hand. "Helen, you've got to listen to me."

"I'm listening. I always have."

"Well, then start taking care of yourself; if not for your sake, then for mine."

"I do everything for you, Raymond. Even the sleeping pills are for you because I can't sleep without you."

"Why don't you go to a doctor?"

"I don't need a doctor, dear. I need you."

He turned away. "Let's not go into that again."

"Sometimes, when I'm sitting home alone waiting for that damned telephone to ring, I ask myself, 'Why did I have to fall in love with a Catholic? Why couldn't it have been a Moslem or a Jew or a Holy Roller?'"

His patience began to show a little. "I've tried to make you understand, Helen."

"I know, a hundred times: no divorce, the Church won't allow it. Church is mother and father, can't disown mother and father."

But she had disowned her own mother and father for him.

69

She didn't go home any more. She hardly ever wrote. And on their fiftieth anniversary, when she should have been there celebrating with them, she was sleeping a weekend with him.

She pushed the coffee away from her and stood up. "I'm tired, Raymond, I'm going home to bed."

He rose, protesting. "But, Helen, I've got most of the day."

"Sorry, dear. I won't be needing you today. I'm sleeping with a couple of pills."

There had been times when she could hate him like that and push him away from her. That day, and others like it, she wished there was something she could do that would hurt him, really hurt him. In those unreasonable bitter moments, she thought of many things but the one that appealed to her most was to give him a social disease; go out and sleep with some horror and then sleep with him and give it to him. She veered from that to the other extreme. She'd stop ranting about him and his Church long enough to ask herself why it couldn't do as much for her as it was doing for him. If it could let him have his cake and eat it, too, there might be something in it for her; resignation would be enough.

She went to a few masses. They were impressive but alien. She'd sit in the dark corners of a cathedral, trying to absorb the quiet holiness, waiting for the spirit and the understanding to seek her out. But all she felt was a sense of rejection. It was too far a cry from her simple Congregationalism. Raymond's church was too mysterious, too heavy with ritual, too cluttered with trappings. It had seemed to her that you had to push aside too many veils to find God.

So she had given up her small attempt at religion and stuck with the sleeping pills. It was the honest way; there was too much horse trading with the good Lord, anyway, and He must be pretty sick of it. A sleeping pill was effective and you asked nothing of it but oblivion; no harps, no ambrosia. Maybe therein lay the crux of the conflict between science and religion; all wrapped up in one little sleeping pill . . . *The sleeping pills!* She had forgotten them. She was sure of it. If she

70

could remember packing anything, it would be the pills. Now, what was she going to do? There wouldn't be anything like a sleeping pill in the house. Her poor mother had never used them. She and Pop were simple people who worked hard and slept hard. Bertram? He wouldn't have enough imagination for a sedative. Evie? Evie was too normal: married, children. The only one who held out any hope was young Jubel. If actors were anything like authors, Jubel might very well eat the things. But he was so young and he was a man. Well, if worse came to worst, she wouldn't sleep. The whole business annoyed her, anyhow. Why should she be so concerned with sleeping? It was becoming a fetish with her. Here she was, going home at last. Her mother was dead. She should be wrapped in sorrow. Her whole life, all that was childhood and mother to her, should be streaming back to her. She should feel guilt and remorse; God knows she hadn't been a good daughter. And she should be worried about Pop, too. But all she could think about was sleep and Raymond, sleep and Raymond and they were both one and the same because they both meant bed.

Couldn't she think about anything else? What about her kitten, for instance? Wasn't he getting too old to be kept? He was a shade over a year, now, and she usually gave them away before a year. If she had had the time, she would have arranged to give him to someone instead of leaving him with the vet until she got back. This one, Tinker, was really cute; it would bother her a little to give him away. But she couldn't stand having an old cat around and she'd get over it just as soon as she got herself another kitten. She did have a special feeling about Tinker, though. She'd never forget what he did to Raymond that night last winter; Raymond wouldn't, either. He was drowsing on the couch and Tinker, who had a habit of jumping up out of nowhere, suddenly leaped, and landed on him. Raymond yelled.

"That damned cat of yours! He jumped right on my face. How am I going to explain these scratches to my wife?"

She laughed at it now, although it didn't seem funny at the

71

time. She supposed that was one of the oddities of life: that something scary or tragic at one time on the ground in the city of Boston could be amusing six months later in the air as your plane circled over New York. That was perhaps the only hurt Raymond had had in their affair and it was accidental and not of her own doing. It seemed to her, in her forced perspective, that the hurts had been all hers, that even in their outside experiences—the ones that had nothing to do with their relationship—he was always failing her. This morning, on the phone, when she had told him her mother had died, all she could get out of him was an "Oh, my dear, I'm sorry." She had waited through a night to talk to him, to tell him, to have his shoulder, and that's all she could get out of him. Of course, she had wanted him to drop everything and come running to her but no, he had authors in his office. Damn him and his authors and his office. When he had come to her to save himself and his authors and his office, when he needed money to keep all of them going, she hadn't failed him. She gave him three thousand dollars, every penny she had, and the things she had kept going kept him away from her.

The plane touched the earth, skipped the rope of gravity a few times and rolled to a stop near the Administration Building. If she had those three thousand dollars now, she might never go back to Boston. She might stay away completely and be done with him. That was the only way but it took a long time to save three thousand dollars when you stopped caring about tomorrow.

They picked up passengers and she drew a man. He was about fifty with bright cheeks that looked as though they had been pinched and kissed red by young children.

"Hope you're not going to mind a fellow passenger," he said.

"Not at all."

He looked over the plane and the people, and approved of everything. "It's a wonderful day for flying. Did you come down from Boston?"

72

"Yes, I did."

"How are the winds upstairs?"

"I hadn't noticed any."

"Fine. I knew it."

They took off and he admired the skill of the pilot, exclaimed over the mechanical progress of the century and began pointing out the landmarks of the great city; the thick rows of apartment houses particularly interested him.

"Seems hardly possible, doesn't it, there should be humanity in all that brick and steel. Funny thing about airplanes, you see everything from them and you see nothing. Cities and towns and plowed fields but you don't see the people who made them. Eerie, isn't it? One person has more substance for me than all that stuff. But it's amazing . . . amazing."

He laughed at himself. "You won't have to take very much of me. I'm going only to Harrisburg."

"I am, too. And I don't mind your talking at all." She didn't. The man had a refreshing quality. He talked what he thought without seeming to think about it. He didn't plant words, expecting to grow situations. "I think you're very interesting."

The man glowed. He seemed to swell with pleasure and he tugged at his vest to hide it. "You know, that's about the nicest thing you could say to me. I've always loved people. They're about the best things there are in the world, and I like to be . . . well, among the best of the best."

"I think that's very nice."

"You know," he went on quickly, "I think you're lovely looking, charming. That gray hair of yours . . . it's beautiful."

She laughed. "You didn't have to say that."

"I wanted to."

"All right . . . What are you going to Harrisburg for, business?"

"No, just visiting my grandchildren. I'm a widower, you know; lost my wife five years ago." He looked at her hand. "You're not married, are you?"

73

"No."

"I didn't think so; at least, I was pretty sure you didn't have any children."

"How did you know?"

"A little theory of mine. Childless women have a wonderful childlike quality about them."

She thought about that, recalling all the childless women she knew. There was something to what he said, she decided; they did have a childlike quality about them. In many of them she could see the brat but he wouldn't know about that.

"Your family in Harrisburg?"

"About twenty miles away. I'm going home for a funeral. My mother died yesterday."

He was stricken. His sympathy was genuine and comforting; more than she had gotten out of Raymond.

The trip went quickly. When they said good-bye at the airport, he gave her his card.

"Please stop off at New York on the way back and call me. We'll have dinner together. I do want to know you better."

She said she would and left him. She thought about him, driving the rest of the way to the house on the bus. He was a charming man; certainly good and obviously substantial. A woman might do very well to cultivate him. A man like that breathed comfort and security and even a chance for someone to love him. She opened her bag for his card. It wasn't there. She went through the bag several times. Then she looked in her pockets. No card. Funny, she thought, she knew he had given it to her, she remembered taking it. She wondered what could have happened to it.

They had come home, all of them. He had told Agnew they would. A man knows his own children. They might be grown, they might be men and women with children of their own, with lives and problems of their own, but in a time of crisis they knew their way home.

He looked around the table. They were all there: Bertram and his wife, Ella, Helen, young Jubel and Evie, even Evie's little ones. The only one missing was Neal, and Jubel could understand why Neal couldn't make it. After all, when a man had a business to run——especially a twenty-four-hour business like an auto court——you couldn't expect him to shut down. Amy would have understood that, and Amy would have been pleased for today.

"Wasn't it nice that all the neighbors could come, Pop?"

"Yes, Evie. I was a little proud of it. Seemed to me the whole town was there."

The whole town and even folks from other towns: distant cousins and old friends who stood for parts of your life you had almost forgotten, faces like creased pages that needed spreading out to be remembered.

"Pass the potatoes, Pop, will you?"

"Wait, Jubel, I'll get you some more." Ella took the dish and started for the kitchen.

"Better add a little cream to them," Evie called after her. "What do you mean, a little? A lot."

It was good to see young Jubel with such an appetite. He was a puny eater as a boy. Amy always had to keep after him. It would do her heart good to watch him now. But he was still thin and he had all that height to fill. Bertram, on the other hand, didn't eat very much—just picked at his food from time to time—but he had a well-fed heaviness about him. Maybe it was a matter of disposition or just something simple and old fashioned like having a good wife to feed and take care of him. It might be all right for a young man to live alone, especially a young actor man with his uncertain hours and seasons, and it must be fine to have the good friends that young Jubel had . . . that man, for instance, who drove him right to the house all the way from New York. It was too bad he didn't have time to stop by. Friends like that had great value. He was sure Helen had many friends of the same high calibre. Of course, Helen came home by plane and bus but he knew there were people who would have been glad to drive her home. A girl like Helen, so attractive and well-dressed and living for so long in a big city like Boston must have many many friends.

It was odd in a way how the years had paired the different children. You'd think that Evie and young Jubel, because they had always seemed to him so much alike, not only in looks but temperament too, would have found the same kind of levels; either both married and settled or both having careers for themselves. But Evie had her family and young Jubel his acting. The same with Helen and Bertram, but somehow it didn't work out that way; even to the point of traveling, with Evie and Bertram arriving by car. Poor Evie, it had been a trial for her. The others had all been home by Saturday evening. First, Bertram and Ella came late in the morning, then Helen after noon and young Jubel just before dark. It was like having the children born all over again, even if the order was a little mixed up. They all knew Evie would be late; she had much farther to travel, but when she hadn't arrived by late Sunday afternoon, he began to get a little worried.

76

"You don't think anything could have happened, do you, Bertram?"

They had been out on the porch; Helen sitting on a chair beside him, young Jubel on the top step and Bertram moving restlessly around. It was one of those moments when the tap of condolence callers had been turned off.

"I'm sure I don't know. Hillbillies take their time. She may get in by next week."

Young Jubel's head had snapped up at that. "Evie's no hillbilly."

"She's married to one and she's been down there long enough to be one."

"Oh, Bertram, don't be a fool."

He turned to Helen. "Pop asked me a question and I answered him. I don't see why you have to stick your nose into it."

"Do I have a nice nose, Pop?"

"Of course, you have, Helen."

"Then it should help whatever it sticks into, shouldn't it?"

He had to laugh at that, young Jubel, too; everyone but Bertram.

"Don't worry, Pop, she'll be along. It's a big trip. I'm watching the road."

"I don't understand it. She must have received the telegram Friday night and here it is almost Sunday night. If she weren't coming, we would have heard from her."

"Evie's coming, Pop. You can bet on that. She'd come if she had to walk."

Bertram snorted. "Chances are that's exactly what she's doing. That old jalopy of theirs couldn't make the trip."

"What do you want from Evie? Why don't you let her get here first before you light into her?"

"Bertram's just so anxious to see her, Helen."

"I don't want anything from Evie. I don't want anything from anybody. She just ought to be here, that's all. And if she had married the kind of man she should have married, you

77

wouldn't have to be worrying whether there were four wheels on her car."

"We can't all afford limousines like yours."

"I don't have a limousine. I have a car that gets me where I want to go. That's the least a girl can get out of a marriage; a car that gets her where she wants to go."

"You've got a lot to learn about girls. I'm sure Ella must be very happy."

"Don't you worry about Ella."

It was strange to listen to them talk that way. They were grown now but it wasn't much different from what it used to be when they were youngsters.

"I don't think we ought to argue this way, children. We're all waiting for Evie, and we're all a little worried about her. Let's not be so upset that we lose track of what's upsetting us."

Young Jubel laughed in open admiration. "Ain't he a great one! Pop, you're all right." He had to, just had to, get up and hug the old man by the shoulders.

Bertram moved away from them. "You're trying to make it look as though I'm against Evie. I'm the only one for her. She's too good to be tied up with a cracker. Mark my words, some day she's going to be sorry, if she isn't already, and sorrier that she has two kids to hold her to him, too."

Helen was exasperated. "Oh, really, Bertram! Why don't you go inside and help Ella peel a potato or something?"

He had looked her up and down. "It wouldn't do you a bit of harm to help Ella."

"I don't cook."

"I suppose it's beneath you."

"It isn't beneath me. I'm not up to it. I just help with the dishes."

He went into the house and less than five minutes later Evie drove up. The car pulled up in front, seemed to lean against the curbstone and expire. Young Jubel leaped down the steps, vaulted the fence and began tearing open the car doors. He was leaning into kisses when Helen joined him and then he was

78

handing out the children. Evie came last, looking tired, but when she saw him standing on the porch, she ran from young Jubel.

"Pa, are you all right?"

"Of course, I'm all right. We were worried about you."

She had hugged him and kissed him. "I'm all right, Pop. It just took so long, so long to get home."

It had taken them all a long time but here they were, sitting around the dining-room table, looking as natural and belonging as though they had never been away. It was even possible to think that Amy was somewhere out there in the kitchen and that she'd be back in a minute. But Amy was always around the house. He'd look up and think he'd see her standing in the doorway or hear her calling to him from upstairs. There were shadows and sounds and even shafts of light that were Amy. And Pitch would stare at nothing, start at silence and sniff at the odorless air with his cold wet nose. Now the cat was perched on the sideboard in his Egyptian pose, his paws tucked under him, his ears pointed, listening to the talk around the table, his golden eyes nodding smiles to the family. He would miss them, too.

"I suppose," he said rather haltingly, "I suppose you'll all be going home tomorrow."

He thought they looked hurt and surprised, he didn't mean them to be.

"Oh, no, Pop." Evie reached across the table for his hand. "We'll be here for a few days." She looked at her brothers and sister.

Bertram was quick. "Not me. I've got to get home. I was thinking of leaving tonight."

"Bertram, we're not driving at night."

He looked at Ella with the intimate hostility of a husband. "You know I've got to see Weston tomorrow."

"It can wait."

He turned back to his food. "Then you'll have to get up at six in the morning."

79

It lay there like some untidy animal on its back, twitching until it expired quietly.

Helen pushed it away. "I'm sorry, Pop, but I have a job. I do have to get back."

"Sure, you do. No one has to stay. I just asked."

Young Jubel cleared his throat. "Of course, it's the season for me. Things are starting up again after a long summer." He paused, laughed out loud at himself and made a "pooh" with his hand. "But what's a day or two."

Evie kissed him. "Good boy!"

"Mommy, are we going to stay with Grandpa Jubel forever?"

"No, Jinny, just for a few more days."

The little girl turned to her grandfather. "You're going to be all alone here when we go home, aren't you, Grandpa?"

"Yes, dear, all alone. I will have my friends, though: Agnew, next door, and all his family and Mr. and Mrs. Peters and . . . oh, all the neighbors."

"But they won't live with you."

"No, dear, just visit. Agnew's coming in after a while and we'll sit and talk."

The child started to say something more but her mother quieted her by patting her head.

"Dear, wouldn't you like to walk down to the store for an ice-cream cone with Grandpa Jubel? . . . Pop, you wouldn't mind, would you?"

"No, I don't mind. I think it's a very good idea, don't you, Jinny? A little walk after dinner is always good."

"Now, you have that twenty-five cents that Aunt Helen gave you, Jinny. You buy yourself a cone and one for Grandpa, or maybe a cigar."

"That won't be necessary, will it dear? Young ladies never have to pay their own way, especially when they're out with their grandfathers."

He took her hand and they walked out through the living

room. Evie went with them just far enough to look at the baby who was sleeping on the couch.

When she came back, she said it. "Well, what are we going to do? We can't sneak off, one by one, and leave him here alone."

"Why not? What else is there to do?" Bertram was creasing the tablecloth with the blunt side of his knife.

"Why, you wouldn't do that to a dog, Bertram. It isn't human, it isn't decent. It's just 'I don't give a damn.' "

"I agree with you, Evie. It's been bothering the hell out of me ever since I got here."

Bertram looked at his brother. "You want to take care of him?"

"I'm having a little trouble taking care of myself."

"You, Evie?"

"God, I wish I could. I haven't even got the money to get home. The kids ate milk and frankfurters all the way." She shook her head viciously. "Oh, hell!"

Bertram twisted his mouth and nose contemptuously. "There you are. It's always the ones who talk the loudest who can do the least."

"I haven't said anything at all, Bertram, but neither have you. What can you do?"

"Nothing, Helen. Ella and I haven't even been able to afford a child. What do you expect me to do?"

Young Jubel slapped the table. "Let's all show our bank books."

"That's not very funny, Jubel."

He shrugged. "I'm sorry, Evie, but this isn't very constructive." He turned to his sister-in-law. "Ella, you're just enough in and out of this to say something helpful."

She shook her head. "I don't know. It's tragic. That poor old man, all alone . . ."

He wanted to say, "Thank you very much, Mrs. Bertram Watson, for your great contribution," but he didn't.

"Look," Evie said, "we're four of us, all grown, all men and

81

women. He raised us, took care of us, all of us, and all four of us can't take care of one of him." She turned to Bertram. "You've been here since Saturday. Did you ask how things were with him? Did you ask him once how he was fixed?"

"I never ask people how they're fixed; they might tell me."

"Your father isn't 'people.' He's your father."

"I think Bertram puts it badly, Evie. I've been here since Saturday and I didn't ask him. Helen didn't ask him, either. For one thing, I guess we've always taken it for granted that things were all right with Pop. He never had to come to any of us." He stopped, sighed and looked down at his empty plate. "And then, I guess, there's the business of guilt. I think we're all a little ashamed. He's so proud of us. I can't tell him I've been out of work for two months. I can't tell him I had to hitch a ride down here. Jesus, I just can't!"

He looked around at them as though he had made his confessional and was waiting for them to join him but Bertram wouldn't have it that way.

"I don't have to ask the old man how he's doing. I can see for myself. He's getting along. I've been over the house. He's got a mess of junk here, that's all, but he manages to sell some of the stuff once in a while. The rooms are cluttered with it. I doubt whether the whole lot is worth more than a couple of hundred. Of course, if he was a businessman . . ." He shrugged off the whole matter.

Helen pushed herself away from the table. "All this is so much nonsense. It isn't a matter of money alone, which we don't have anyhow. But if we gave Pop a million dollars and left him here alone, what would we be doing for him? Just buying our way out of our responsibilities, that's all. The point is, who wants to live here with him or who wants to take him home with them?"

She walked around the table. No one answered her.

Finally, young Jubel rose and took her arm.

"Helen, you're the only one here with any liquid assets. Take me down to a bar and get me drunk, will you?"

82

vii

Bars were shipshape places, young Jubel said. You walked into them and it was like stepping on board. There was a square-rigged air about them, a scrubbed-down neatness, an orderliness and a kind of damp, yet water tight, discipline that was handed out along with the drinks by the white coated skipper who ran the show. Close the bulkhead behind you and you shut out the world. You chose your course and your sea —Scotch, Bourbon or rye—and you sailed away on it.

"I wouldn't know about that," Helen said. "I'm not much on bars or ships." She looked over the tavern. "Seems more like an amber bead to me, a round, glistening amber bead."

Jubel followed her eyes. He could see what she meant. The globes over the lights were amber, the bar, the booths, the tables were brownish, the walls yellowish. The whole effect could be amber if you had had enough muds in your eye and they had.

She held up her glass of rye and water. "Even this."

He clinked it with his own. "Even this."

"Yes, sir, Helen, you sure gave us hell back there."

"I gave me hell, too. We stink, just stink, all of us." She took off her hat and laid it on the table; it seemed to have a tendency to lean. "Nothing personal, of course. Maybe as people we're all right but as children we just stink."

"What about people?"

"What about them?"

"What's the difference between children and people?"

"Two different animals. But I've got a theory."

"What's that?"

"Did you ever stop to think that being born is like slavery?"

"No, not exactly."

"Well, it is and even if you love your masters, you've got to get away from them. You have to fly on your own. When you're old enough, you start buying your freedom even if you don't know what you're doing. As soon as you start giving money home, you're buying your way out."

"That's very interesting, very interesting." It was growing on him.

"It's like anything else if you say it fast and don't think about it too much."

She waved at the bartender who brought them two more. There had been a twenty-dollar bill on the table when they started; now they had watered it down to two fives and change.

"Now, wait a minute, Helen." Jubel's gestures were liquid. "I won't let you disparage yourself that way. You just made a brilliant statement. That business about slavery . . . brilliant."

"Are you a good actor, Jubel?"

He laughed. "I think I'm the best goddam actor in the world. So far, I'm a lonely man."

"Pop always said you were doing fine."

"Pop always said *you* were doing fine."

They smiled.

"You've got all the equipment. You look like one, you talk like one, you even act like one."

"Sure. There's only one trouble, though. My fate hasn't caught up to me."

"Why don't you try Hollywood?"

"Hollywood. The land of the outstretched palm and me with

84

my hands in my pockets." He shook his head sadly and diddled a finger in a pool of wetness. "No, they've got to ask for you out there. You can't go looking."

She patted his hand. "Don't worry, they'll come looking for you."

He shrugged. "Ah, we'll put a three-cent stamp on it and send it home."

"What does that mean?"

"Army expression." He took a drink. "Funny thing about army expressions, they don't mean the same out here. Now, that stamp thing. Whenever one of the Joes would start bitching, someone would say, 'Aw, put a three-cent stamp on it and send it home.' It doesn't mean the same now. It used to have significance. I remember a kid in the outfit. I don't even remember his name. We were in Germany, Aachen. Never forget that town . . . Well, anyway, this kid got hit. When I got to him, he said, 'I'm hurt, Jubel, bad.' I could see that he was but I said the usual, 'Aw, put a three-cent stamp on it and send it home.' The kid was going fast. He said, 'I guess you'll have to put that three-cent stamp on me, Jubel.' "

He stopped and gulped. "But you know the funny thing about that, Helen? We couldn't put a three-cent stamp on him and send him home. The poor bastard never had a home: no mother, no father, no home, no nothing." He blew his nose. "I often think of that kid . . . Does that story have a point, Helen? Does it? I often think about it."

"I don't know. Maybe if I was sober I could tell you. Save it and tell it to me some other time."

"Can't do it. Think about it only when I'm drunk."

"You're not drunk. You're just drinking."

He hit the table with his fist. "Wait a minute. I've got it! . . . But let me get it straight. Yeah, yeah. It's this way, Helen: I'm sad for this kid."

"What kid?"

"The kid in Aachen."

"Oh, yeah. Go ahead."

"I'm sitting here, crying my eyes out because he didn't have a home, no mother or father we could send him to. And here I am being sad because I *do* have a home and a father." He stopped and shook his head. "No, that's not it, is it, Helen. It's not the same."

"No, it's not the same."

"Well, it was a good try."

"On the other hand, it's almost the same. The sadness is the same. The difference is the reasons: diametrically opposite."

"What do you mean?"

"You're sad for him because he didn't have a home. You're sad for yourself because you do have a home. It's like being sad because you've got a wife or you haven't got a wife, or because you have money or you haven't got money. Relativity."

"Exactly. You know, Helen, you've got a hell of a good mind. That's the point: relativity. That's almost as good as what you said about slavery. Brilliant. Brilliant."

"All right, it's brilliant. What good does it do? Does it take care of Pop? Does it make it easier for him or for Bertram or Evie or us?"

"Poor Evie. The kid's having a tough time."

"Maybe not any more than you or me or Bertram."

"Maybe, but it shows on her. It doesn't seem right for her to be stuck off away down there. Evie likes people; she's alive. She has no business running an auto court."

"You sound just like Bertram."

"I don't sound like Bertram; our motives are different. All Bertram cares about is money. If Evie had money, Bertram wouldn't care where she was or who she was married to as long as he could borrow some of it once in a while . . . Wave at the bartender. I'm thirsty."

She waved at the bartender. "Why doesn't anyone feel sorry for Bertram?"

"Bertram does. I feel sorry for Ella."

"Oh, you. Every man feels sorry for every other man's wife."

"That go for women, too?"

86

"Sure . . . Make it the same, bartender . . . And it doesn't pay to be sorry for anybody. If they don't like what they are bad enough, they'll change it."

"You, too?"

"Especially me."

"How about Pop?"

She thought about Pop for a minute. "That's the trouble with talk, Jubel."

She opened her bag for a mirror. "Jesus, look at me." She took out lipstick. "I can remember when I thought that stuff was sinful. Now, it's sinful to be without it." She made up her mouth quickly without fussing.

"You can always tell a woman by the way she puts on her lipstick; clue to character. I don't know what it shows exactly but if you like it, you might like her."

She snapped her bag shut and looked up abruptly. "I suppose I'm the logical one to take care of Pop, aren't I?"

"You? Why you more than I or Bertram or Evie?"

"Because I'm a woman and I'm alone; no obvious ties. Just a job and I can give that up and come home and keep house for Pop."

"You can't keep house."

"That's beside the point."

"Pop wouldn't let you."

"Also beside the point."

"Now, wait a minute, Helen. You can't give up your life that way."

She took his hand and held onto it. "Talk me out of it, Jubel. Please talk me out of it. I can't, you know I can't. I've got to have a life of my own."

"Of course you have, baby. No one expects you to do that."

"I expect it of myself. That's the miserable, rotten part of it and I'm just not up to it. Besides, I couldn't stand that cat of Pop's. I hate old cats."

He let her cry for a few minutes. "We all feel the same; even Bertram, I suppose. But there's a difference between feeling

87

and doing. Hell, if anyone ought to stay home with Pop, it's me. I haven't even got a job."

"No, Jubel, you can't. This is your time. You can't waste it."

"Okay, that settles it. We talked each other out of it. Let's have a drink." This time he waved at the bartender. "Why aren't you married, Helen?"

She wiped her eyes. "Because I'm in love. I've been in love for years, damn it."

"Married?"

"Not only married. A Catholic, too."

"Hopeless case."

"You're telling me. Only sometimes I feel I'm the hopeless case."

"Here. Drink this up. You'll feel better."

"Jubel, do you have any sleeping pills? I haven't had a wink in two nights. I left mine home."

"As bad as that?"

"As bad and worse. And it won't get any better because I won't let it."

"Drink your drink."

She drank her drink. "Why don't *you* get married, Jubel?"

"I've got news for you, Helen. I *am* married."

"You're not!"

"I am."

"You're drunk."

"Maybe, but I'm also married."

"I don't believe it. How long?"

"Six months and four days."

"Jubel, why didn't you tell us?"

He put a finger to his lips. "It's a secret."

"For heaven's sake, why?"

"She doesn't want anyone to know. She's ashamed of me. Doesn't want to tell her father she married a broken-down actor."

"She's got a nerve. Who does she think she is?"

88

"Toby Sheffield, that's who. Her old man has a million dollars worth of million dollars. Filthy."

"That's still no excuse."

"It is for her."

"But why didn't you tell us? We would have been glad to know."

"Couldn't. Promised not to. Secret all around . . . I feel so lousy about Mom not knowing."

"You didn't lie to her, did you?"

"Lie? What for?"

"She knew you were an actor."

"Listen, she knew everything. She knew I was an actor. She knew I didn't have a dime. We had it all out the other night. We're through, finished. I am, anyhow."

"But she still loves you."

"In her own peculiar way."

"And you?"

"Look, Helen, what do you expect me to do? Give up my work because it's not, as the French say, *recherché?* Everybody can't be a millionaire. There have to be some poor people who . . ."

"Does she know about Mom?"

"Huh? . . . No. I found the wire after I took her home."

"And you haven't called her, told her anything?"

"I told you I was through, finished."

"You go right to that phone and call her now."

"Won't do it."

"Then I will. What's her number?"

"Now, wait a minute, Helen. This is none of your business."

"It certainly is. I won't sit here and see a marriage go on the rocks over some foolishness. She's your wife, Jubel. You've got to tell her. You should have brought her down here with you."

He had to laugh at that. "You don't know Toby. I'll tell you what, go ahead and call her. Tell her you're my sister and tell her what's happened. Then see what she says."

He wrote Toby's name and number on a match cover and

89

pushed it over to Helen. She picked up all her change from the table and carried it to the telephone booth. He finished his drink, and hers too, before she came back.

"You're a fool, Jubel. That girl was worried sick about you."

"What did you tell her?"

"I told her what happened, that's all. I didn't let on that I knew a thing."

"What did she say?"

"She wanted to come right down. Even asked me about planes. I told her it wasn't necessary. You'd be home in a day or two."

"Yeah."

"Now, when you get home, you call her first thing. Do you hear me?"

"I hear you."

"And get this foolishness settled."

"Helen, you won't say anything to anyone about this, will you?"

"Not until you tell me to."

"Thanks. I'll try to clear it up somehow; one way or the other. Can I call someone for you?"

"A call won't do *me* any good."

"Then let's have another drink."

"No, let's go out and find me a sleeping pill. I'm going to worry about Pop all night if I don't close my eyes."

viii

"Pop said she died here, sitting right at the table." Evie wiped a dinner plate and put it down on the spot. "Just as though she were falling asleep."

Ella turned down the water in the sink; the splashing was almost a joyous sound. "It couldn't have been a better way as long as it had to be. I hope it happens to me like that."

Evie went around to the side of the sink so that she could look at her. Ella was wrist-high in suds.

"You're absolutely silly to talk that way."

"Why? Don't you ever think of it, Evie?"

"Never."

"I'm glad. You must be happy."

"Or busy or just not built that way, I guess."

"Maybe it's a family trait. I don't think Bertram ever does, or Jubel either. I'm not sure about Helen, though. Are you?"

"I don't know. I'm not sure I know Helen too well any more. She looks wonderful, doesn't she?"

"Wonderful. I suppose city life and having an important job and not being a housewife . . . I suppose it all helps, doesn't it, Evie?"

"Sure. We could be as glamorous as all hell if we didn't have to slave over a sink."

"You should have gone with them."

91

"And leave you here with the dishes alone?"

"I wouldn't have minded."

Evie shuttled back and forth between the sink and the table, building her stacks of dried dishes. "No. Besides, it isn't proper for a mother of two children to go out and get drunk. But I hope they do. I hope they get plastered. They'll feel better."

"It won't do any good."

"That sounds as though you should have gone."

Ella laughed. "I can just see Bertram giving his approval to that."

"Does he have to?"

"No, but it helps. You ought to know that."

"Yes. Aren't they the beasts? Where is Bertram?"

"Snooping around. You know him. He probably thinks your mother left him a fortune under an old mattress cover."

"What is the matter with him?"

"Bertram?" Ella turned around. "He's a man without a nickel who doesn't want a nickel. He wants a million dollars."

"Must be a devil to live with."

"Sometimes." She went back to the dishes. "I hate him for some things, I try to understand him for others and I love him for what he was or could be if he only gave himself a chance."

"Ain't it the truth."

"But I imagine you know Bertram pretty well. People don't change much over the years."

Evie opened the cupboards. "I wish I could remember how Mom kept things. It all seems different. I guess the plates go here. If we hadn't used every dish in the house, I'd have something to go by. Well, I suppose it doesn't matter."

She came back to Ella. "I don't think I know Bertram pretty well, or Helen or young Jubel. I don't think they know me. You know each other as children. You know that one's blond and one's dark and the color of their eyes and their birthdays and which like showers and which baths and who you like best. You know them as children but that's not beginning to know

92

them. Why, I look at Jinny, my own Jinny, and I ask myself what kind of a girl, what kind of a woman, she's going to grow into, and I don't know, Ella, I don't know."

"You don't have to worry about Jinny. She'll be all right."

"It isn't that. Jinny will be what she has to be. It's just how little we really know our own brothers and sisters, our parents, even our own children. Sometimes it bothers the hell out of me."

"I guess the only ones we really know are our husbands."

"Why? Because we sleep with them?"

"Sleep with them, eat with them, the whole day and night business of living with and without them for years."

"And then wake up some day and discover you don't know them at all . . . or they don't know you."

"Usually the latter. Don't you know? That's why they say they can't understand us or depend on us or count on us to make up our minds. It isn't that we're so complicated; we're just more human. A man's different. You surround a man with a certain set of circumstances and you know exactly how he'll react because he knows what's expected of him. That's why I wanted to have a family."

"That doesn't do it, Ella. Marriages stuck together by spit and children don't amount to much."

"If they stick together at all, for any reason, it's an accomplishment. Sometimes I think the whole business of staying together depends on how many obstacles to divorce you can accumulate: you stuff this break with children, that one with habits, the other one with possessions . . ."

She stopped herself abruptly. Bertram was coming.

He walked into the kitchen as though he had paced the last step of his cell but he didn't turn around.

"I never saw a house with so much junk in it."

"You can talk to your wife like that, Bertram, but I take exception."

"You know what I'm talking about."

"You never did have much of a sense of humor."

"I can live without it. This place is like a museum, a cheap one."

"No one asked you to take an inventory."

"I was just looking around."

"Well, there's nothing in the sugar bowl. I've already looked."

He colored. "You always did have a quick mouth, Evie."

She went over to him, put her hand on his shoulder. "I'm sorry, Bertram. Let's not get into an argument about nothing. Let's talk about Pop."

"What's there to talk about?"

"You're going home tomorrow. Don't you care what becomes of him?"

"Helen's going home tomorrow, too. Jubel, the day after. You're going home, yourself, in a couple of days."

"But I can't take care of him, Bertram, I can't."

"No one's asking you to. Besides, why should we talk about it? This is Helen's and Jubel's headache, too. You can't let them walk out on it because they have the price of a drink."

"We're the only family ones. We're the only ones with homes."

He walked away from her. "I won't be penalized because I happen to be married. That's all it amounts to; just being married. Why don't you look at it from the other side? We're the ones with the responsibilities. Why should we be expected to take on another one?" He came back to her. "All this is talk, Evie, just talk and what's the good of it? When it's time for you to go home, go home."

"Why can't we talk to Pop? Why can't we ask him what he wants to do?"

"Not me. That's as good as an invitation."

The door bell rang. Bertram peered through the hall as though he could possibly see who was standing on the porch. "Now, who is that?" He started for the door, stopped, turned around and talked to Ella. "And don't forget. We're leaving at six in the morning."

94

The women looked at each other. Evie sat down, the dish towel still in her hand.

"What am I going to do, Ella? I'll be the last one here. Then I'll have to go, and how am I going to leave him?"

Bertram walked to the door thinking: Goddam women! Why do they always have to go sticking their necks out? Talking, talking, when it doesn't do any good to talk. You could always depend on them to make things difficult. Here they were faced with a situation: Mom was gone, Pop was left alone. That was it, that was all of it, without tears, without slop. The old man had a house, a business. No matter how good or bad they were, he had them. What was all the fuss about? Sure, he was going to be alone. But what was so wrong in being alone? A lot better, lots of times, than having a houseful of family and a houseful of trouble. Why couldn't Evie and Helen see it that way and leave it alone? Why did they have to go wetting it down with tears and sentimentality? As far as young Jubel was concerned, he was just blowing with the wind. If the girls were sensible, there wouldn't be a peep out of him.

He opened the door. It was Agnew, his father's friend.

"Evening, Bertram. Your father in?"

"No, but he'll be back in a little while. He's down to the store."

He had to step back into the hall to let Agnew in. God, he thought, how do people let themselves get so fat. It made him think of an elephant walking with the hide jiggling. You had to watch yourself; sitting on a porch in a small town, rocking back and forth, would do it. Or just being happy and not giving a damn about pushing anywhere.

"Left my dog home this time, Bertram. Wanted to have a quiet talk with Jubel, and you never know how your pa's cat is going to act up when I take him along."

He waved at the girls in the kitchen as he cut across the hall to the living room. "Hello, Evie . . . Ella. How are the ladies?" He stopped in the middle of the room with Bertram

95

right behind him. "Never know which chair I want to sit down in when I come in here."

"It is a little crowded, isn't it?"

"Oh, no. It isn't that at all. You see, I've got to pick me a chair that I can get out of after I'm in it." He gave an amused giggle. "And it isn't only that, Bertram. I've got favorites; chairs I like to sit in, chairs I like to look at."

Oh, for Christ sake, sit down and get it over with. Bertram headed for a chair, hoping it would set an example.

"No, Bertram, please. That's one I like to look at. You sit over in that Sheraton. I'll take this bastard Napoleon. I'm in a looking mood tonight."

Bertram sat in the Sheraton. He had sat in the chair a number of times in the past few days but he had never been aware that it had a name; not that it made any difference whether they *called* this stuff or not. He looked over at Agnew who teetered on the edge of the "bastard Napoleon," shifting his stomach from one thigh to the other. The old guy had a nerve telling him where to sit in his own father's house. He might have been more annoyed with him except that he was a little surprised by Agnew's appreciation of his father's stock.

"Don't suppose you noticed me calling my dog, Lady, a *he* when I came in, did you, Bertram?"

"No, I didn't."

"Well, Lady's a lady, you know, but I find myself doing that every once in a while. Throw-back to my father. He used to call every dog a *him* and every cat a *her*. Made things easier for him. Now, your pa, he's different."

"Is that so."

"Why, you know that. He makes a great distinction. Not only divides cats and dogs into their proper genders, he treats them like people. Says each one has a personality. To me, a dog's a dog and a cat's a cat, hunting or mousing or just watching the house. Not your pa, though."

Damned if he was going to make the polite responses. He never liked small talk and this was an example of how big you

96

could make it. Sit on a porch and rock in a small town and an ant became an elephant.

"Or your mother, either. She was a great cat woman, Bertram. Always had a cat in the house, and two or three around the house. Always got more out of a cat than any man, woman or child I ever saw. I always figure a person's got something extra when they can do anything with a cat. Of course, your mother was a grand woman, had a man's mind and a woman's heart.

"You could talk to her, Bertram. I remember one day I came in here and Amy was working away in the kitchen. It was during the war and we got to talking, as we always did, about how it was going to be like after, whether the world was going to be any better for it. And, finally, she turned to me and she said, 'Agnew, if we do have a better world, a perfect one, it's just going to make it so much harder to die and leave it.' She said that, mind you, while she was standing there baking a huckleberry pie. I say a woman who can talk like that while she's making a huckleberry pie is quite a woman."

"Yes."

"Well, you don't need me to tell you that, Bertram. You saw all those people at the funeral. That speaks for itself."

He wished his father would come home and take Agnew off his hands. This business of exhuming the dead for a sentimental autopsy was the kind of thing he wanted to avoid. It was bad enough without having outside windbags come in to stir up the air. The only thing worse than sitting here, listening to him, would be to have Evie or Helen listening, too.

"And now Amy's gone and Jubel's left alone."

Oh, hell! You, too? Why did people have to be so consistently stupid!

Agnew shifted his stomach around and came closer to the edge of his chair. "Have you children had a talk with your pa yet, Bertram?"

"Talk? About what?" Each word had a chip on its shoulder but Agnew didn't seem to notice.

97

"About what he's going to do. He's an old man, Bertram. We're apt to forget our people get old."

"I suppose he's not going to do anything." Because he was old that was more the reason for him not doing anything. "He's got a home, a business. He'll stay right here, of course."

"Alone?"

Alone, alone, alone! Of course, alone. What did he need, an army?

"Your pa's a quiet man, doesn't talk much. But I know him as well as you, maybe better. You can't cut a hole in him without filling it up with something. Jubel's a family man. He needs family around him. I told him, before you came, anyone of you would be glad to take him home with you."

Sure. Take him home with us. What do you care? Be generous with your nose, stick it into other people's lives. Be bighearted, charitable, liberal. It doesn't cost you anything. You haven't got a thing to lose. Makes you look good, too. You can rock on your rocker for the rest of your life and think how nice it was of you to take care of old Jubel, get him settled down with his children.

Bertram took it out on the arms of his chair, squeezing them in his fists.

"I made him an offer, you know."

Always meddling, always busybodying . . . "Offer! Offer for what?"

"Why for this place, of course." Agnew waved at the room. "The house, everything in it, the whole business."

Bertram felt himself stiffen and almost rise. It was a peculiar sensation, as though he weren't sitting at all but squatting with nothing under him, supporting himself in mid-air by gripping the chair arms.

"You want to buy my father's business?"

It was more incredulous than he had wanted it to sound. He mustn't give himself away like that.

"Didn't your pa tell you?"

He had to be careful. He didn't know what they were talking

98

their way into. It couldn't have been much of an offer, small enough not to even be taken seriously or even mentioned, most likely. On the other hand, maybe the old man didn't want to mention it. It might have been just big enough to want to make him keep his mouth shut, afraid of all the hungry children. But it couldn't have been that big. Agnew wouldn't have that kind of money. Yet, you couldn't tell what people had or didn't have. Country people, small-town people, led deceptive lives. He remembered reading somewhere that there were small-town lawyers who made as much as twenty thousand dollars a year, and a lot of farmers were small millionaires. They might not talk much but they had sharp eyes and they knew a good thing when they saw it. Live in a town, grow up with it, spot a good thing—a store, a business, real estate—invest your money, and you could sit and rock on the interest for the rest of your life.

"I say, Bertram, didn't your pa tell you?"

"Frankly, Agnew, I don't really remember. You can imagine that we've been pretty upset around here. I doubt that Pop gave it a thought. If he did and he did say something . . . Well, I just didn't pay any attention to it."

"More than likely."

A man like Agnew might just have plenty salted away. You didn't want to buy a house and a business at his age without having a solid cushion to lean against. Didn't he own the hardware store in town years ago, sell it and buy something else? What was it? He couldn't remember but it was some other kind of business. Besides, he had a house of his own next door. That would mean two houses and who knows how many others he might have. He couldn't have offered the old man too little. After all, the house and the land it was on was real property. And the business, it was worth something; it must be if the man wanted to buy it.

"Well, I made him an offer, all right. A good, solid, businesslike offer." He giggled a little. "I'm Jubel's good friend but business is business, you know."

Now, it seemed to Bertram, he was no longer squatting on

99

air but eggs. So Agnew had made a "good offer." Five thousand? Ten thousand? The house alone was worth almost that and then there was the business. He had to find out. He had to ask him. But could he? Would Agnew tell him?

"Of course, what I'd buy, if I bought it, would be possibilities; based on what I would do with the business if I had it. Your pa isn't much of a businessman, Bertram. He's more on the craftsman type, what we used to call in the old days an artisan. Antiques don't mean a thing to him. Only went into the business because he was getting along and your ma wanted him to."

Agnew's stock as a trader was going up by the minute but he needn't think he was dealing with a boy.

"But that doesn't detract from the intrinsic value of the business, Agnew."

Agnew's jowls gave an inch. "Yes and no, Bertram. Antique business is an odd business. That chair you're sitting on, genuine Sheraton. Your pa picked it up for twelve dollars. It's worth ten times as much. Old Jubel would probably ask fifty dollars for it and have a guilty conscience. I could get two hundred and fifty."

Two hundred and fifty dollars! For this chair! He stared down at it with new eyes. His hands trembled along its arms.

"But you must remember, it isn't worth two fifty unless you can get two fifty. That's the kind of business this is."

Agnew was right about that. The old man wouldn't have the nerve to ask such a price. He had a sense of giddiness; as though he had been running full speed in one direction, stopped short and had to whirl completely around. His mind was popping with half-formed ideas. He felt that he was sitting on something more valuable than even this two hundred and fifty dollar chair, and much more delicate.

The old man hadn't said a word about this, not to him, not to Evie, Helen or young Jubel. If he had, there wouldn't have been all that to-do around the dinner table. It was either because Agnew's offer hadn't been big enough to take seriously or because it was big enough to be kept quiet about. You wouldn't think the old man would pull a stunt like that, especially on his own children.

Agnew was pointing for his attention. "Look there, Bertram. That's my favorite." He was nodding over a pint-sized occasional chair whose upholstery was puffed out beyond a delicately carved wooden frame.

Bertram looked at it without being impressed. The top carving reminded him of an admiral's fancy hat or maybe the suggestion of an eagle sitting on top of the flag. It had a flaring military flavor, especially with the two side pieces which looked like scepters topped by a pair of enlarged epaulets. To make it more confusing, there was a rich cluster of meaty acorns set in the middle. Certainly, nothing to get excited about.

"That's a pre-Federal piece, Bertram. Never seen a stick that yells *period* quite as loud as that. I could get five hundred from the right party for that one."

Bertram stared hard at the chair, trying to see the five hundred dollars in it. Agnew wasn't a fool. He wouldn't talk up the price of what he wanted to buy. The chair must be worth five hundred. If he couldn't see it, well he couldn't see the foolishness in stamps or coins either.

"I don't know that I'd sell it, though." Agnew rocked back and forth on his thighs. "I'm mighty fond of that one."

Bertram looked around the room. Two hundred and fifty for the chair he sat on, five hundred for the one Agnew nodded over, and the parlor was crowded with pieces. Maybe that smell in the house was not must but money.

"Now, don't go getting the idea all this stuff is valuable, Bertram. It isn't. Most of it's junk. Your pa knows it and I know it. Of course, you can make money on junk too if you sell it right."

That was realistic, sensible. It came close to his own evaluation of the old man's stock. Most of it was junk. Sure, he might make a mistake about an item or two, and maybe there were a couple of other pieces scattered around the house that weren't total losses but, on the whole, it certainly wasn't a gold mine. It would be silly even to think about going into the business with the old man; even though he could certainly help him realize more out of it. A proposition like this, though, while it was a little better than penny-profit stuff, still wasn't for him. It was small-town, small-league and always hustling to make it go unless you wanted to sit still, like the old man did, and wait for it to come to you. No, a deal like Weston's was more in his line; something where you could make a killing, not kill yourself making. Maybe work hard for a year or so but then you could sit back and watch it roll in. Now, if Agnew, over there, would put enough on the line to make a sale worth while, he might be able to talk the old man into it.

"What kind of an offer did you make for the house and the business, Agnew?"

"A good offer, a solid, business-like offer. Seventeen thousand, five hundred for the whole shebang."

Dollars, of course! That was whistling money. He wondered, suddenly, if they had been talking too loud, if Evie, or even Ella, might have heard them in the kitchen. Jesus, what he could do with that kind of money; ten thousand to Weston and seventy-five hundred left over to play around with. He had to organize himself, get his thoughts lined up, plan a way to carry this off. If he had only the old man to worry about, it wouldn't bother him but there were Helen and Evie and young Jubel. They might see red if they smelled that money. Christ, he was lucky to have stumbled on it alone. He felt like going over and shaking Agnew by the hand. The thing to do now was keep it to himself, keep it to himself until he could have it to himself.

"That sound like a fair offer to you, Bertram?"

"Well, I don't know enough about the business to say yes or no. The house, alone, should be worth twelve or fifteen thousand, especially in these times."

"I'm not interested in the house alone. Besides, you're three or four thousand overboard. Couldn't get more than nine or ten for it; maybe not even that."

This was dangerous ground. Once you started cutting a proposition down the middle, it could work both ways. Agnew might decide he wanted the business without the house, and where would that leave him. Agnew could move the stuff next door without so much as a backache. The most you could expect for the business, then, would be seventy-five hundred; small compared to the seventeen and a half thousand. But he was borrowing trouble, looking for it. Agnew wasn't a fool. He must have thought of that. What he wanted was the house and the business, all in one package. Maybe he was going to sell his own place after he took this one over; that might even halve the price for him. Whatever his reasons, he must have them. So no sense raising obstacles. Best to drop it fast.

"What did my father say? Was he interested?"

"That's just the point, he didn't say and I don't know if he is interested. I thought he might have talked it over with you kids and made some plans."

That's what *he* had to make, plans. If he had only known this the day he came, or even yesterday. But he had just gotten finished telling Ella—in front of Evie, too—to be ready to leave at six in the morning. He had taken a firm, unyielding stand. He couldn't back down now without tipping his hand. But that's exactly what he had to do because he wouldn't have the time or the opportunities to get the old man alone and talk to him; not between now and six o'clock tomorrow morning.

He'd have to stay on longer than the rest. He'd have to reverse himself, change his mind on one pretext or another, and get them all out of the way. Helen would be no problem; she was leaving in the morning, anyway. He could push young Jubel around and get him going, too. But Evie, she was going to hang around for a while and give him trouble. He'd have to figure out something for her; maybe a couple of bucks and Ella's co-operation to speed her on her way. He'd have to be smart for this, no doubt. A little of that acting ability young

Jubel was supposed to have wouldn't hurt but he'd manage; might even be good enough to teach his young brother a trick or two. He supposed he should feel sorry for them, or a little guilty about what he was planning. But he was the oldest one and, besides, the money would be wasted on the others. Give part of it to Helen? What for? She was getting along. To young Jubel and let him piddle it away trying to become an actor? Or Evie for that cracker husband of hers to sink in a bottle of corn liquor or a crap game? It'd be throwing the money away. Actually, he was going to do them a favor. Once Weston's proposition started paying off, there'd be enough for everybody and he'd see to it that they'd never have to worry about where their next meal was coming from.

"I'll tell you what, Agnew, I'll talk to Pop and let you know."

He had to keep him from talking about it any more. Any minute, from the sounds in the kitchen, Evie and Ella would be coming into the room. He wished there were some way he could get Agnew out of the house.

"Where's your sister, Helen? I think she ought to talk to your pa, too. She's a smart woman, Helen; got a business head on her. Takes after your ma."

"Yes." He pulled out his watch. It was after eight. Didn't people out in the country go to bed early?

"I planned to talk to Helen, talk to all of them but first to Pop. No use getting everybody all excited until we find out what Pop wants to do. You know how families are."

Agnew giggled. "Yes, yes, I know. Got one of them myself. Only I thought all of you talking to him might help him make up his mind. But you're the oldest one of the bunch, Bertram, and I guess you know how to handle it."

There were steps coming up the front porch and for a moment Bertram had the sick fear of Helen and young Jubel coming back.

"Yes, I can handle it. Why don't we just leave it that way and I'll let you know tomorrow."

But it was only the old man and Evie's kid, and he breathed

104

easier. Evie and Ella came into the room almost at the same time.

"What have you got there, darling?" Evie picked up her daughter, kissed her.

"Pretzels. I had ice cream, too, but the ice cream melts and I had to eat it fast. Grandpa Jubel said you used to eat pretzels and ice cream when you were a little girl."

"Yes, and they were delicious; so salty and sweet and icy all at the same time. Oh, they were good!"

"I didn't give her too much, Evie; just enough."

"Of course you didn't, Pop. You know all about children. You brought up four of us."

Jubel turned to his friend. "You never know about the younger generation, do you, Agnew. I'm sure many a child could tell his pa he didn't do right by him . . . Have you been waiting long?" He sat down beside him.

"Not too long, Jubel. Been talking here with Bertram . . ."

Bertram jumped up. "What do you say we all go into town and get some pretzels and ice cream for ourselves? You girls have been working too hard in the kitchen. You need a little refreshment."

Ella and Evie looked at him, startled.

"We'll take Jinny with us, too. She could stand a little more ice cream to finish off that pretzel. Couldn't you, honey?"

Evie shook her head. "But I've got the baby here."

"Oh, Pop will keep an ear open for him. Won't you, Pop?" He took Jinny's hand and began herding them to the door.

"Sure. You go on ahead. I'll sit right here with Agnew."

He had them out of the house without another word and even though he could feel Ella's bewilderment, he wasn't bothered about that. He was worried only about Helen and young Jubel coming home too early. But, he figured philosophically as he piled them into his car, there were risks in any venture, and you just had to take them and hope for the best.

Ella sat at the dressing table, creaming her face. She wore a nightgown and robe and she was almost ready for bed. Across the room, Bertram filled a scoop chair to overflowing. He was fully clothed and he had an unhappy look of stalled transiency about him; as though he had just stopped by for a minute and was about to go some place.

"Don't you think you ought to get ready for bed, Bertram?" She had asked him that half a dozen times already. It had taken her four askings to get him upstairs.

"In a minute." She must have asked him that a dozen times already but he wasn't annoyed; he couldn't afford to be annoyed. For all she knew, they were still leaving at six in the morning and she had every right to want to hurry him to bed.

He had thought by now he'd have everything arranged in his mind: his excuses for staying on, how he was going to break the news to his dear sisters and brother and, finally, how he was going to get them off and away. But nothing had jelled. After he had rushed Evie and Ella out of the house, he had spent the time counting off seventeen thousand, five hundred crisp new one dollar bills, seventeen hundred and fifty crisp new ten dollar bills or eight hundred and seventy-five crisp new twenties. It was pleasant thinking but it was either that or worrying about Helen and young Jubel getting back to the house before Agnew was gone and the old man went to bed. As it turned out, he didn't have to worry. Here it was after eleven and they still weren't home. This was one time he approved of drinking; not that he ever thought about it for most people but he suspected that young Jubel and Helen, especially young Jubel, couldn't be relied on to hold their liquor. However, that was danger past and no use thinking about it. It was still his secret, not one of the others knew about it. He could be reasonably certain that Agnew had talked further about the sale with the old man but that wasn't important, whether he said yes or no. If he said yes, it made his own job easier. No, would mean a little persuasion on his part. The important thing was secrecy and so far it had been kept. What would happen when he did his about-face and told them he was staying on for a while, he didn't know. He ought to try it on Ella and see what happened; go through a sort of dress rehearsal or dry run with her.

Ella was looking at him in the mirror. She had finished with her face and he thought she was going to ask him about bed again but she didn't hold his eye. Instead, she leaned back a little, sighed and looked around the room.

"You know, I kind of hate to leave this place. It happens every time I come here. When the night before comes up, I get such a feeling of sadness." She shrugged a little and looked up. "I don't know what it is. Maybe it's just these vaulted ceilings; they do something to me."

Now, what the hell was there so special about a vaulted ceiling? The world was full of houses with vaulted ceilings. Not that he was complaining about her wanting to stay; not now, anyhow. But, Jesus, there ought to be a more valid reason than that. He could just picture himself telling Helen and Evie and young Jubel that he was staying on for a while because he couldn't bear to leave the vaulted ceilings in the house. The least she could do was come up with a good reason, a good excuse, for him.

"Well." She tidied up the table. "You really should get to

107

bed, Bertram, unless you're going to stay up all night. It's not too far away from six now. You'll need sleep if we're driving all that way tomorrow."

He shifted his weight around in the chair. "Maybe we're not going home tomorrow."

He watched her start and turn around. "What did you say?"

"I've been thinking it over. Maybe we're not going home tomorrow."

She was looking at him carefully, trying to see if he meant it. He smiled at her.

"I've decided it isn't right to run off in such a hurry. We can wait a couple of days."

"Suddenly?"

"Suddenly."

"What about Weston? What about that big proposition of yours that couldn't wait another day?"

"It'll keep."

She stood up and crossed the room to him. Her floor-touching robe cut even her small height but he could get no comfort from that; he was watching her face.

"Bertram, what are you up to?"

See? It was going to be no good. Not that this mattered—he was going to have to tell Ella anyway—but the about-face was too complete, too sudden, even though that was the only way it could be and he guessed the others would see it, too. Still, this was an interesting experiment.

"Do I have to be up to anything? I've changed my mind, that's all."

"That's not all. That's not even the beginning. A few hours ago, right after dinner, you said we were leaving at six in the morning. You said it at dinner, too. That's all you've been thinking about ever since we got here; leaving, leaving, and now you're not leaving."

"So?"

She was thinking. He could see her assembling her thoughts in an orderly sequence.

108

"What did you and Agnew talk about? What did he tell you?"

"What makes you think he told me anything?" She was either being very smart or it was all too obvious.

"*You* taking Evie and me down for ice cream! *You* worrying about us working too hard and having some refreshment! I think I'm beginning to see it, Bertram, and I'll bet there's money in it somewhere."

There was no sense in going on with this. Ella saw it, all right. He'd have to tell her now. Besides, from the looks of it, he was going to need her help. He smiled and as he opened his mouth to speak, the front door slammed downstairs.

"You got to watch that door, Helen. You're making a hell of a racket."

"I ain't making the racket. It's the damn door. I just closed it."

They bumped through the dark hall, thick with furniture, blackness and walls.

"You need radar to find the kitchen in this place."

"How about a match?" She mixed around in her bag without luck. "It's darker inside this damn bag than it is in the house."

"Forget it. It's straight ahead."

"Straight ahead! You couldn't walk a white line in sunlight."

But they found the kitchen and even the light on the wall. They popped into being like small children tossed out of sleep, eyes and knees blinking.

"Oh, I feel awful." She put a hand out to the wall.

"You'll feel better if I can find some coffee."

"Who wants to feel! If I had only gotten one of those damn sleeping pills, we wouldn't have had to go back to the bar."

Pitch wandered into the kitchen from one of the dark corners of the house. He sat in the middle of the floor and looked them over.

"Maybe she knows where the coffee is."

109

"She's a he."

"All right, he. Where's the coffee, Pitch?"

The cat yawned in their faces; a red and white circle of teeth and tongue and whiskers.

"Did I tell you I have a cat, Jubel?"

"Like Pitch?"

"No, this is a kitten. Always have kittens. Can't stand old cats around. I'm the only one around who gets old and I can't give me away."

"You're not old, Helen."

"I'm old."

"Naw. Old is Pop. Old is Agnew. Old is sixty."

"Old is twenty when you're ten and forty when you're twenty. When you're forty and you're me, you're old. Get me that coffee, will you, Jubel?"

"Sure. Sure." He staggered to a closet and rattled around among jars and paper bags. "Here! I've got it!" But not before a tin of biscuits clattered to the floor.

"You'll wake everybody in the house."

"All I need now is the coffee pot."

He stopped and listened. The wail of Evie's baby seemed to come from a long way off, like the voice of a cat in a closet.

"Sshhh, Tommy." Evie reached out her hand to pat him back to sleep but the motion jolted her awake.

She opened her eyes, scared. At first, she thought she had been dreaming but she couldn't remember a dream. As she came wider awake she realized there was revulsion as well as fright, as though the bed she was lying in were unclean. Tommy quieted and she got up. The small night light was burning so she didn't have to hunt for cigarettes. Now, she knew what it was. She was back at that auto court with the traveler again. She felt better; as long as she knew what it was, she could feel better.

She lighted up and found a chair. Funny how you could intelligently reason a thing out of your mind and then find it

110

stealing back, when you weren't looking, to hit you over the head. And just moving her hand in the dark would do it. There were some people who could go through an experience like that, or any unpleasant experience for that matter, and convince themselves it had never happened. There were others who would live with it night and day and go out of their minds. Where did she come in? Somewhere in between? No use looking for a pigeonhole for herself. She was just trying to be honest about it. No excuses, no alibis. She had been desperate. She did what she thought she had to do at the time. Maybe if the sun had been shining, if she hadn't been so tired, so utterly alone, she would have done something else. But that was all *if* thinking. She did what she had to do and that's all there was to it. She wouldn't make her children pay for it or her husband pay for it. It was her own woe and she would keep it to wake her in the night, scared and sick.

She heard the sounds from downstairs, Helen and young Jubel in the kitchen. She hoped they were good and drunk and thinking about anything but Pop and leaving him alone. No one was facing up to that problem; least of all, she. If anything, she had been putting it off, even letting Bertram talk her out of it, salving her own guilt by staying a few days longer than the rest. It wouldn't make the going any easier for herself or for Pop. Was she staying on only because she would have to ask him for the money to get home? Was she making it so hard, so unbearably difficult, for herself that in the end she would say, "Come on home with us, Pop. Close up the house and live with Neal and me and the children."

Sounded fine. Sounded wonderful. She'd do it in a minute. She'd do it now if she could. But how could she say, "Come and live with Neal," when Neal didn't want any part of him. You couldn't ask someone into your house, especially your father, and then give him a hell instead of a home. You couldn't do that to your husband, either. It was his home whether he was right or wrong, and he did have the right to say who was going to live in it. That was the trouble with

111

marriage and partners; you kept having to look in their eyes
for yeses or noes. Everything was consent, consent. You
couldn't buy a dress and he couldn't buy a pair of shoes without thinking about it, and you either bought it for him or in
spite of him.

What was it Ella said down there in the kitchen this evening: you stuff this break with possessions, the other with children? But sometimes the stuffing was the thing that broke it.
She had her own children to think about, too. She could say
to Neal, to hell with you, and not go home. You couldn't
make fatherless children out of Jinny and Tommy when they
had their whole lives ahead of them. The whole nut of living
was selfishness. You were forever being torn, forever having to
make a choice between best and next best, closest and next
closest. You couldn't be a mother and a child both. Maybe it
was easier if you were like Bertram, not a parent and not so
much of a child either.

Helen and young Jubel were making an awful racket downstairs. Now, that she listened, most of the house seemed to be
awake. Wasn't that hum Bertram's and Ella's voices down the
hall?

"I should think you'd be ashamed to even tell me this."

"Why should I be ashamed? What I want to do is as much
for you as it is for me. Besides, do you want me to keep things
from you?"

"I'm sure you would if I didn't have to know."

"Listen, Ella, let's not complicate matters. Let's not make
them any more difficult than they are or have to be. This is
a very simple situation: Agnew wants to buy my father's house
and business. He's offering seventeen thousand, five hundred
dollars. I think the old man should take it and come to live
with us."

"So that you can take it from him."

"Well, he won't need it if he's living with us, will he?"

"Bertram, don't you see that's dishonest? It'll be his money

112

if he decides to sell this place, his whole lifetime of money. You can't take it away from him."

"All I've been hearing ever since I got here was 'Poor Pop. He's going to be all alone, no one to live with, no one to take care of him.' From you, from Evie, from Helen, from Jubel, all singing the same song. All right, he's not going to be alone, he is going to have someone to take care of him: you, me, us. That solves the problem, doesn't it?"

"Just your problem."

"That's all I'm interested in."

"I know, but what about Helen and Evie and young Jubel? They happen to be children, too. That money, if your father decides to part with it, belongs just as much to them as it does to you."

"Who are you married to, Ella, them or me?"

"It's a cheap confidence game, that's all it is, and you want to play it on your own family, your own father, your own brother and sisters."

"What do you want me to do, give my brother some of it so that he can piddle it away trying to become a ham actor? Give it to Evie for her cracker husband to drink up?"

"Why do you keep saying Neal drinks? You don't know."

"All those crackers drink. And as far as Helen is concerned, she doesn't need the money."

"Just you."

"Just me. Listen, Ella, let's stop this nonsense. I'm going to convince my father that the best thing for him to do is sell the house and the business and come to live with us."

"Why do you think everything is coming to you, Bertram?"

"Because I'm the oldest one. Because I'm over forty. Because when a man gets to be forty-five he either inherits the world or the world inherits him."

She watched him pace the floor without moving an inch. He still sat there, smothering the chair, but his mind was walking all over the house and everyone in it. She couldn't imagine him inheriting the world, not even the small one he hoped for.

113

She wondered under what dim stalactite he had been born, under what unhappy sign of quicksilver that left his reaching hands always empty. She felt sorry for him, sorry and guilty because if a wife can take credit for the good in her husband, she must take it for the bad, too. Even if this quirk were born in him, she should have straightened it out. Somewhere along the line she should have helped him see that it was just plain simple for him to suppose the only sure way to make money was to be underhanded or crafty or out-and-out crooked about it. The jails and poorhouses were full of people who thought in that kind of rut.

"Did you ever stop and think that your brother and sisters might not see it your way?"

"I don't expect them to see it any way. They're not going to know about it."

She had to laugh at him. "And how are you going to keep them from knowing about it, the way you kept me from knowing?"

"You're a lot smarter than they are, Ella. You know me better. You caught on fast."

"Just turn around and tell them you've decided to stay. Just tell them you want your father to come home with you and watch their ears go up, watch how smart they become, watch how fast they catch on. They know you, Bertram."

"That's why I told you about it; because they do know me and because they will catch on."

"Don't put me into this. I don't want to hear any more. I wish you wouldn't involve me in all your schemes. Don't tell me anything. Don't confide in me. Keep all your secrets to yourself. Just leave me alone, please."

"You've got to help me, Ella. This may be my last chance. How else can I get that money for Weston? You can make it so easy."

"No."

"Whatever you think about it, it'll take care of Pop. It'll solve his problems."

114

"No."

"It'll be simple, nothing to it, a minimum of lying."

"No, I tell you."

"It's just a matter of one of us being sick, you or I, it doesn't matter as long as we stick together on it and as long as it keeps us here after the others have gone. And it isn't even as hard as that. Helen leaves first thing in the morning. Jubel will go the next day. All we really have to worry about is Evie. You'll help me with her, won't you, Ella?"

"I can't. I won't." She watched his face begin to crumble, the dry tears begin to come.

"You've got to help me. You're the only one who can help me. You're my wife, you've got to." For the first time, he released the chair and came over to her. "Whatever we do, we mustn't let them know we've changed our minds, that we're not leaving. One of us will get sick in the morning. That's all there is to it, Ella, just that at the very last moment."

There was a din of crashing pots and pans from the kitchen.

"If they're making coffee down there, I want some." She knotted her robe about her and headed for the door.

Bertram followed her. "Stick by me, Ella. I need you. You'll ruin me if you don't."

They went out into the hall and met Evie at the stairs.

"Now, look what you've done. And still no coffee. Oh, and I feel so awful."

"Well, all I've been doing is trying to find the damned percolator. The hell with it. We'll boil the stuff. Coffee's coffee."

"Coffee's coffee but give me some."

"Never mind, Jubel. I'll take care of it." Evie came into the kitchen with Ella and Bertram behind her.

"All that racket and no coffee?"

"We've been here hours. First it was the coffee and he couldn't find the damn stuff. Then it was the percolator and all we got was a pot and that's just what I feel like, a pot."

"You're just tired, dear, that's all."

"We tried to get me a sleeping pill—didn't we Jubel?—but the damn druggist wouldn't sell us any. What else could we do but go back to the tavern and get drunker?"

"You certainly did a fine job. I hope you didn't make fools of yourselves."

"Oh, what if they did, Bertram? I'm sure it won't hurt your reputation any."

Helen focused her eyes on him. "Why, you're not even undressed, Bertram. Or is it time for you to go home?"

"We should have had Bertram down to the tavern with us, Helen. I would like to see Bertram on a tear, jaggin' himself on a tootin' hellbender."

"I don't think I'd care to do that on the night of my mother's funeral." He was satisfied with the silence. He walked to the kitchen window and gave them his back.

Young Jubel staggered up. "You don't have to be so goddam self-righteous about it, Bertram. Sure, I got drunk but I had time for it. I'm not running out at six o'clock tomorrow morning. I'll be around for a couple of days."

Bertram turned to him. He wouldn't let himself look at Ella. "I happen to have business to get back to. Besides, my conscience doesn't bother me."

"My conscience doesn't bother me, either. I just happen to have more corpuscles in my blood."

"More alcohol, I'd say. If I had been in the army as long as you were, I would have learned to carry my liquor a little better."

"You're just a goddam ignorant civilian. You think every soldier's a drunk. Of course, you've never been in the army. You managed to live through two wars without getting into one."

"I was a little young for the first. They didn't want me for your war."

"I didn't notice you fighting to get in."

"If I had gotten in, I would have come out with a little more than you did."

"Come out with what?"

"With something hard and solid, like money. I know boys who came back from Italy and Germany with enough to take care of their fathers in their old age."

"I was too busy fighting to peddle soap. You would have been good at that, though."

Evie came between them. "I wish you two big grown-up men could hear what you sound like. A couple of kids, that's all, just kids. Why, my Jinny sounds more intelligent. Now, sit down, both of you, and have some coffee."

They all moved to the table. Evie poured. They stood around her with their cups in their hands.

Helen waved at Bertram. "What's this about taking care of fathers in their old age? We didn't have a war for that, did we?"

Evie answered her. "Of course not, Helen. It was just a manner of speaking. Drink your coffee. You'll feel better."

"I don't see how it solves our problem, the war. Here we are, I'm going home tomorrow morning, Bertram's going home tomorrow morning. You and Jubel will be leaving in a couple of days and Pop's still going to be left alone."

Bertram shifted his cup and saucer. "Let's not go into that again."

"Why not? It makes better conversation than the war and you don't know a hell of a lot about that."

"I know enough about this to know it'll get us nowhere."

"Someone's got to worry about Pop. You aren't."

"All right, so you are. If you're so worried and you're such a big shot, why don't you stay here and take care of him?"

"You know I can't do that."

"Then stop talking about it."

Helen was shaking her head. "I suppose I'm the one who should stay with Pop."

"That's nonsense, Helen." Evie patted her head.

"Of course, it's nonsense. It's all nonsense. Why you keep talking about it, I don't know. The world is full of old people.

117

They either live by themselves or they go into homes for the aged."

Evie put down her cup. "That's a stinking thing even to think."

"What does he care? He's going home tomorrow."

"Bertram's not going home tomorrow. He's going to stay here until you're all gone."

"Ella!"

"Then he's going to make your father sell his house and his business to Agnew for seventeen thousand, five hundred dollars."

"Oh, no!"

"Yes."

"What a cheap lousy trick."

"I thought you were low, Bertram, but you could crawl under a snake without trying."

"You're not going to get away with it."

"We won't let you."

"That's a swindle if ever I heard one."

"It's just plain stealing."

They didn't see their father standing at the kitchen door. He was in his nightgown and his feet were bare.

"Children . . . Children . . ."

Their heads turned. Evie ran to him.

"Pop, what is it? What's the matter?"

"You're making too much noise. You'll wake your mother."

He didn't linger. He turned and left them. They stood there, shocked, silent, listening to him go back upstairs, up to bed.

It was Evie, finally, who turned to them. Her whisper was a controlled scream.

"We can't leave him! Don't you see! We can't leave him!"

All along the road the country had the faded yellow and orange look of fall; not bleak yet but with the dry straw color that came before the hoar-frost. There was still green in some of the fields and Jubel supposed that from the air, the way Helen traveled, the land must seem like somber patchwork. Here, riding along in the car with Bertram and Ella, he could only get a hint of it. He wondered about Evie driving home with the children in her car. Evie was going south, heading into the country that was still green, while he and Bertram and Ella were traveling west. Winters were colder out here. He could remember all the nights of winters, back home with Amy and the newspaper, when they'd sit and read of the storms and the first snows and check the weather reports, the temperature highs and lows and the precipitations, wherever the children were. It was odd, sometimes, what a difference there could be between such close places as Boston and New York, and how a city like Columbus, Ohio, could suffer through a severe winter and then be the first to report a crocus. Atlanta, that was as close as they could come to Evie's town, was always a surprise; even though you learned to expect a ten or fifteen degree difference.

"Do you suppose Evie and the children might be home by now, Bertram?"

He had to speak up again, this time louder, because Bertram had his window open a little and there was a rush of air by his ears.

"No, I don't think so, Pop. She's got a longer way to go, even though she left before we did."

That was so. Anyway, she must be down through Virginia; maybe even the Carolinas by now, depending how much of a hurry she was in, although he told her to be sure and drive carefully and not at night. He remembered, years ago, when Evie and Neal first moved down south. They were living in Atlanta then—that was before the auto court—and Evie called on Christmas Eve.

"It's like spring down here, Pop," her voice said from far away. "I was out today without a coat. Merry Christmas."

And they had had snow on the ground.

Helen called one year, too, to tell them about a holiday blizzard. That was the year young Jubel was overseas and there was that terrible business in the Belgian Bulge. He and Amy didn't know just how cold it was over there, or how much snow they were having, but there were pictures in the papers of the frozen forests and you read that Europe was having one of its worst winters.

"Are you warm enough back there, Pop?"

"Plenty warm, Ella, thank you."

"If you're not, Bertram can close his window a little."

"No, everything's just fine."

He did nudge the blanket a little closer to Pitch, though; not that it made any real difference, he guessed—the cat had been sleeping for almost two days and one night solid on the road—but you could never get them too warm. Pitch rumbled a purr under his hand. It was nice to have a cat who could travel. So many cats were unhappy in cars. Not Pitch. As long as it was comfortable and warm and he had his family with him, he didn't mind where he was off to. It seemed that everyone was off to someplace—by now, Helen and young Jubel were back in Boston and New York—and the house was left alone.

120

Of course, Agnew was there, but not one bit of family left.

He was homesick. He had had to cut too many roots. He was too old to leave a home and start a new kind of living. But what could he do in the face of all of them? They wouldn't take his no, they insisted, they wouldn't listen to what he had to say.

He had come down early the morning Bertram and Helen were supposed to leave but they weren't leaving. Helen was still in bed. As a matter of fact, Evie said Helen wasn't feeling well. But Bertram was there, and not going, and young Jubel, too, even though he looked as though he should have been in bed.

"None of us are going home, Pop; not yet, anyhow."

"Well, I know about you, Evie, and young Jubel, but Bertram is going. Aren't you, Bertram?"

"Not right away."

He would have been very happy with that news except there was an odd look on Bertram's face. Evie and young Jubel looked strange, too, but in a different way.

"Of course, I'm glad you're staying, as long as there's nothing wrong."

Young Jubel had taken his arm and walked with him to the table.

"Nothing's wrong, Pop. Here, have some coffee. It's just that we all had a little talk last night and decided we were going to have to do something about you."

Somehow, that had sounded funny and he had laughed. "Afraid I'll get into mischief? You don't have to worry. I'm a little too old for shenanigans."

"You never can tell. I've seen some pretty wild old ones. New York is full of them."

"Not as old as me."

"Older than you."

"All right, Jubel," Evie elbowed him out of the way. "Let's not go into a song and dance."

"Pop, why didn't you tell us Agnew wants to buy the house and the business?"

"No reason to. I'm not going to sell it. When did he tell you about it?"

"He didn't tell me. He told Bertram."

Bertram had sat down then. "It's a very good offer, Pop. Seventeen thousand, five hundred."

"I know what the price is but what do I need it for? I won't have a house, I won't have a business, I won't have anything."

"Bertram thinks you ought to sell and go to live with him."

He had looked at his oldest son and then at Evie and young Jubel, going over their faces. He thought of Helen lying in bed upstairs, and of his two grandchildren sleeping in his house. This was family. This was the thickness of blood, of sharing and taking responsibilities and being one. He felt such a fullness of love for them, such complete satisfaction in what he had given in his time, that if nothing else happened, if the world stopped where it was, it would be enough.

"You'd be happy with us, Pop. Ella and I would make a good home for you. You'd never have to worry about another thing and you wouldn't have to be alone."

"I don't know, Bertram, I don't know. Your mother never believed in parents moving in with children. Separate lives, she always used to say, separate lives."

"But we want you. We're asking you. We've got a nice little house, Ella's a good cook. You won't have to lift a finger."

"It doesn't work out. I've never known it to work out."

It seemed as though young Jubel and Evie were waiting for Bertram to say something more but he didn't. He tried. He began to speak, stopped, licked his lips and then let it drop unhappily.

"I don't want you to think I don't appreciate this, Bertram. It's generous, more than generous, but it's dangerous, too. You take someone into your house, even your father, and you go through the close business of rubbing lives together . . . Somehow, it doesn't work out. It should but it doesn't. Besides . . ." Now, there was some other thing he had wanted to say but it had slipped away. He was beginning to lose the thread of his thoughts more often these days.

"What is it, Pop?"

"Oh, yes. Besides, it's too big a step to take. It's too permanent. Suppose, after a while, you decide you don't want me any more or I don't want to live with you any more. Those things happen, Bertram. You mustn't forget them in a rush of good feeling and generosity. What then? Where would I go?"

Evie leaned in close. "I want you, too, Pop. I want you to come to live with Neal and the children and me."

"Oh, now, Evie."

"Me, too, Pop. I haven't got a lot of room but there's a double bed and you might get a kick out of living in New York."

"Helen wants you, Pop. She told me to tell you."

"All my children. All of them." He had laughed and cried a little because he was so in love with them and because they wanted him.

"It's just that you can't stay on here alone. We'll all be worried sick about you."

"I'm afraid, Evie. I'm afraid of just going with one of you. It might not work out and it could mean losing the rest of you."

"We won't let you lose us."

How could he talk against four children? They had overwhelmed him. They wouldn't listen to him. But he didn't give all the way in. He gave them just so much of their way. He wouldn't live with any one of them for good. Instead, he'd try visiting for a year; three months with each of them. And he wouldn't sell the house and the business. He'd make an arrangement with Agnew to take it over for twelve months, rent it to him, and at the end of that time, make up his mind. Time enough then to sell, time enough then to decide whether his children wanted him or whether he was better off alone.

That's the way he was. He would have it no other way. But it didn't help the homesickness. It didn't take the edge off each mile that Bertram was putting between him and Amy. That was what he couldn't say to them because they wouldn't have understood it: how can I leave your mother all alone? It was

123

an unreasonable thought, an unreasonable argument; so unreasonable he didn't even mention it. They might have sensed it because they did say he could come home between each visit, before going from one to the other, but Agnew would be living in the house and it wouldn't be the same. Although he did think he might go to the cemetery and see to it that Amy's grave was kept fresh every three months.

He couldn't say no to them, anyhow; not the way Bertram looked when he did say it. Bertram was so anxious to have him, so crushed when he had hesitated, so almost in despair when he had wavered. On the whole, he was glad he had said yes. All the children were happy; especially Bertram and so he had to go with him first. He wasn't sorry. Bertram and Ella had made the trip an extremely pleasant one. He knew that Bertram liked to drive fast but Bertram wasn't driving fast. He knew that Bertram could have made the trip in a little more than a day's drive but Bertram was taking two days. They had stopped overnight in that nice hotel in Wheeling, had a fine dinner with wine and a good night's rest on a firm bed. Bertram had even ordered chicken so that he could save some for Pitch to eat, and he had packed it carefully into a cellophane cigarette wrapper so that it would be in good condition when he took it up to his room.

It was interesting, too, to see how the world had changed since he had traveled around in it, how mere towns had grown into cities and what fine improvements they had made in the hotels. It made him feel a little easier about Evie's traveling. He wondered if he had given her enough money; things were high on the road these days. He did want to give her more than the fifty dollars but she wouldn't take it. She seemed embarrassed even about that but there was no need to be. When a girl couldn't ask her own father for money, it would be a mighty sorry world.

He began to doze on that. The monotony of the car's motion and the endless countryside gently patting at his eyes put him to sleep.

"We'll be home in about an hour, Pop."

Ella's voice prodded him awake but for only a second; he was too tired to answer.

"The poor man's asleep. I guess it must be a long trip for him."

"He's a lot better off than if he went with any of the others."

He was, too. If the old man had had to ride with Evie or hitch with young Jubel or fly with Helen, he could be a lot worse off. Here, at least, with them he was making it in easy stages, sleeping on a good bed and having some pretty fine meals on the way. It's true the ride was a long one for an old man but any ride was bound to be long for an old man.

And the old man was really old; now, he realized it. When Agnew sat with him in the living room and told him his father was getting on, it didn't mean anything. But when he saw him walking in his nightgown, his mind wandering around, talking about Mom as though she were alive, he could see it for himself. In a way it was like watching a house begin to crumble. Well, the old man was reeling around in his seventies and you couldn't live forever. He guessed his mother's death had weakened him. Sad. Sad. And yet what were you going to do, what could you do? It was life. It was the old business of the watch running down, the tired tree falling when you took away the fence. It was a good thing the old man was coming with them. He needed some comfort and security now, not just a roof over his head and a houseful of trouble which was all Evie could offer him, or a ham sandwich and a closet with young Jubel and Helen. An old man had to walk into an orderly home. He had to live with solid, mature, feet-on-the-ground people who could take care of him and not bother him with their troubles, and even see to it that his own affairs were put in order.

It was strange how that messy, typical family squabble in the kitchen, when they had all turned on him after Ella had blabbered about selling the house and the business and him wanting to take the old man changed his whole perspective. Not that that was all of it but that and Pop coming down in

125

his nightgown certainly put a new light on things. It slowed him up. It said, here now, take it easy, there's no hurry. The poor man's tired and old, tired and old and he hasn't much more to go. Why hadn't he had sense enough to see it before? Why hadn't he been smart enough to size up the whole simple situation before it became involved and dirtied by all the fingers reaching? If he had been foolish and sentimental, if he had felt like Evie and Helen and young Jubel and gone one step further, yielded and asked the old man home right from the start, in short, if he had been foolish instead of smart, he would have been smart instead of foolish. Some of the smartest things in the world were done by foolish people: a waitress in a hash joint listens to a deadbeat's hard-luck story, lets him get away with a check and twenty years later the deadbeat leaves her a million dollars, or a good-natured slob picks up a tramp on the road, gives him a ride, a free meal, a couple of bucks and the tramp turns out to be somebody's rich nephew who inherits a gold mine and splits it with his benefactor. Foolish people doing foolish things but winding up on the smart end. It didn't make them less foolish in the long run because the percentage was so small and for that one waitress and for that one benefactor there would be a million others who would have to pay the checks out of their own pocket or might get murdered or robbed on the road. Yet, it was stories like that that kept people doing it.

There was no figuring it out and it was easy, only after it was over, to know what was smart and what wasn't. In his case it hadn't been quite so cut and dried or lucky; he should have known a little something about antiques and what they might be worth. But you can't know everything in the world and a man had to guard his own life jealously and be selfish about his own interests. As it worked out, it was all right. He had no complaints. He was even glad that Ella had brought the whole business to a head. Of course, it hurt to hear his own brother and sisters call him down and curse him out. But if that's the way they felt about him, it was best to have it out in the open

126

anyhow. He was a great believer in the theory that what you said or did in heat was what you thought about in cold quiet.

"It's good to know what you think about me, anyhow." He had said that after his father had left them and went back upstairs.

They were ignoring him. Evie, young Jubel and Helen stared at each other as though they were in shock. Even Ella looked stunned. Evie moved toward the hall.

"No, Evie. Don't follow him."

She stopped. "I'm scared. He might fall."

"He'll be all right." Young Jubel took her hand and brought her back.

"But what is it, Jubel? You heard what he said."

Helen put down her cup. "He talked about Mom just as though she were alive."

"I know."

"What was it, Jubel? Was he sleepwalking?"

"I don't know. I guess it was a kind of mind wandering. Jesus, I don't know."

Ella had cut in then. "I think it was a lot of things: dreaming a little, remembering. You've got to realize, Evie, he's had a great shock. He's been hiding it from us but it comes out."

"He can't be left alone. He just can't be, that's all."

Then Bertram had said what he had thought sensible and certainly in line with the events. "Pop isn't going to be alone. He'll be living with Ella and me."

Evie was a fury. "Aren't you ashamed! Aren't you ashamed of being the miserable, rotten creature! And after what you've seen with your own eyes!"

Young Jubel stepped up to him. "You're not going to get away with it."

"I must say I don't understand you. This morning you would have been on my neck, weeping with joy."

"This is twelve hours and seventeen thousand, five hundred dollars later."

"Talk. Talk. Ella's hysterical and everybody jumps to con-

127

clusions. There's no seventeen thousand, five hundred dollars. There hasn't been any sale. No money has passed hands and yet you accuse me of wanting something that isn't even in existence. But, as I say, I'm glad to know what you think of me, anyhow."

It was Evie's turn. "What do you expect us to think of you? What do you want, a medal?"

Helen picked up her cup and put it down, picked it up and put it down. "He talked about Mom just as though she were alive."

"I don't want anything. I don't want anything, just an end to this jabbering. You take him home. Go on, take him home to your drunken husband and your squawling brats." He turned on his brother and Helen. "Or you take him home to whatever you've got; your furnished rooms and your dirty living."

Evie whirled him around by the arm. "Sure, I'll take him home to my drunken husband and my squawling brats. At least, he won't have his eye teeth stolen."

"Yes, and I'll take him, too. For seventeen thousand, five hundred I can get a penthouse overlooking Central Park with air conditioning, and he won't have to sleep with a gun under his pillow."

Helen stood up. "Wait a minute. Wait a minute." She seemed clearer, now. "In the first place, you're making too much noise. You're going to have Pop coming down again. In the second place, it isn't what any of us want. It's what he wants. I'll take him, if I have to, because he can't be alone."

She staggered a little. "You talk to him. I'm going to bed. I won't be going back tomorrow. Ask him which one of us he wants. And don't tell him about Bertram. He won't believe it and, besides, Pop deserves better than that. Good night."

Ella had had to help her up to bed. He and Evie and young Jubel sat up the rest of the night, drinking coffee, waiting for morning and for the old man to come down. Most of the time, he felt as though they were keeping their eyes on him and

128

when they did speak, it was as though he weren't in the room.

"What do you think we ought to do, Evie, warn him?"

"I don't know. I think maybe Helen's right. What's the use and he does deserve better."

Minutes later, young Jubel said, "All right. But now that we know what he's up to, we'll watch it."

They watched it but in the end, his father chose him anyhow. They felt easier about it because it would only be for three months and each of them would have their turn. Besides, there was no immediate sale of the house and the business and so the old man's potentiality as a plum was put off. It had been a long way to home, but he was getting there.

"Town looks good, doesn't it, Ella?"

"Do you think the house will be warm enough for your father? You may have to start the fire."

"We'll start it anyhow, just to make sure."

She was amazed and baffled by him. From the moment she had opened her mouth in the kitchen and told Evie and Helen and young Jubel what she thought Bertram was up to, she had expected the storm. It never came. It began to look as though it never would. It hadn't been easy to tell on him; a wife had her loyalty. There were do's and don'ts that weren't written into the marriage ceremony. You don't expose your husband to abuse; not if you live with him, if you expect to go on living with him. But that's exactly what she had done, and to the abuse of his own family: even worse! She did it because she had to—a woman had to live with herself as well as her husband—and there was something so low and unholy about taking from your own old father while the rest of the family wasn't looking.

It was right if she had been right, but was she? If she had been right and she had snatched money from Bertram's hands, would he have forgiven her so quickly? Not if she knew Bertram, and she thought she knew him. The money she thought he wanted—it was an intangible now. His father hadn't sold and he was only going to visit with them for three months. So

129

Bertram didn't get what she thought he was after, but he was acting as though he had. There hadn't been a word from him about it, not one since he had turned to her in the kitchen with that stabbed-in-the-heart look, and said, "Ella!" It was as though the whole episode hadn't happened, and what she found out, she found out from Evie.

"Pop's going home with you, Ella."

That was the next day, after it had all been decided.

"You're not letting him!"

"Oh, yes. He wants to. Didn't Bertram tell you?"

"I haven't talked to Bertram about it."

Evie smiled at her. "You know, Ella, I love you for what you did last night."

"I'm not so sure I was right."

"It doesn't matter. I love you for it anyhow."

"I'll let you love me. I'm sure Bertram doesn't."

"It was one of the quietest, bravest things I've seen in my life. I'm sure Jubel, in all the war, didn't see anything to equal it. But he didn't understand it. You have to be a married woman to understand it."

"Nonsense. Why are you letting him come home with us?"

"It's all worked out, Ella. Pop's not selling the business or the house. He's letting Agnew take over for a year, and you're going to have him for three months. Then he'll move on to the next of us."

"But why Bertram first?"

"It's more convenient that way and Bertram wants him most." She sighed, "I guess the rest of us aren't quite ready for him yet. We sort of have to prepare the way. I know I've got a lot of preparing to do."

"Do you trust Bertram?"

"I don't have to trust him. You'll be there."

Either Bertram thought he told her about the arrangements, or thought one of the others did or just took it for granted that she knew, but he never said a word. In a way, it was better because it left out any ugliness that might have been brought up with it. Ugliness was something Bertram seemed to want to do without for the time being; it would be foreign to his attitude of the last few days. He was a sweet, even-tempered, lovable man. He treated his father as though he was the dearest thing in his life. He worried about his comfort. He spent money on him.

She wished she could accept the beautiful father-son relationship without worrying about it, without suspicion, without wondering what Bertram might be up to. It bothered her. She felt responsible. She stayed up nights thinking about it. It colored everything she thought about or said. She knew she was borrowing trouble at an exorbitant rate of interest but she couldn't help it.

Bertram drove into the driveway and up to the house. He jumped out of the car and pulled open the back door. He held out his hands to his father.

"Here we are, Pop. Welcome home."

xi

On the second Sunday home, they went to church with his father. The Reverend Mr. Lambert called upon the Old Testament for the text of his sermon: "He that maketh haste to be rich shall not be innocent."

Somehow, that seemed particularly suitable, Bertram thought. He didn't pay much attention to the text itself because he was quite intrigued by the business of haste and riches. Not that he was one to take sermons and churches and reverends seriously—everyone was trying to make a buck in the world—but the appropriateness of the words themselves to his own situation seemed coincidental. Lately he had been thinking a lot about haste. The word, or one similar to it, would pop into his mind in the form of a maxim or a snatch of a maxim: "Marry in haste . . . Fools rush in . . . Haste makes waste . . . Without haste! without rest!" Things like that and while they had no significance in themselves—for instance, he hadn't married in haste and repented in leisure, Ella was all right even though there were things about her, sometimes, that he wished might not be what they were or a little different from what they were—they had certain associations. He would think, many times since they had come home from his father's house, of haste and its opposite, leisure.

Haste and leisure, he would say to himself, haste and leisure, and he would sit for hours mulling over their relative values. Sometimes, when he had a sales call to make, he'd start thinking about them and get so involved and fascinated by their consequences, that he'd pull over to the side of the road and let his thoughts play instead of tending to business. He knew what brought all this on; it wasn't old age or softening of the brain. He came home to find that Mr. Weston and his proposition were temporarily out of town. This gave him pause, after the first few hours of panic in which he thought he had lost his last chance at big money, and he realized how silly it was for him to have been in such a hurry to get home in the first place. Then Mr. Weston came back and announced a delay in his project.

"It's this way, Bertram. I saw a couple of kinks in the program that I thought ought to be ironed out."

"It sounded pretty good to me, Mr. Weston."

"Exactly. It sounded good but I don't believe in doing business by ear; not in this day and age, anyhow. Mind you, I'm not saying the basic proposition is unsound, not at all. It is sound. It's a good solid idea with just enough imagination to it to give it flare."

"But there were kinks?"

"Well, not exactly kinks. Let's call them reservations. You see, Bertram, I never like to do anything half-baked; that's why I've been asking men like yourself for ten thousand dollars. I maintain you get out of a business what you put into it, and in a shoestring business, you get just that—a shoestring. Now, as far as those reservations are concerned. I went ahead and wrote to fifty editors on my list; a nice friendly letter, suitable for country newspapermen, outlining my service and asking them if they'd be interested in it."

"What did they say?"

"Some said yes, some said no, some said yes with reservations. It's those reservations I have to find out about. That's the margin of difference between success and failure or just ordinary success and big success."

"What are you going to do?"

"This is an age of pre-testing, Bertram, of polls and surveys. I'm going out into the field and talk to these editors, tell them what I have to offer and find out what they want. It'll take time and some money but there's no sense being hasty about it."

That word again, and a good thing, too, because it had eased him down to a walk. Haste could be a dangerous pace to set for one's self; many a hasty-pudding in life turned out to be just a bowl of meal mush. And he had had enough of meal mush. He wanted some of the delicacies for a change. When you stopped and thought about it, the really big fortunes had been built on solid foundations and, besides, all the arrows, all the little indications, were pointing to an easy, cautious tempo.

This, of course, wasn't abstract thinking, not a conclusion reached by a churchman's sermon or a businessman's hesitation. It came out of the solid rock of knowledge, the comfortable security that his father was a walking equity of at least seventeen thousand, five hundred dollars. That was money, that was a solid, round, pocket-stuffing sum you could lean back on and figure with. It was contemplation money, consideration money. After his talk with Weston, he wasn't even sure that he'd invest any of it in the editorial syndicate. Now, he could take his time, look at it from all angles and make a right decision. If he went in now there'd be no doubt about success but he could afford not to be hasty.

Living began to take on a satin-quilted texture. Having the old man in the house had many of the aspects of playing caretaker to a nice kind of property. Besides, he found himself getting rather fond of the old codger. Take that business of room and board, after the first week, when he came to him and Ella with fifteen dollars in his hand.

"Bertram, I've been figuring out what it must cost you to keep me here and I think it amounts to about fifteen dollars a week."

"Oh, Pop, we couldn't take any money from you. Could we, Bertram?"

134

Ella had given him the prompter's eye and nudge but it wasn't necessary; he didn't expect anything from the old man.

"It's not money, Ella. It's just expenses. It would cost me money to live home."

"But you're our guest, Pop, and Ella's right."

"Family is never guest. Family should pay its way all the time."

"But you've never taken money from your children."

"That's different, Ella. A mother and father bargain for children; it's part of the luxury of having them. Children don't owe their parents anything except maybe a little love if they have it coming to them."

"You're a dear, Pop, but we couldn't take it. You're making Bertram very unhappy."

"Now, look here, children. This is all nonsense. I'm staying with you for three months and then I'm going on to Helen or young Jubel or Evie. I'm going to pay my way all along or I don't go. So let's not make a fuss."

Pop had laughed as he pushed the money into his hand. "Besides, Bertram, this doesn't even include the cat's food."

Of course, he had to take it. You could see the old man felt pretty strongly about it, and there was no sense in making him unhappy or driving him away, as he told Ella later on.

"Then you shouldn't have taken the whole fifteen; five or ten, maybe, at the most."

"Oh, what's the difference if it makes him happy. Anyhow, you heard what he said, he wouldn't stay."

She went on to rationalize: actually, it didn't cost any more for food—Pop ate so little—and the spare room was there and the whole thing was ridiculous. But she left out the human element and the contrariness of old age.

"Well, save it, then. Put it away. Christmas isn't far off. We ought to be able to buy him a handsome gift with it."

But that was silly. The old man didn't want anything, didn't need anything. She couldn't name a suitable gift to add up to the two months of his room and board that would accumulate before the holidays.

"You just leave it to me. I'll take care of everything."

She had given him an "I'm-sure-you-will" look and dropped it. But it didn't bother him. It was all a small tempest, anyway. The sixty dollars a month that would come from the fifteen dollars a week would just about pay the rent on the house, and if the old man wanted to make that his contribution to their living, all well and good. It was an unexpected little blessing; it also eased some of the ordinary pressure of living, the trial of stretching dollars and days at the end of each month. It was something to be appreciated but not taken advantage of the way his sisters or brother might, once they knew the old man was paying his own way. He could just see young Jubel or Evie pricking up their eyes at the sight of sixty dollars a month and wondering how they could ask for more. It was a good thing he had gotten him first; no telling if the old man would have anything left by the time the hungry members of the family got through with him.

The ideal situation would be not to let them have a chance to get through with him; not even have the chance to get to him. Sure, it was supposed to be the year, split up four ways among them, but there was no reason why it had to come off. Plans were made to be postponed or ignored altogether for a good enough reason or for any reason. Any number of things might happen to prevent his father from going on to the rest of the children: he might get sick, the long trip to New York or Boston or Georgia might be too much for him at his age or, best and easiest of all, he might decide he liked living right here with him and Ella so much, he just wouldn't want to go on to the others. In that case, his own worries would be over and he could count on the money, one way or another. And there was something else in his favor; the others didn't really want their father. They talked about him and worried about him but no one had made a move for him until the issue of the money came up. And even then, it seemed to him, they were all

136

glad not to have him first because of the intrusion on their lives. He could understand Evie's reluctance; she was having a tough enough time with that sot husband of hers and the kids, but with young Jubel and Helen, it must be something different. Who knew what either of them were up to, what kind of lives they led, and how much of an inconvenience it might be to have their father around? He might put them into a position of leading normal, decent lives. But, in spite of their reluctance, they were going to take him, anyhow. It was wonderful what changes you could suffer through for the promise of money. It was the common denominator, the mighty leveler. It made everybody a little echo of everybody else in this world.

But he had the inside track; he had him first and he would make the most of it. Besides, it was best for the old man, regardless of the money. Why, he didn't talk to him about it for almost a month after he came to live with them. He wanted him to relax in his new change of scenery, not think about home or the children or business or anything else; just become part of a new pattern. And when the money did come up, it was the old man himself who brought it about.

It was on Thanksgiving day, right after a dinner that was good enough for a king. He had told Ella to go ahead and make it the best—he even gave her extra money for it—and the table had the look and the weight of cornucopia. There was the extravagant fifteen-pound turkey with all the traditional expensive accessories that made the buying of the bird seem almost negligible: a three-dollar bottle of wine, a couple of dollars worth of chrysanthemums and a cold, bleak day with a touch of snow that must have cost him an extra half-ton of coal to keep the house comfortable. At any rate, it was an old-fashioned, father-kind of Thanksgiving and well worth it all because the old man had second helpings of everything and it was funny that the more a man put into himself the more he came out of himself. For the first time, his father seemed almost cheerful.

They had their coffee out in the living room; a touch he

always liked because it was one of the few things that gave you a sense of elegance without costing anything.

"That was a wonderful dinner, Ella, a wonderful dinner." He sat by the window, in the big chair, with the cat stretched out across his lap.

"Thanks, Pop. I hoped you'd like it."

"Ella really outdid herself."

"Oh, no, Ella always cooks well. I've had some wonderful meals since I've been here."

"Well, come to think of it, Ella is a pretty good cook. She's much better than Evie, and Helen doesn't cook at all."

"Evie's a very good cook, Bertram. I'm sure your father thinks so, too."

"As a matter of fact, I'm not sure I know Evie's cooking. She never did much of it when she was home. You know, Bertram, your mother never forced any of you children."

"In the case of the girls, I don't think it would have done any harm."

The old man turned and looked out of the window. "It's been a long time since I've seen snow on Thanksgiving."

"The seasons are a little advanced out here. We get an earlier winter but we get an earlier spring, too. Personally, I like the mid-west. It isn't too beat down by civilization. Nature still has a chance out here. I think you'll like it after a while, Pop."

"I like it fine, now."

"It's a lot better than those big, dirty eastern cities like Boston and New York. You have a chance to breathe out here. On the other hand, it's still part of the country and the world, not a God-forsaken hole like Georgia."

"I suppose all places have their faults and good points, too."

"But some more than others."

"It's simply a matter of taste, Bertram. I'm sure if we lived in New York, we'd like it well enough."

"No." He slammed the door on Ella's reasonableness. If she couldn't help, he didn't want her to hinder him. Then he remembered; he hadn't told her he wanted his father to stay on

138

beyond the three months. Why had he let the conversation slip away to weather and places to live? He had a point, sure, but it was a debatable one. Now, with cooking there wasn't any room for argument; on that score Ella was head and shoulders above Evie and Helen.

"After a meal like this one, Pop, do you wonder what it's going to be like living with Helen or young Jubel?"

"No, but I imagine it'll be very nice visiting with them for a while."

"But Helen can't cook, Pop."

"I suppose we'll manage."

"I hate to think of you eating that rotten restaurant food, day in and day out. It can be pretty bad even for a young man."

"I'm sure there are a lot of fine restaurants in places like Boston and New York. It might even be pleasant for a change."

"Maybe once or twice but not day in and day out, Pop. I know; I've been on the road. You have to have a cast-iron stomach."

Ella stuck in her two cents' worth. "I'm sure Helen will take good care of your father."

He was going to have to have a talk with her.

"If worse comes to worst, I can always fry an egg and bacon. I used to do it at home every once in a while. By the way, Bertram, I had a note from Agnew yesterday. Did Ella tell you?"

He looked at her sharply. "No, she didn't." It must have come in the middle of the day; he saw all the morning mail.

"It slipped my mind. I meant to."

"It was nothing important. Agnew sold one of my Sheratons for two hundred and fifty dollars." He laughed. "The man has no conscience. I wouldn't have had the nerve to ask more than a hundred for it."

"Did he send you the money?"

"Not yet. We have an accounting the first of the month."

"You trust Agnew, do you?"

The old man looked surprised. "Why, of course, Bertram.

139

Agnew's a friend and a neighbor, a good friend and neighbor."

"He might have gotten three hundred for it and told you only two fifty." He stopped when he saw the look in his father's face. "Well, he might have. It's been done before."

"You have to trust people. You have to trust them and believe in them."

"I still think you would have been better off to sell it to him outright."

"No. I might want to go back."

"You'd have solid cash now. You never know what'll happen to a business in a year."

"You know more about a business than you do about cash. Besides, I've got to think about the future; I'm not going to be here forever."

"But, Pop, that's silly."

"No, Ella, just common sense."

"What do you mean, about the future?"

"I want to leave something for my children, as much as I possibly can. My grandchildren, too."

Good Lord! Six now instead of four to haggle and fight for it. He hadn't given Evie's kids a thought but apparently the old man had. And grandfathers were notorious. He had heard of many a grandfather who thought more of his children's children than he did of his own. Sometimes they left everything to their grandchildren.

"Southern kids don't need much. Some of them don't even wear shoes."

His father laughed as though he had made a joke.

"It would have been nice if Evie and the little ones could have been here today. That Jinny, now, she's quite a little lady, isn't she? And the boy's going to grow up into something fine, too."

"They're lovely children, Pop."

"Yes, they are. You take Jinny, you can talk to her just like a grown person. She's going to be a smart girl and a pretty one."

140

Trash and sentimental nonsense. What was the old man thinking of? What was he planning to do? He could fight the others, Helen and young Jubel and even Evie alone, but the children were something else. How do you fight an old man's soft-headed affections? What do you do to direct his senile foolishness?

"I've often wondered why you and Ella never had any children, Bertram."

"What? What did you say?"

"I've often wondered why you and Ella never had any children."

"Where are you going, Bertram? Bertram!"

"Out for a walk."

xii

You can live with a man for fifteen years or you can live fifteen years for a man and not have what time and a husband should give you. And then, suddenly, from outside both of you, and in defiance of time, you find yourself receiving on a silver platter what you ached to suffer through.

"Why should you be so startled, Ella? It's something you've wanted, isn't it? You've hounded me for years for one, haven't you?"

"But you've never wanted a baby, Bertram. When I could have one, you didn't want one. Now, you want one so badly, you're even willing to adopt one."

"I didn't say I wanted one. I'm merely asking you how you feel about it. . . . Well?"

"I don't know what to say. I don't know how I feel about it."

He waited for her to make up her mind. But that was Bertram: snap a judgment for him in thirty seconds on something that was as big as life itself. He stood there, his eyes blinking impatiently.

"Well, do you or don't you?"

"I guess I do."

His eyes stopped, rested. "You know why I'm thinking about it, don't you?"

She nodded but it didn't satisfy him.

142

"It's for the old man's sake. He wants us to have a child. It would make him happy." His mouth wrinkled on the bitter words. "Maybe make him happy enough to stay with us instead of going on to the others, worrying about his hillbilly grand-children."

"Have you done anything about it yet?"

"Just thought about it, that's all; and asked around a little."

It's a man's world, all right, she said to herself. A woman can't have a baby herself, not even an adopted one. For fifteen years she had wanted and he had said no. Now, for five min-utes, he said yes and she said yes. It was a man's world, all right, and a woman just stood by and waited for the nod. All you had to do was look at Helen and you knew it was a man's world. Helen had everything, beautiful emancipation and free-dom and she wore them well, like the latest Paris creation with accessories, but a woman without a man was hunger looking for a stomach to live in.

"But can we afford a child, Bertram?" Now, she was asking him.

"We've got to. If he wants one, we'll afford it."

"It won't be his own grandchild if we adopt one."

"I didn't say we were going to *adopt* one. We could board one for a while. See how it works out. There are a million kids who need a home. You get paid for it, too. I've been looking into it for a couple of weeks now; since Thanksgiving."

She was glad he was being honest for a change. He was as much as telling her that it was just a dodge, a trick, to get his father's money and that was as much as she could expect from Bertram. No use pointing out the ironies to him, reminding him that if they had had the baby she had wanted, he wouldn't have to go scurrying around for a ready-made one now. No use throwing an old moccasin into his face. But standing there, listening to him, was something like listening to a joke being told back to you and you were expected to laugh.

"You see, Ella, I'm not making any mistakes this time. I'm not keeping anything from you. I'm telling you the truth. I'm

143

not trying to be smart. I'm doing what I have to do to protect my own interests. The others would do the same. Besides, it's what the old man wants." He had an afterthought. "I'm not saying we're not going to adopt one. I'll see how things work out."

"It still won't be his grandchild."

"I told you I wasn't going to make any mistakes, didn't I? I'm going to have a talk with the old man."

He went off to find his father but not before he stopped in the dining room for a drink and decided it was good to talk with Ella. It wasn't that she told him anything he didn't know but she was helpful in developing his own thoughts, in testing and airing them. He supposed that was one of the real reasons for wives; to act as a sort of mirrored sounding board. All men, great or small, had to have someone to talk to, someone to reflect themselves in. And it had to be a wife, not just anyone or any wife, but a wife who was a counterpart of the husband. That was what love was, not the attractive opposite but the discovery of yourself in someone else.

He found his father in his room, answering a letter from Helen.

"It's all decided, Bertram. I'm to go to Helen next." He smiled. "I'm beginning to feel like a sacred cow going the round of green pastures."

"What's their hurry? You've been here only a month."

"A month and a half. And before we know it, it'll be Christmas and a new year. The children have been writing each other and now it's decided."

"You don't have to go any place. As a matter of fact, I don't think you should leave here at all; that is, if you like it here."

"I do like it, Bertram." He looked away. "You've made a nice little home for yourself, you and Ella. You're a good son. You've made me feel at home."

He could see, the old man was breaking up over it. Poor Pop, it was a shame, a shame. He leaned over and playfully poked at him.

144

"We love you, Pop. It's good to have you around. Now, you just forget about tramping all over the country, living in furnished rooms, eating in restaurants. You've got to think of yourself."

"I know, but they want me, Bertram. I can't say no."

With a little encouragement, maybe some argument, he felt the old man could be coaxed into staying. But there was plenty of time for that. There might not even be a need for that in another month or so.

"Well, we'll see, Pop." He nodded at the letter. "But don't commit yourself to anything. Don't make any definite plans. You've got plenty of time."

"Yes." His father pushed at the writing with an old finger. "You know, Bertram, I've become quite a letter writer."

"That so?"

"Yes. Never used to do much of it. Your mother did most of the corresponding."

"I don't care for it, myself. I wouldn't bother with it if I were you. Ella writes to the girls."

"Oh, no. I like it. It's a funny thing. It's part of my new living, my retirement, so to speak. I was always afraid of retirement. I never wanted to have nothing to do. But when you stop doing, life has a way of slowing down. It's pace, that's all. You take the time to do things you never did before, and the things you do, you do slowly. You relish them. You make them important, somehow. Writing a letter, or receiving one, becomes an event. Walking down to the mail box or the store —it's a kind of ritual. You take longer to dress and shave. It's pace, Bertram. You just slow down."

"You'll have a tough time slowing down in Boston or New York. Those big cities are mad. And you might find it too slow with Evie. Guess you'd better stay here, after all."

"But it'll be nice to see Evie and the children when I get to them. I don't know my grandchildren too well, you know. Seen them only a few times. It should be nice to stay for a while and get acquainted."

145

"That reminds me, Pop. I wanted to talk with you about something."

"What's that?"

He found himself suddenly embarrassed. The idea of becoming a father, even an adopted one, seemed so out of character for him, so extreme, that for a moment he almost decided to stall and think about it a little more. On the other hand, what did he have to lose? It would be just talk.

"What did you want to talk about, Bertram?"

"Well, in a way it's sort of silly, Pop, but you know, Ella and I have never been able to have any children. Ella has always wanted one and I was thinking . . . How do you feel about an adopted child, Pop?"

There wasn't even a flicker of hesitation. "I think all children are wonderful, adopted or otherwise."

"I'm not talking about children generally, Pop. I'm thinking about an adopted child for Ella and me."

"I know what you're thinking and it's a wonderful idea. I'm all for it."

"But there are a lot of problems involved. Frankly, I'm a little afraid of it. God alone knows, sometimes it's hard enough with your own, I hear."

"It's worth it. To get you've got to give."

"I don't know how I'll feel about someone else's child."

The old man pulled up his chair a little closer. He seemed a little excited, almost eager.

"Let me tell you something, Bertram. Chances are, you know all about it already but haven't stopped to think. In most cases, it's easy enough to have children; sometimes too easy for people who don't want them, and personally I think there are too many unwanted children in the world. A natural father and mother are blessed but the father and mother who adopt a child and give it their love and care are twice blessed."

"Sometimes it doesn't work out."

"Nothing works out all the time. But if you want this to work, it will. You and Ella are two good people. You'd make wonderful parents. You should have a child."

"I'll tell you what I was thinking, Pop. I was thinking of taking in a child, boarding it for a while and then . . ."

"No." The old man almost snapped at him.

"Why not? It seems to me that would be the safest way to do it. That way, there'd be no mistakes. We could try it for a while and if we wanted it . . ."

His father was shaking his head at him. "No, Bertram, if you're going to do it, do it. You can't expect you or Ella, especially Ella, to have a child around and not grow fond of it. It's dangerous to fool around with emotions. You've got to love your child all the way, with no reservation and no thought that it's only a trial and that in another year you might not have it. Absolutely no! If you don't adopt one, don't do anything."

He was a little surprised by the old man. He certainly had very strong feelings about it. If he hadn't gone right to him from Ella, he might have thought she had been talking to him. But he supposed when you got as old as the old man, you accumulated some opinions.

"All right, then, if you feel that way about it, tell me this: how are *you* going to feel about an adopted grandchild?"

The old man seemed to be searching for the right words. "Bertram, I don't know if you'll believe it, but, if anything, I'll love him more because he'll need more love."

He was talking about a "him."

Well, that was one advantage of adopting a child. You could name the sex and even the color of the hair and eyes.

"Would you love him more than Evie's kids?"

"I would love him more. I'd feel he'd have it coming to him."

He stood up. "All right, Pop. Just remember that because we'll adopt one, then, and you'll pick him out. And we'll give him to Ella for a Christmas present."

147

xiii

He had written to Helen before the holidays; a short note without even a salutation:

> *Thought you might like to know Ella and I are adopting a three-year-old child. He'll be home with us for Christmas. Pop is very happy about it.*
>
> *As a matter of fact, Pop is very happy about being here, altogether, and I don't think it would be a good idea to uproot him all over again. Besides, traveling won't do him any good at his age. I'm willing to keep him here with me.*

He had signed it and sent it off. That was more than two weeks ago and here they were well into the month of January and the answer was hot in his hand. He had thought while he wrote it, and many times after he had sent it off, whether it would have been more politic to have mushed it up a little, made it the long flowery note of a loving brother to his dear sister. He might have been more successful if he had. Or he might have been more successful if he hadn't written at all; if he had let Ella do the writing.

148

As it was, the letter he held in his hand wasn't from Helen. It was his own note passed around from Helen to young Jubel and an answer on the back from Evie; not even a different piece of stationery. Didn't those hillbillies know the fundamental decencies of society? Or didn't she and her drunken husband have the price of a piece of writing paper? A strip of brown wrapping would have been better.

Anyhow, the comment from Helen was, "What do you think of this?" Young Jubel had written, "I think it smells." And then there followed the letter from Evie on the other side:

> *Dear Bertram,*
>
> *You have either gone out of your mind or you're trying to be very clever. I don't know which but it doesn't matter because you're not fooling anybody.*
>
> *I feel sorry for your adopted son unless Ella can make up for all you lack. The only thing I can say for the kid is that he won't inherit any of your characteristics.*
>
> *About Pop, you can start packing his bags now. If you don't send him on his way to Helen's, she or young Jubel or I, if I have to, will come for him. Better give up the fight gracefully.*
>
> Love,
> Evie

It was a dirty letter, the kind that left you exposed and bleeding and the dirtiest part of it was the way they had passed it around with their obscene comments. But they weren't going to get away with it. Let them have their cheap, temporary satisfaction for what it was worth. He still had the old man. That's more than they had; what's more, they'd have to get him away. But he didn't want them coming down here, shooting off their mouths to the old man, not any of them.

He went upstairs to find Ella. She was in the bedroom with

149

the baby, turning a book of pictures for him. The room was sprinkled with toys, and he had a flash of their cost; twenty dollars if a dime.

"I thought you left, Bertram."

The baby broke away from her and ran to his knees, waving his book at him.

"Pictures, Daddy."

Bertram looked down at him. There was no denying he was cute and the way Ella dressed him, the corduroy overalls and striped shirts—and those ran into money, too—he was a big little man.

"Pick him up, Bertram. He wants you to."

"Just a minute." He walked over to her, the baby following him. "I want you to read this, first."

"All right, Teddy." He picked up the boy, carried him to a chair and placed him on his lap.

He had never handled a child in his life—not since he was a boy, anyhow, and fooled with young Jubel—but it was certainly strange how quickly you could get used to them.

"Horses, Daddy."

"Yes, a whole bookful of them. Do you like horses?"

"I like horses."

He was a smart boy and talked well for his age. Somehow, he didn't think three-year-olds had any vocabulary at all. He wondered if he could talk when he was three. Teddy leaned his head against his shoulder. He felt warm and comfortable on his lap. Children were the damndest things; the way they snuggled up to you and gave you the unaccountable feeling of need and reliance. He had to admit, the old man had picked a good one. It wasn't only the old man, though, he and Ella and the people at the orphan home had something to say, too. They were careful, mighty careful, and if he hadn't taken as many steps as he had, there were times when he would have dropped the whole idea, right in the middle. It wasn't the routine investigation he had minded so much—his job and character references, although he did resent everyone in the

150

world knowing what his business was—but the personal going over they gave you. Sometimes, he had the feeling they were running him through a psychiatric wringer, and he'd wonder who was doing the adopting, he or the child.

"Try to do a little good in the world and see what they put you through," he had told his father bitterly.

"Now, Bertram, it's only to be expected. They have to be very careful and, besides, there isn't much more to it. You'll forget the unpleasantness after it's over. It'll be worth it, too."

He guessed it was because the old man was so happy about it. Ella, too, but that was to be expected. What he didn't expect was to get a child who even looked a little like him. And it wasn't an accident, either. The people at the home went out of their way to find a three-year-old boy who matched; eyes and hair and a vague sort of resemblance that seemed less vague every day he was in the house. The only thing he wasn't completely pleased with was the boy's name, Theodore. But when the old man told him what it meant—gift of God—he resigned himself to it. Maybe, in a way, it was symbolic; a sign that everything was going to work out all right and the gifts would come rolling in.

He looked at Ella. "Haven't you finished it yet?"

"In a minute."

She had read it and reread it. Now, when he turned away, she looked at him and their son. They were an amazing sight, the two of them together. She had been afraid, so afraid, when it had all started. It was no way to adopt a child; to use, to exploit him for selfish reasons. It wasn't going to work out. It couldn't work out. Once you used someone, whether what you used them for failed or succeeded, you were through with them. They had outlived their purpose, but a child's life had a long way to go. Leave out her own feelings, leave out the hurts she would suffer from the arrangement, and there was still the child. But what could she do? Bertram had wanted it, whatever his reasons. Bertram's father had wanted it and she, herself, had wanted it whatever her fears. Somewhere in her mind she must have had a hope that it would turn out well but she didn't even know about that until it happened. And then she almost didn't believe it because there was so much that could have gone wrong. Most of all, she had been afraid that the boy would distrust Bertram, dislike him and fear him. Next to that, she dreaded Bertram's impatience and the time when he couldn't stand it any more to have him around. But Teddy didn't know about these things and so they didn't affect him. He took to Bertram as he took to everybody else. He loved him. When he found out he was his "Daddy," he loved him more. It was that simple. As for Bertram, he had yielded, let down the bars and given in to his instinct which she knew he had had all the time. She was sure that Bertram in his own way, and with his own capacity, loved the boy.

It was just the premise that bothered her, the reason, in the first place, for having him at all. What was going to happen to Bertram if his plans didn't turn out? How was he going to feel then about the boy?

She turned the letter over again, on its back, to Evie's note. It wasn't nice of them. Helen could have written the answer. She might have written to the others first, if she had wanted to, but she should have been the one to answer. Or, if it was left to Evie, as it was, Evie shouldn't have done it this way. It was unnecessarily cruel, aside from the issue. But the issue was the problem. It was no time for Bertram's father to leave. It was too soon. There'd be no telling what would happen if he left and left Bertram up in the air. All that business of the money—she tossed it aside with her head, it was so trivial. The only important thing was their child and what his life meant to them.

"Well, what do you think? Haven't they got a nerve!"

"It isn't exactly a nice kind of letter."

"Nice! It's putrid. It stinks. It's dirty."

"Bertram." She nodded at the child and shook her head.

"Oh, all right." He gently tipped the boy off his lap. "Go on over to the window, Teddy, and look at . . ." He looked

152

at the window, himself. "Oh, look at the sky or the birds or something."

The boy obeyed happily. He went to the window and looked at the sky or the birds or something. That was the wonderful quality of him, she thought. He wasn't hurt; no child tears, no fleeing legs. He accepted. It was behavior one would hardly expect even from a child born to a normal home.

"What am I going to do, Ella?"

"I've been trying to think."

"You know what's going to happen once he leaves here and they get their hooks into him." He paced a circle and came back. "Don't you?"

She knew. She didn't care but she knew. Once Bertram's father left, he would take with him the peace and quiet and the sugar-coated love. It wasn't what was going to happen to him; what was going to happen to them? She wasn't sure about Bertram any more, not sure of his goodness or his badness. His father and the child had confused her and she would look at Bertram and wonder how much of him was real and how much pink and blue camouflage. You could turn on a child just as easily as you could turn to him; it was only a matter of perspective.

"We've got to think of something, Ella. We've got to keep them away from here." He spun around on a thought. "I know. You call Evie. Tell her the old man doesn't want to leave here."

"I don't know that Evie has a phone."

"Well, call Helen then. Tell her and let her write to Evie."

"It's not the way, Bertram."

"Why not? What else can we do?"

"The three of them can come down here at once. They can come with fire engines but it won't do any good if your father doesn't want to leave. He's the one to talk to, Bertram."

"But the old man doesn't want to go."

"Did he tell you that?"

"No . . . no, he didn't actually tell me that."

"You just took it for granted."

153

"Well, why not? What does he want to go to them for? Live with young Jubel and Helen in two-by-four apartments, swill around with Evie and her tribe? He's an old man. He's got to take care of himself."

"Don't tell it to me. Tell it to him."

"I have told it to him."

"I don't think he's convinced."

"Why?"

"Just my impression. Things he's said. I think he's going, Bertram."

"And leave me here holding the bag?"

She knew what that meant. The bag was Teddy and all that Teddy had cost him. Teddy was also an investment and, while you don't throw an investment away, what do you do with it when it's a bag, too?

"Does it really make any difference, Bertram?"

"Just about twenty thousand dollars' worth of difference. You'll admit that's a difference, won't you?"

When Bertram argued tangibles, you didn't counter with talk of love and happiness and family.

"Yes, that's a difference."

The child came back to him. "Can I stop looking at something now, Daddy? Grandpa's coming."

He looked at her. "I didn't know he was out of the house."

"Of course. He went out for a walk."

"You think I ought to talk to him, then?"

"I think so."

He waited for the sound of the downstairs door, and started out of the room.

"Daddy, take me."

He stopped to tell him no but then he asked himself, why not? It might be a very smart thing to take the boy along; the old man's pride and joy. He scooped him up into his arms and they went down the stairs together.

The old man stood just inside the door, still wrapped in coat and hat, letting down packages from his arms. There was a big

154

hullabaloo of greeting between him and the boy when they came together. You'd think they hadn't seen each other in a year, Bertram thought, but it was all to the good as far as he was concerned. He accomplished the feat of getting rid of his father's coat, scarf and packages without separating the two of them.

"Didn't know you'd still be home, Bertram. Aren't you working today?"

"Oh, I've got a few calls to make but nothing special."

The boy titillated against the old man's cheek. "Cold, Grandpa."

Bertram followed them into the living room. "What are all these packages, Pop?"

"Well, one of them's for Teddy." He put the boy down. "This one." He unwrapped a toy duck mounted on wheels that flapped its wings on a miniature xylophone as the boy pulled it around the room. They watched him until he trailed the din out into the kitchen.

Christmas seemed to go on forever with the old man in the house. Bertram eyed the other packages on the floor.

"Those are just some things I got to take along to Helen."

Helen. Just some things he got to take along to Helen. There it was without even asking for it; a puff of breeze demolishing his carefully built future. He felt himself go cold, as though the pit of his stomach, and especially his navel, were deep frozen, packed in ice.

"What's the matter, Bertram? Is there anything wrong with you?"

"Nothing. I'm all right."

He guessed he really didn't believe it when Ella told him. It was unbelievable even now. After all he had done, all the trouble he had gone through, the money he had spent, even adopting a child for him, after everything, the old man was just going to pick himself up politely and go. Well, he wasn't; not if he could help it, he wasn't. No one was going to make that much of a fool out of him.

155

"I must say, you don't look very well, Bertram. Are you sure you're all right?"

"Listen, Pop, forget about me. I'm all right. I want to talk about you."

But he didn't talk right away. He caught himself in time. Wait a minute, he said, Ella was right again. He hadn't really talked to the old man about leaving; not enough so that it was ever decided either way. In his own mind, it was settled but he never did hear his father say, "All right, Bertram, I'll stay here. I won't go on to Helen's or Evie's." So there was no use going off half-cocked. Settle it now, that's all, for everyone. Maybe the old man wanted to be coaxed or something. Maybe, because he himself had thought it was arranged, he had neglected to make it plain to his father, or let him know how much they wanted him. He thawed a little.

"Pop, I don't know if I told you, but Ella and I—and even Teddy, now—have been counting on you to stay on with us. We want you to stay with us." He leaned on the word, want, and bent his body as he said it.

"Why, I know that, Bertram. You told me that a while ago."

"Then you're not going to Helen's!"

The old man smiled. "But I am, Bertram. Helen's expecting me. They're all expecting me."

"But, Pop . . ."

"Oh, I know how you feel, Bertram, but really there's nothing to worry about. Restaurant food can't be that bad and I'll manage, however the children put me up."

"You can't stand the trip."

His father laughed. "Nonsense. I've been down to the depot; even looked over some of the trains that were standing around. Accommodations seem very comfortable."

"You'll be alone. No one to talk to. Helen works all day."

"I'll get along. I don't mind being alone. Besides, I make friends rather easily."

"You can't make friends in a big city. They'll rob you."

The old man laughed at him.

156

"Pop, you can't go. You've got to stay here."

The old man stopped and looked at him. "Bertram, you really don't look well at all."

"Pop, we made a home for you here."

"Why don't you go upstairs and lie down for a while?"

"Pop, we adopted a baby for you."

"Ella! Ella!"

She came running down the stairs and into the room. When she saw Bertram slumped in his chair, silent, tragic, weeping with dry eyes, she said, "When are you leaving for Helen's, Pop?"

He had tried everything—everything in God's world that he could think of—and here he was driving the old man into Boston himself. That could be a laugh if he had a sense of humor; you do all you can to hold a man to you and you end up by "driving him away." But it wasn't as preposterous as it seemed. He hadn't given up; not completely, even though they were into the city and heading for Helen's street. When they had started, and even before, he had hoped that something would happen, something that would keep the old man with them. Aside from actual effort, like the call Ella made to Helen which didn't work, there was always the unexpected possibility: the old man might get sick, Helen might get sick, something might happen in Helen's life that could change her plans. She might have to leave town, go away on a business trip, something, anything. But with all those possibilities, and a hundred more he was sure he hadn't thought of, nothing came to pass. The preparations and the days went on until, finally, it was time to go and he knew he would have to go with him, drive him there. There was always the one final hope that when he got there, when he saw what city and apartment living was, he'd want to turn around and come right back, and Bertram wanted to be right there to take him back. He even went so far as to plan the trip with an eye to the time of arrival; the

158

middle of the day when Helen would be at work and coming to a strange city and a strange house with nobody home might do the trick. It would help, anyhow.

Nothing up to now had worked, but you never could tell. All along the way, he had hoped the old man wouldn't be up to the trip, that somewhere along the line, it would be too much for him and he'd have to ask to be taken back. No such luck, though; he had weathered it fine despite the long drive, the not too particular restaurants, and the general discomforts of the road, and seemed to be enjoying himself when he wasn't sleeping away with the cat on his lap. Even the city itself didn't discourage him. He was bright and alert to it as they drove through the crowded downtown district, admiring the buildings, the stores and theatres, the enormous numbers of people. And he was thoroughly amused by the damned foolishness of naming one part of a street Milk and the other, Water; one part Spring and the other, Summer.

"I think this city has a sense of humor, Bertram."

"If it has, it's the English kind. You won't understand it. They might have thrown the tea overboard but they've kept everything else."

"It should be almost as good as going abroad, then."

"I spent a week here once. This is a town that can't make up its mind. It's like an old seagull trying to flap along with the rest of the world but it can't because its feet are tied down by phony tradition and culture. You won't like it, Pop."

"I can't see how that would be true, Bertram. After all, there are a number of well-known schools here, the history is genuine enough—even that Tea Party—and it's a big insurance town. I told you I have my policy with a Boston firm."

The old man was determined to like it. You couldn't talk him out of anything. If he didn't know him better, he'd think he was rubbing it in about the insurance policy.

"I've been refreshing myself on American history the past few weeks. It should be interesting to see all the old places: Bunker Hill, the Old North Church, the Massacre, Faneuil Hall."

159

"That Faneuil Hall always sounded like a men's lavatory to me."

"You shouldn't talk that way, Bertram. The Hall was a place of great historical importance." He laughed to himself. "I think I'm going to have a time for myself, nosing around."

I suppose, he thought bitterly, if I had built a museum for him he would have stayed.

"Bertram," his father's voice had that end-of-a-journey quality to it, the last-chance-of-being-alone tone. "I want you to promise me to do something when you get back to Ella and the baby."

His ears pricked up. He had reached the stage now where everything the old man said had significance, where even a change of voice held out a hope for a change of mind. "Promise you what?"

"That you'll see a doctor when you get home. You're not well, Bertram. You're nervous, irritable, high strung. You're not yourself."

That again. Jesus Christ. And he thought it might be something good for a change. That's all he had been hearing from the old man for a week: doctor, doctor, is there a doctor in the house, in the automobile?

"You've not only got a wife now, Bertram, you have a child, too, and you owe it to them to take good care of yourself."

Why did old men have to keep repeating themselves? He had said that, too. That had been during the final stage when he had tried everything in God's world he could think of to make him stay. There was so little time, he gave up going into the office and made only the most necessary calls. He had to talk to him but he could only say so much without giving himself away. In desperation, he had gone out of character and tried two frontal attacks; no tricks, no beating around the bush, just upped and asked him outright.

"Pop, I need some money."

He had lain awake with those words all night, tossed and turned them around after pushing aside the soft-cushioned

160

ones. Indirection had gotten him nowhere. After that decision, which came somewhere around two in the morning, he tried to plot the rest of the conversation: what his father would say to that, how he would say it and where it would lead to. He even tried to frame the old man's questions, "How much money do you need, Bertram?" or "Why do you need money, Bertram?" and his own answers, "Ten thousand dollars right now," or "Because I'm pressed, with the baby and everything, and I've got a chance to go into business for myself."

He had it all worked out but, in the morning, when he got to the old man and dropped the naked statement in his lap, his father said, "What? What did you say, Bertram?"

And that wasn't what he had expected, so he had to repeat himself. "I said I needed some money. I need it bad."

That was his mistake, to rephrase it, but how was he supposed to know the old man wouldn't hear him the first time.

"It's never good to need money desperately, Bertram."

"It may not be good but it just so happens that I do need it desperately." He couldn't backtrack after that. Could he say he didn't need it desperately. Might as well say he didn't need it at all.

"I've found that 'desperate' money somehow never materializes. When you look for money too hard, you find trouble."

Hell, he didn't want a lecture. All this because he had gotten off on the wrong foot, because the old man didn't have his ears open when he had talked to him. Stay up a night and plan a conversation—questions, answers—and take it to a pair of deaf ears.

"Why do you need money so desperately, Bertram?"

Here was the track, after all. Maybe it wasn't a waste of time.

"Because I'm pressed, with the baby and everything, and I've got a chance to go into business for myself."

"How much money do you need?"

"Ten thousand dollars."

"Is it a good business?"

161

It didn't surprise the old man. His hopes were booming. "The best. There's no telling what I can make out of it."

"Have you tried the banks for a loan?"

"I can't get it from the banks."

"Then maybe it isn't a very good business."

"It's a wonderful business, I tell you. That's why I came to you."

"You want me to lend you the money? Ten thousand dollars?"

"Why not? You could sell your house and your business to Agnew——that seventeen thousand, five hundred's a good price. Pop——stay on here with us and help me run my new business."

"I couldn't do that, Bertram."

"Of course, you could. It's a perfect arrangement."

"It wouldn't be fair to the other children."

"Why, Pop, we'd make enough money to take care of everybody."

"I can't do it, Bertram. I'm sorry."

He argued and pleaded with him but the old man wouldn't be moved. "It wouldn't be fair to the other children," he kept saying. Finally, Bertram gave up. He slumped in his chair.

"I'll tell you what I will do for you, though."

He didn't ask him what. He just looked at him and waited.

"I've got a ten-thousand-dollar life insurance policy with a Boston company. When I get up to Helen's, I'll borrow a thousand on it and send it to you."

He didn't say anything to that and very little after that. Truthfully, the news of the insurance policy had proved to be a bit of shock to him. He felt that it called for re-evaluation. In three months his father had jumped from an obvious burden to a man of property with a house and business worth seventeen thousand, five hundred plus a ten-thousand-dollar insurance policy. Talk to him some more and who knows what else might turn up: safe deposit boxes or gilt-edged stocks and bonds. It wasn't too improbable to think that his mother might have had an insurance policy, too.

162

It was something to think about and he had thought about it until the night before they left for Helen's. Then he made his other direct approach.

"Pop," he said, after Ella had taken the baby up to bed, "that insurance policy of yours—Mom was the beneficiary of it, wasn't she?"

"That's right. She still is. I haven't gotten around to changing it. One of the things I want to do when I get up to Boston."

"You didn't have to wait for that. You could have done it through your agent, you know."

"I know. Just put it off. Figured as long as I was going, I'd take care of it personally."

"It's been three months. A lot can happen in three months."

"Not too much. Even if I passed along, I expect," he was amused and he stopped to laugh a little, "I expect there wouldn't be a cat and dog fight over my estate."

"People shouldn't leave money indiscriminately."

"It isn't indiscriminate, Bertram, if you leave it to your children."

"But children are people, Pop. Some deserve it and some don't." He had to watch his voice; it was getting out of hand.

"Not in our family, Bertram."

"Well, some people don't know what to do with money. It's a shame and a sin to give it to them."

His father had looked at him for a quiet moment. "I don't know of any sin that was ever committed by giving. . . . Good night, Bertram."

Good night was right. Only it wasn't a good night for him and he hadn't had a good night since. He wondered, as they drove along Helen's street looking for her house number, whether he'd ever have a good one thinking about it. When he got back home with Ella, they'd have to put their heads together and come up with something. He had told her to do some thinking about it before he left but she was so wrapped up in the baby. Wonder if the kid misses me at all, he asked himself.

163

"If the numbers run right, Bertram, that should be the house just ahead."

It was; an old three-story brick, nothing like what he had expected. He thought Helen would live in a large, noisy apartment house surrounded by a city full of automobile horns.

"It's a nice, quiet neighborhood."

"Chances are, she lives on the top floor. Climbing won't be good for you, Pop."

But he didn't go up first to see if Helen was really on the top floor or whether she was at home at all at a little after three in the afternoon. He took his father's two bags and followed him and the cat up the stoop. It wasn't going to be pleasant for him to find no one home but that's the way it had to be.

"Pop! You're here!"

It was Helen at the door before they had a chance to touch her bell. From the light behind her, he could tell her apartment was on the first floor. He felt cheated, double-crossed. She had no right being home this time of day. How did she know when they'd be coming? She looked as though she had been sitting and waiting for them for hours; smoking a cigarette, reading a magazine, completely dressed and groomed, not caught in the act of anything. He stared down at the bags in his hands while the kissing greeting went on.

"Come in, Bertram. How are you?"

She led the way into her apartment. It, too, looked as though it were expecting them: clean, neat, even a vase of fresh flowers in the carefully furnished living room.

"You've got a lovely place here, Helen."

"I'm glad you like it, Pop. Sit down, both of you." She took their coats.

"I can't stay. I've got to be getting back."

"I'll make you a drink. Scotch?"

"All right."

She mixed it from a little portable bar. "You're looking wonderful, Pop. Bertram must have taken good care of you."

"Bertram and Ella both. They were very good to me."

164

She brought the drink to Bertram. "How is Ella?"

"Fine." He didn't want to say it but he did: "You look very well, Helen."

"Thanks. Tell me about the baby. Somehow, I can't imagine you as a father."

"It's a beautiful baby, Helen. He even looks a little like Bertram."

She thought that was very funny and laughed.

"Aren't you working these days, Helen?"

"Of course, I just took the day off because I was expecting you and Pop."

There was a meow from the end of the room and Helen's kitten came trotting in. He had a hopefully exciting moment as he watched Pitch leap from the old man's lap. The cats met in the middle of the room with their backs up.

"Pitch! Pitch!" the old man called.

Leave him alone, he thought. If the fur flies, maybe you or your cat won't be able to stay here. But it was a short-lived hope. Either Pitch understood his status as a guest, or the kitten just seemed too small to take seriously, but he quieted down. In a minute, they were sniffing and pawing at each other with contemptuous familiarity.

"They'll be all right, Pop. Don't worry." She stood up. "Come on, I'll show you the rest of the place. Want to come along, Bertram?"

"No, I'm all right here."

She came back for a moment. "Angry with me?"

He thought of his letter and how she had sent it around to Evie and young Jubel and what it looked like when it got back to him. He shook his head.

They went out of the room. He sat there, looking around the apartment, staring at the glass in his hand, listening to their voices talking and laughing. It gave him a peculiar sensation: for a minute, he envied the old man staying on here with Helen.

A man, old Jubel said to himself after four days of living in Boston with Helen, is necessarily confined by living and by being just a man. If he were dead and a spirit, he could be any place at any time. Being a man, however, and being fettered by the necessities of the flesh, he must make a place for himself in the world and in making it, he builds a small narrow cubicle for himself and his family and he tolerates only those who have built small narrow cubicles near and like his own. So the farmer knows only his soil and his sky, the city man his office and his flat. Any circle, no matter how large and how freely you move in it, is still a circle.

He talked to himself as he wandered the streets of the city. At first, he walked around the block. Then up and down a street as far as he dared to go. Then followed an avenue until he was almost lost. Each time he widened his circle but it was still a circle bound by the limits of the neighborhood and the city and the infirmities of old legs and a tired body. When he was a young man, a long long time ago, he had the same feeling about the world. It amused him to see how little he had progressed or changed. The in-between years, the squirrel years of activity and production, didn't leave much time for thinking, he guessed. In the early time of his marriage, he would talk about it with Amy. Now, he had only himself to talk to.

It wasn't that he would have done his own life any differently but maybe the children's. Still they weren't his own alone; Amy had something to say about them and they for themselves. It wasn't that he was dissatisfied with them, either. They were living their own lives. Only, if he had been able to give them anything as children, it might have been a sense of freedom, of not being harried or pressured, which they all seemed to be for one reason or another, no matter where or what they were.

When he was at Bertram's, he would wonder quite a bit what was going on at home. He would see the village and the house and think about Agnew. He would remember the rooms, shaded now and empty, and every once in a while he would be sick for them and want to know, at a precise moment, how they looked and how it would feel to be in them again. Here at Helen's he thought of Bertram and Ella and the baby. He would look at the clock and remind himself that they were sitting down to dinner or getting ready to put the baby to bed. He missed them and Bertram bothered him. He didn't like to see him worried and desperate about money; he would have to get around to the insurance company and send him the thousand dollars. Then, he supposed, when he would leave Helen and go on to young Jubel or Evie, he would think of her as well as his own home and Bertram's. And so it would go. But the odd thing was that now he thought less of home and more of Bertram and when he would leave Helen, he would think more about her than of Bertram and even less of home. The trouble with the small circles was that they pressed the people in them. Or was it that the people pulled them tighter to themselves? Maybe circles should stand up on their rims and roll instead of lying flat on their backs, stagnant, going nowhere.

He liked it at Helen's; not that it was better than Bertram's; it was just different. He had put his circle on its rim and it had moved. In the few days he had been with her, he had become aware of the city-world. It was different from the town-world or the country-world; as different as looking at the same object through the opposite ends of a telescope. The country-world magnified everything and everybody. The commonplace was an event. In the city-world, a giant became a pygmy. There were so many people doing so many things, it took a large event to make small talk. In the few days he had been with Helen, he became part of the moving routine of her life. They had established an easy, affectionate relationship in which some of each was rubbed off on the other and there was much giving and taking and he didn't feel as much of a guest as he had at Bertram's. Maybe it was because he could do things for Helen; not in the way of money or gifts but in usefulness to her.

For one thing, he put an end to her nonsense of leaving the house without breakfast in the morning. He reminded her of what her mother used to say, "Breakfast is the most important meal of the day and the difference between a good breakfast and a bad one, or none at all, is the difference between getting out of bed on the right or the wrong foot." There was no real excuse for it now that he was around. She had told him she didn't sleep well, that she didn't usually close her eyes until it was almost time to open them and so she was always late for the office and, besides, she sent out for a container of coffee. But he made it plain what he thought about melted cardboard and the flannel taste of coffee in containers. It was a ridiculous habit for her to have gotten into and he proceeded to change it.

It was no trouble at all for him to get up early enough to put together a working girl's breakfast. He was an early riser anyhow and it was just a matter of getting the hang of the coffee pot and the toaster and the orange squeezer, and synchronizing all their operations with Helen's shower bath and make-up time so that everything came out even and she was sitting down at the kitchen table by the time the last ten-minute bubble bounced to the top of the percolator. Of course, there were protestations about "too much to eat," and "all the bother," but in the end, when she was grabbing for her coat and bag, she stopped for a kiss and a pinch on the cheek and a "You're a good kid, Pop."

It was very rewarding and if he had been more of a cook he might have gone on from there to make dinner every night. But he enjoyed eating out too much. Boston was a good eating town. The restaurant food, in spite of Bertram's warnings, was delicious and it was a delightful treat to be served and waited on by waiters who knew their business. He wasn't a man who relished servility but he liked the comfortable luxury of having his chair pushed up to the table, of having his water glass constantly filled and the other countless observances of dining. At first, he felt a little self-conscious and guilty about it but Helen explained it to him: "But it is right, Pop. You pay for the service as well as the food. Besides, you're such an elegant looking gentleman, everyone wants to do things for you." That was all butter and honey but it was nice to hear, anyhow. Just as it was nice to hear her say, when they walked down the street together or into a restaurant and people looked at them: "They think you're my sugar daddy, Pop."

He reminded her of that when she tried to pay the check the first night.

"Sugar daddies are supposed to pay the bills, Helen. That's their function."

"Not mine. He's different. I pay his bills."

But he wouldn't hear of it. Later on, they came to an agreement. They would alternate paying for dinners with one stipulation he insisted on: he would always select the restaurant. On her nights, he chose the modest inexpensive places. On his nights, they dined at the hotels. And even though he was sure Helen knew what he was doing, she let him have his fun. But he didn't get as much pleasure out of that as he did making breakfast for her or having her call him, as she did now and then, to ask him to pick up a dress for her at the cleaner's or to expect a package from one of the department stores. Or, as he was doing now, putting together the mixings of a Martini for her because she liked a cocktail when she got home from the office.

Let's see, three parts gin to one vermouth. He wasn't making

169

a mistake this time. He had gotten them mixed up on his first try and Helen made a horrible face when she tasted it. After that, he had it fixed in his mind and now he was pretty good at it. A twist of lemon peel and add the ice when Helen was walking in the door, stir—not shake because she said shaking *bruised* the gin—and there you had it, a first-rate Martini, a perfectly vile drink. He had tried a sip of it but it wasn't for him. A little Port wine just to keep her company was good enough and it was good for the stomach's sake, too.

He looked at his watch. Helen would be coming up the street in about ten minutes. He took his seat by the window so that he could see her coming. The cats bounced into the room; Pitch and Helen's little tiger. There was a flurry of furred bodies whirling and cuffing in silent turmoil. After a bit of it, the tiger broke away and, while there was no damage done, it was easy enough to see which cat was ruling the roost. Pitch had certainly taken over in the cat department and, watching him, he wondered if he hadn't in a subtle way done almost the same thing; with as little sound and less fury, but almost the same thing. He had moved into his daughter's house and here he was, in the fashion of fathers, inflicting himself upon her; for one thing, telling her when, what and where to eat, sleeping in her bedroom—even though she had insisted on it—preparing cocktails each evening, expecting to go to dinner with her every night.

Small, even subtle insinuations, each not amounting to much but added all together they might amount to an imposition. He didn't want to impose upon Helen; he didn't want to impose upon any of his children. He didn't want them to start making their lives over again to suit him, or even to change them a little. Yet, he wondered if that wasn't what he was doing without really knowing it. He thought back for a minute to Bertram. Was there anything he had done while he was there that might have made Bertram, or Ella, unhappy or uncomfortable? Were things much different when he left from what they were when he had arrived? Only the baby, that was all and that was all

170

to the good. And Bertram did want him to stay. Sometimes he had been almost violent about it but he suspected that was part of Bertram's nervous temperament, and the things he did, and sometimes said, could be attributed to it. On the whole, he guessed he hadn't been too terrible an influence on Bertram's family and that, by now, they must be back to normal again. It wasn't quite the same with Helen. She was alone and he was moving *into* her life; with Bertram and Ella, he had just moved in *with* them. He had been only a third of the family there, here he was a full half of it. It would be the same with young Jubel. With Evie he wouldn't have to worry at all; only a fifth there. And then back home to be a whole family in himself.

But to get back to Helen. Somehow, he felt he had to watch himself with her, not just go treading in everywhere like an old fool. Now, take that phone call this afternoon. He had been quite annoyed by the man and he had been planning to ask Helen just what it was all about. After all, when you pick up a telephone in a house in which you feel very much at home, you don't expect a voice to say, "Who *is* this?" in a tone that accused you of being a housebreaker or an interloper or whatever.

He was glad he had had the presence of mind not to answer the question but to ask in return, "Who is *this?*" The man was the caller. It was up to him to say who he was first. But there was a confused and surprised silence.

"Hello. I said, who is this?"

"Is this Kenmore 8749?"

He had checked the number on the dial as the voice said it. "Yes, this is Kenmore 8749."

Then carefully, "Is this the residence of Miss Helen Watson?"

"This is the residence of Miss Helen Watson."

"Well, then, who is this?" The man was demanding.

"My dear sir. You are calling this number. It is customary for a caller to announce himself."

More silence and then almost a feeling that he was going to hang up but he didn't.

171

"My name is Raymond Oliver. I'm a friend of Miss Watson."

"This is Miss Watson's father."

"Oh." A laugh of relief and a river of charm. "I'm very sorry, sir. I didn't realize. I'd forgotten that Helen said you'd be visiting her."

"Yes. I'll be here for several months."

"Good. I hope you're enjoying your stay in our city."

"I like it very much."

"Fine."

"Helen isn't at home. She's at the office."

"Really? I called her there but they said she was out. I thought she might be home. She's well?"

"Oh, yes, very well."

"Good. I'll call her again."

"What did you say your name was?"

"Raymond Oliver."

"Raymond Oliver. I'll tell her you called."

"Thank you and I do hope to see you soon, Mr. Watson."

He had been planning to talk to Helen about that call; find out who the man was and why he had acted so peculiarly, as though he had a right to be disturbed when someone else answered the phone. It wasn't that he had any business asking Helen, just curiosity, but now he wasn't sure that he'd do more than mention it to her. He ought to think a little ahead about his behavior with Helen and not make any mistakes. He'd be very unhappy if he did. But he didn't get the chance to do any thinking at the moment because Helen was coming up the steps and he had to hustle to get the ice in the cocktail shaker and open the door for her.

"Pop, do you know what a lucky man you are to be able to stay home and make Martinis?" She had kicked off her shoes and had her first taste of the drink.

"Why? Bad day at the office?"

"Not at the office. I wasn't in much today. Running around like a cockroach trying to placate a woman's club."

"How do you placate a woman's club?"

172

"You don't, you just try. These ladies had a perfectly good client of ours scheduled to speak to them tomorrow afternoon. He's a man who wrote a very interesting book on Egypt. This morning they called—this morning, mind you—and said they didn't want to hear about Egypt. They didn't think it would be stimulating enough and didn't we have one of those southern authors. Have we got southern authors! I told them we practically run an underground railway for southern authors. It was just that time was so short. Well, anyway, I fixed everything up but my little Egypt man is going to be very unhappy tomorrow."

He liked to hear Helen talk about her work. In spite of her complaints, he knew she enjoyed it. There seemed always to be a lot of unexpected excitement in it. He didn't understand what it was all about but it was interesting; the kind of work he'd never know anything about if his daughter weren't in it.

"What makes a southern author stimulating, more so than a man who writes a book about Egypt?"

"I used to wonder about that myself, Pop, but I found out. It's the Negro Problem. To a lot of northern ladies who don't have anything to worry about, the Negro Problem becomes a sort of conscience. They can cheat on their husbands, neglect their children, gossip about their neighbors, but as long as they can be righteously upset about the southern Negro, they feel fine."

He filled her glass again.

"And I even discovered the trick of being a successful southern author."

"Really?"

"Yes, it's very simple. You take your black and white characters. You make all your blacks white and all your whites black. Presto, you have a best seller and a million speaking engagements—in the north, of course."

She achieved the olive at the bottom of the glass. "Well, enough shop talk. How about you, Pop? You have a nice day?"

"Very pleasant. Took a walk this morning, wrote a note to

Bertram, had a nap this afternoon. Oh, you had a call today, Helen."

"I did? Who was it?"

He tried to remember the man's name but it had slipped away from him. That was annoying when he had been thinking about it only a few minutes ago. He went for the telephone pad and brought it back with him. "A Mr. Raymond Oliver."

"Oh, Raymond. What did he call here for?"

"He said he had tried to get you at the office but you weren't in."

"Raymond never leaves his name at the office. He's a competitor of ours, runs a lecture bureau of his own. He was my first boss."

"He said he was a friend of yours."

"He is. Make me another drink, will you, Pop?"

Three parts gin, one vermouth. Helen never had more than the one batch of Martini, not since he had been here, and he wondered if he should make the full amount or cut the formula in half. But he didn't want to ask her. She wanted another drink and that's all there was to it. She could have as much or as little as she liked.

"Did Mr. Oliver seem surprised when you answered the phone?"

"Yes, quite surprised."

"Raymond takes everything for granted . . . Thanks, Pop . . . I hope you didn't tell him you were my father."

"But I did."

"Too bad. A little jealousy wouldn't hurt him."

"Do you see him socially?"

She laughed. "In a secluded sort of way. He's a married man, Pop."

She didn't look at him when she said that and he was glad for it because he could imagine his face. What does a father feel when his daughter gives him news like that? Angry? Indignant? No, just glad that her mother never knew and sorry for her, very sorry.

174

"Are you shocked, Pop?"

"You're a big girl, Helen."

"Big enough and old enough. Almost forty, Pop."

"You don't look it."

"I feel it and more."

"How long have you known him?"

"Years."

He wanted to ask her more but it wasn't really important. She would tell him when she was ready to. He might feel less depressed about it if he could at least be angry with this Mr. Oliver. But Helen obviously loved him.

"Don't take it so hard, Pop. Come on, we'll go out to dinner. I'll fill in all the gory details so that you can be proud of me."

She left him to clean her face.

xvi

When you live alone for a long time, and you get used to it, you guard your loneliness like a good companion and you resent losing it to an intruder; even your own father. Over the years, Loneliness becomes family, friends and part lover and even if there is a real lover who comes and goes, you hold it closer to you because Loneliness is a house of mirrors.

She hadn't looked forward to her father's visit. She felt she had been trapped into it; more by herself than by anyone, more by her emotions, her weakness and then by the togetherness of family. She wondered if her father wasn't the conscience of all of them, if all fathers, all parents, weren't the consciences of all children. It would seem that way with everyone but Bertram but maybe Bertram didn't have a conscience. She wasn't interested in her father's money. She would just as soon have let him stay with Bertram if he wanted him or his money that badly but Evie and young Jubel wouldn't hear of it and she supposed they were right. All of them knew what Bertram was after and it would be plain silly to let him get away with it; just on general principles and ethics. You don't let people take advantage of you even if you aren't too interested in the advantages. Certainly, she was not indifferent to money but there were all kinds of money: good and bad; old and new; blood money and honest money.

176

In the daydream of becoming an heiress, the dream that everyone has, it was always a shadowy uncle twice removed who did the dying; no one whose money was dampened by your own tears, never your father. Right now, money to her had only the vaguest importance. She couldn't honestly say it would change her life in any way. She wouldn't give up her job—that was most of her life—so she wouldn't sleep late or luxuriate herself in idleness. She might buy a few more clothes and permit herself the indulgences of more plays, more books, more concerts, more of the fillers to round out the corners of living, but not enough difference even to bother with a star wish. She sometimes thought, but not seriously and only in her times of depression, that if she had the money she'd leave Boston and Raymond. Or was it Raymond and Boston? That was the convenience of money: it could take you away physically, keep you from facing a situation, from having anything to do with people or things once they became too much for you. You just picked yourself up and left town. It called for no resolution, no strength of character. You bought your ticket, packed your bags and went away. Still, having the money and not the resolution or the strength of character, you might just as easily buy another ticket, pack your bags again and return. The point was to have just enough money to get far enough away so that you couldn't return. And she had that if she wanted it. She didn't want it. She guessed she didn't want anything but to stay where she was and keep picking up the crumbs of Raymond Oliver that fell from his wife's table. Someday, when she would be old, older than her father was now, and sitting alone, a little girl would come to her—just as little boys came to old men to inquire about wars and blizzards—and ask her, "And what did you do all your life, Mistress Watson?" She would answer, "I sat and waited like a dog, living off the left-overs of a man." "And were the left-overs good, Mistress Watson?" "Very good but they didn't make me feel less of a dog."

If she had been the kind of a girl—woman—she hoped she

177

was, she would have welcomed her father's visit. It was a heaven-sent opportunity to quit Raymond for three months and see if she could stand it. But she didn't want to give it a chance; misery could be heaven-sent, too. She knew what visits were like, even small ones from old schoolgirl friends who were passing through Boston. It was always the night they stayed that Raymond could get away. She would tell herself, what difference one night over the years. Surely, you can spare it. Be generous, hospitable, gracious and she was, even though she was so mad she could spit. Such a waste of pearls! With her own father, though, it should have been different; blood and water. And she had gone through that adolescent stage, years ago, of family rejection. She loved her father, really loved him now. She had been miserable at the thought of his being alone and she wasn't sure, even now, that she wouldn't have fallen apart and taken him home with her for good if they all hadn't discovered Bertram and the money and come to this arrangement. After that, you'd think she'd have been pleased; only three months when she might have had years. And those three months were three months away, three months at Bertram's first. There was time to relax and prepare herself for her father's visit. It didn't work out that way. Those had been three months of worry and fretting, of wondering every day while she was worrying, whether it wouldn't have been better to take him first; go through it instead of having to look forward to it, three months' worrying and three months' having.

Bertram's letter, when it came, was welcome hope. It wasn't news to her that he wanted to keep Pop with him and she had no illusions that Evie and young Jubel would let him but, wrong as it was, she hoped for it. Something might have happened to make them change their minds; if young Jubel got himself some work or if Evie's husband, Neal, said absolutely no to her father's coming or if they both saw things in a different light, now that they were away from it. She could hope for it but that's about all she could do. Even though Bertram had written to her, it wasn't up to her, it was a family affair. She thought about writing Evie to tell her she agreed with Bertram but she didn't dare. In the end—and she didn't know whether she was motivated by weakness or strength— she simply scribbled, "What do you think of this?" on Bertram's note and sent it on to young Jubel.

She went to Raymond, too, for help. In a way it was his problem as well as hers. As a matter of fact it was her main topic of conversation with him when they talked at all.

"It seems to me you could at least try to see me more often this month."

She had taken his preoccupied thoughts away from him. "What did you say?"

"My father. He's going to be here in a couple of weeks. Remember?"

"Oh. Your father. God bless him. He's a dear old man, isn't he?"

"Yes." Yes, indeed, he was a dear old man and God bless him, indeed, but she didn't want to discuss him as a person; he wasn't a conversation piece. God wasn't either, for that matter, except that Raymond was forever calling on Him to bless everyone. She still wasn't used to it. It was blasphemous, profane; the same kind of perverted vanity that women displayed when they decorated their bosoms with the cross. She didn't like the sound of God in people's mouths all the time. You spoke to Him and carried Him in your heart. You didn't go around displaying Him.

"He's coming here next month, Raymond. I'm not going to have a life I can call my own."

"It'll only be for a little while."

"Three months! Do you call that a little while?"

"Three months. Oh, my dear, I didn't know."

"I've told you enough times. Three months!"

"Yes, my dear, I know, but there's no sense in getting excited about it."

"What are we going to do?"

He thought about it but when Raymond thought you

couldn't be sure he was thinking about what he was supposed to or whether his mind was on a client, his wife or one of his children. He had the same look for all of them.

"It's . . . It's quite a long time, three months, isn't it?"

"Yes, it's a long time."

"But what about your brothers and sisters? Surely, they can take him just as well as you."

"I have only one sister, I'm the other. And he's staying with one of my brothers now. I'm next on the list. Don't you understand?"

He was tired. She could tell he would much rather have leaned back and relaxed a little, maybe even napped a little.

"But didn't you tell me one of your brothers wanted to keep him?"

She didn't remember that but she must have told him. Weren't any secrets safe? Not that that was a secret but it was amazing the things you told a man.

"I told you." But she had told him again, going back to her mother's death, going back to the house with Evie, Bertram and young Jubel, telling him about her father and his house and his business and even of Agnew.

After he had heard it all, he laughed. "That brother of yours, that Bertram, he's a fox, isn't he?"

"I don't care what he is or what he gets out of it. It's worth every cent to have someone else move in on your life."

"But you have to care, Helen."

"I know I do. The others won't let me out of it."

"Not for the others, for yourself, Helen."

"But I don't care about the money, I tell you. I don't want my father's money."

He came to her across the room.

"Darling, you've got to help me out of this, you've just got to. I won't be able to stand it for three months. I'm entitled to a life of my own at my age."

"Now, Helen, let's be sensible about this. The money, after

180

your father goes, God bless him, will belong to you just as much as it does to any of them."

"I don't want it, Raymond. I want to be left alone."

"Maybe more to you. Maybe your father loves you more than the others."

"I don't want it."

"That's ridiculous. That's like saying you don't want food or rent or clothes on your back. Now, that's a tidy sum of money, Helen, and suppose the dear old man wants to leave most of it to you. You can do things with that money . . . invest it or start a little business of your own. It's security for you and you can't turn your nose up at security."

He should have known better than to throw those cold water words at her. "Raymond!"

"What is it, dearest?"

"I've told you, you don't ever have to worry about me! I'm not your responsibility. I've never taken any money from you, I don't expect any. When I'm too old to work, I'll take poison or go into an old ladies' home."

She had moved away from his soothing hands. That ended it. They didn't talk about it any more. After that, she resigned herself to her father's visit. The days moved on like creeping paralysis, filling her with a hopeless inertia until almost the very last when she suddenly became impatient for them and her father to come and get it over with. But when they did, and he drove up to the door and she saw him climbing the steps, somehow it took no effort at all to throw her arms around him and kiss him and tell him how glad she was to see him. She guessed blood had taken over.

It hadn't been so bad. Pop was a dear, sweet man, a little old darling, and God bless him, she thought, and she laughed as she thought it. She should have known that nothing was ever as bad as you expected it to be. It wasn't that she was able to have Raymond to the house—and it was a month, now —but that she wasn't dying for him as much as she thought she would. Sometimes, she wondered why that was. Could she

181

be getting into the years where companionship meant more than love, or took the place of love? No, she could feel her own body denying that. She needed him, she still needed him badly; every time they had lunch together, she wanted him, every time she put her head to the pillow. But having her father around, coming home to find him there, eating with him, living with him in the house, seemed to take the curse off it. It was odd because it was her father who was keeping them apart and it was her same father who made being apart more bearable. Oh, nuts, she didn't understand it.

She didn't know whether she had made a mistake to tell Pop about Raymond; not for her sake—for his. She didn't know why she had at all except that it seemed so natural to. If Raymond hadn't called the house and they hadn't gotten started on him and if she hadn't been tired and missing him, Pop might never have known about him. But he did call and Pop had spoken to him; one thing just led to another, greased along by a couple of Martinis, of course. Well, it was done and she didn't regret it, wouldn't regret it at all if Pop didn't make so much of it.

"Helen," he'd say, "there's no reason for you to have dinner with me every night. I don't mind eating alone once in a while; especially now since I know my way around."

"Now, Pop, I told you Raymond's a married man. He goes home for dinner every night."

He had made believe it wasn't that at all. She must have other friends she might like having dinner with. No, no other friends. There was a man who had called her from New York, someone, she told him, she had met when she had flown home for Mom's funeral. He was a nice man, not exactly her type, but he was coming down to Boston for a weekend soon and she had promised to go out with him. She had assured her father she would let him know when that would happen and he could have his dinner alone.

Some days later, he talked about spending the night in town at a Turkish bath. "Haven't been to one of them in years," he said.

182

"Oh, Pop, that's silly. You know you never went to Turkish baths."

"I did, too, years ago, before you were born."

"Well, you can't have missed them very badly. Anyhow, I don't think they're good for you. They're too exhausting."

"No such thing. If anything, they're invigorating. Chances are, I'll come out feeling fifty years younger. I remember," and he went on at great length about the steamings, the massages and the rubdowns.

She had let him finish. "All right, if you want to go that much. But there's no reason why you have to spend the night there. You have your days to yourself, you know."

She had expected him to be flustered by that but he wasn't. He spoke as though he had the answer all prepared.

"It's safer to stay the night. Less chance of taking cold."

"Fiddlesticks! You can cool off in an hour or two." She moved to the arm of his chair. "Pop, you're a sweet old thing but if I want you to leave the house or if I want to be alone for a while, I'll give you a quarter and you can go to the movies. How's that?"

He had laughed heartily at that. "I'm afraid I come higher than that unless you think I could sneak in for half price."

"Now, Pop, let's be serious. I know what you're trying to do and I wish you'd stop it. We're both big grown-up people and we can be perfectly honest with ourselves. If I want to have Raymond over here for a visit, I'll tell you."

How civilized language was; over for a *visit*. How nicely an innocent word could cover up, disguise and tie all the human emotions into a neat, innocuous little package with even a ribbon on it.

"All right, Helen, we'll be perfectly honest. I don't really give a hang about Turkish baths. We have a fine bathtub right here in the house and it's good enough for me but it was either the Turkish baths or some other story that wouldn't be quite as convincing."

"It wasn't a bit convincing, not to me, anyhow."

183

"Well, the others weren't half as good. I thought of running into an old friend at the insurance office, someone I could spend the night with."

"What insurance office, Pop?"

"The one I have my policy with. Didn't I tell you?"

He watched her shake her head.

"That's strange. I was sure I told you, Helen. I guess my memory isn't what it used to be."

She wouldn't let him brood about it. "What about the insurance office, Pop?"

"It's a Boston firm. I suppose I should have written to them and had them change my beneficiary right after your mother died—at least, Bertram said I should have done it—but I managed to survive until I got here. Anyway, I took care of it and I also borrowed the money for Bertram on it."

"For Bertram?"

"Didn't I tell you that either?"

"No, Pop."

"Well, Bertram needed some money. He adopted this little boy, you know, and he was talking about going into business for himself. As a matter of fact, he wanted me to sell my house and business and go in with him."

"Did he want you to stay on with him, too?"

"See? I knew I had told you."

"No, Pop, but go on. Did he want you to stay?"

"Yes, he did. Wanted me to stay, wanted me to go in business with him."

"Why didn't you?"

He thought about it for a while, as though he were trying to remember all his reasons. "Well, if Bertram were my only child, I might have. But I have three others, you know. It wouldn't be fair to them." He thought a little more about it. "I know Bertram's had a lot of expenses and jobs aren't what they used to be. You have to hustle around these days to make a living. I borrowed a thousand dollars on my policy and sent it to him. I thought I told you that."

184

"No, Pop."

"It's nothing to worry about. I get money regularly from Agnew and I'll pay it back."

"I'm not worried about it, Pop. I think you should have done exactly what you did. And I think, if you wanted to stay with Bertram, you should have done that, too, and forgotten about the rest of us."

"Oh, no. No, no, no. I wanted to come on to you, Helen."

She let him alone for a minute while he thought thoughts that she couldn't guess at. He came back quickly, though, and rather suddenly.

"I'm very happy here, Helen. You're a good daughter. But I don't want to interfere with your life. I don't want to be in the way."

She had kissed the top of his head. "You're not in my way, Pop, and you're a better father than I am a daughter. I know I'm a disappointment to you. I know I should have been married years ago and given you grandchildren by now." She had to stop because, suddenly, her eyes were brimming.

"No. Helen. As long as you're happy."

"I'm not happy, Pop. I'm not happy. I'm miserable. How can I be happy with a married lover, with a man who isn't my own?"

She didn't expect him to answer. She had stopped because, for a moment, she couldn't speak any more. She had to stand up.

"He's Catholic and he thinks more of his Church than he does of me." She had choked up. "And I'm not big enough to fight the Church." She had run for the bathroom.

The bathroom, now that she thought of it, was about the most emotionally used room in a small city apartment. She ran to it when she was happy to see what joy did to her face in the best mirror in the house, to see what she could do *with* her face after she had cried; to be sick in, to be clean in, to start and finish her wonderful days and her miserable days in. She wondered if all women took their emotions to their bathrooms, if Ella, when she couldn't stand it any more, ran to her bathroom, if Evie ran to hers. But did Evie have a bathroom? Down there in Georgia where she was, there might be only outhouses, and you couldn't run to an outhouse with your troubles. With the troubles Evie had—that husband of hers and the children and the struggle to keep going—she could be in a constant state of emotional diarrhea, outhouse or no. That's why she didn't want to write to her about Bertram and the thousand dollars Pop had borrowed on his insurance policy for him; another upset. She argued it with herself for a week but she finally did write and tell her because she knew how strongly Evie felt about the whole business and that she was entitled to know.

She did make it as painless as possible, though, having learned over the years that the worst kind of news is never as bad as delivering it badly. Instead of making it a special letter, a "what do you think has happened" affair, with black indignation scrawled all over the paper, she made it a simple note. She said that their father was well and passing the time pleasantly. She told them the movies they had seen and the places where they had dined and then, near the end, just a few offhand lines. "By the way, it's just as well Pop came here when he did. I just found out he borrowed a thousand dollars on his insurance policy for Bertram. It's nothing to really worry about because Pop is paying it back. I thought you ought to know so that you could be happy he got off so cheaply."

She wrote the same letter, practically word for word, to young Jubel, too. After she did, she felt much better. It was a load off her shoulders and she had enough of her own troubles to worry about. She had reached the point with Pop, and with Raymond too for that matter, where a meeting between the two was inevitable. Raymond had openly asked for it and her father—while he never remotely suggested it—was naturally curious. Every once in a while he'd ask how Mr. Oliver was or say something in a conversation—like, "Saw a man on the street today who looked very much like your Mr. Oliver, from

186

your description of him"—that would show he was thinking about him. She guessed she didn't need much encouragement to talk about Raymond, either, and between the two of them, Raymond was a good part of their relationship.

But it was Raymond who really forced the issue. After the surprise telephone talk with her father, he always asked for him. As the time passed and she made no move to bring them together, he became annoyed. One day it made for a completely disagreeable lunch at which they talked about nothing else.

"I'm not being unreasonable, Helen. I think you're deliberately keeping me away from your father."

"I'm not deliberately keeping you away. I'm just not doing anything to bring you together."

"Same thing."

"All right. It's the same thing."

She had looked out of the restaurant window. Snow was falling on Tremont Street and on the Commons across the way. Up on Beacon Hill, the golden dome of the State House was being tarnished by it. It was an absurd March snow that had no business falling so close to spring. It made as much sense as this argument they were having. She had better call Pop and tell him not to go out this afternoon; with that east wind blowing, it would be pretty treacherous underfoot.

"Here it is almost time for him to leave. . . . How long has he been here?"

"Two months."

"Two months, and I haven't even set eyes on him. Aren't you ashamed, Helen?"

"I? Ashamed?" She had laughed in his face.

"Well, he knows about me, doesn't he?"

"You know he does."

"Has he said he doesn't want to see me?"

"No. I think he might even be a little curious about you."

"All right, then, why haven't you done anything about it?"

"I'm a little embarrassed, frankly, for your sake."

187

"You don't have to be. If your father, bless him, is everything you say he is, there won't be any embarrassment. Come on, Helen," he had leaned across the table, touching her without moving a hand. "If he didn't know about me at all, it would be another thing. But he does know, and all this is silly."

Perhaps it was silly. She hadn't kept them apart because she was afraid of anything. It was just that she loved each of them so much in different ways and she had put each of them in different parts of her life. What would it be like to have them together in the same room?

"All right, Raymond. Will you have a drink with us tonight? Come over about six. I'll call Pop and tell him to mix double Martinis."

Work, for the rest of the day, was a nuisance she didn't bother with. It would have been silly even to attempt any, the way she felt. She spent the afternoon pushing papers around, working hard at postponing everything that was due for attention. She canceled two appointments—there was no sense in talking to people if you weren't going to know what they or you were talking about—and spent a good deal of her time running to the ladies' room; pure nervousness. All in all, she built up a head-splitting rest-of-the-week for herself. Not that it mattered; nothing mattered but six o'clock this evening. Time and events after that would be only echoes.

She left the office ten minutes early and taxied home. She realized she was acting like a schoolgirl but she couldn't help it. In the cab, she went over her wardrobe and decided on her blue taffeta. That with a touch of white and pearl earrings would do it. She worried about the house. Was it clean? Pop straightened it out a little every day but the girl wasn't coming in until tomorrow. God, she was carrying on like a fool. You'd think she'd never had Raymond over, that he was a new boy friend who had never seen what she or her house could look like. And what about Raymond? Oh, how she hoped he'd behave himself and look handsome. What was he wearing today? A dark suit but he always wore dark. Was it flannel or serge or what? She wanted so much to have Pop like him. And Pop? Oh, dear, stop dithering.

She didn't have to worry about Pop. He was dressed and shining and waiting for her.

"Pop, what did you do to yourself? You look beautiful!"

He was pleased. "Just brushed myself a little and went down to the barber for a shave."

"You look extra pink and white. I'm so proud of you. And that's a new shirt you're wearing. And I love that tie!"

"It isn't every day that an old man gets to meet his daughter's beau."

"You're really sweet, Pop. I've got to rush. Raymond'll be here any minute."

"I made half a drink for you, just in case you needed it."

"I do, I do."

She gulped the drink and whirled into her dressing. She looked radiant in the bathroom mirror. It was fun and Pop was excited, too. She was almost bubbling and she didn't know how long it was since she had bubbled.

Before she was ready and out, she heard Raymond's voice God blessing her father, so she never did know how the meeting came off. But it must have gone well because they were chatting brightly when she came in the room. They both stood up and exclaimed over her.

"You have a very beautiful daughter, Mr. Watson, but I suppose you know that." Raymond was being hearty this evening.

They sat down and she passed the drinks: the Port wine to her father, the Martinis for Raymond and herself. As she came to Raymond, he touched her nose. "A mite too much powder on tonight, my dear."

"Never mind my nose. Take care of your drink." She wanted to tell him not to be so damned possessive.

He took his drink and held it up. "Helen, you're still using that light vermouth. You know I don't like it."

"Oh, quiet, and drink."

They drank silently for a moment.

"Helen tells me you've been visiting one of your other children."

"Yes, my oldest son, Bertram." Pop was so dignified and yet nice.

"Making the rounds, huh?"

"Yes, seeing them all."

"I'll bet none of them are as wonderful as Helen."

"Oh, stop it, Raymond."

Pop took a sip of his Port. "I think all my children are pretty wonderful."

"Even the oldest one, that Bertram?"

Pop gave him a surprised look. "Why, yes." Then he looked at Helen.

"Of course, Bertram's wonderful. He even wanted Pop to stay with him for good and any son who wants that is a pretty wonderful son."

"I agree with you, Helen."

"But I thought . . ."

"Phooey on what you thought. Let's not talk family. Pop is up to his ears in family all the time."

"I don't know about that. Family is mighty important. Don't you think so, Mr. Watson?"

Pop walked the fence on that. "Yes, I suppose so, at times."

"It's the whole foundation of our American way of life."

"That's where we'll leave it then, Raymond, right at the bottom. I'm for a little lighter talk."

He looked hurt. "Sometimes, Helen, I don't understand you."

"You do, don't you, Pop?"

"I try."

"You do."

They traded a short understanding laugh and Pop turned to Raymond.

"I understand you're in the same business that Helen is in, Mr. Oliver."

190

"I gave Helen her start. Didn't she tell you?"

"Yes, she did. You were her first boss here."

She sat and looked at them, not listening. Why wasn't it going right? What was each of them doing to each other? The room was square and hard with corners everywhere; even the words had corners. Now they were talking about business; what it used to be in the old days. There wasn't any hostility —the talk was civilized, polite, interesting—but no warmth, either. Now, it was Boston, old historical Boston with all the landmarks and the romance of the Revolution. All good conversation along with the remarks her father made about the Gettysburg battlefields, but it was all high-surface, brittle, with not a drop of humanity in it; or only as much as you could find in a museum. What was it? They seemed to be walking on eggs—old eggs. That was it—*old* eggs. Not a word about tomorrow or the future. Was it because there was no future for Raymond and herself? How could he talk about tomorrow when tonight, in a little while, he would be home with his wife and his children?

She stood up. "Raymond, you've got to go."

He looked at his watch. "Oh, my God, yes!" He hurried to the closet for his hat and coat with the panic of the late and guilty husband.

"It's been wonderful meeting you, Mr. Watson. I'll see you again before you leave. God bless you."

She took him to the door and said good night to him there. She wished there were some way she could get to the bathroom without seeing her father.

191

xvii

Mr. Harry Lunning came up from New York about two weeks after Raymond's visit to the house. It was almost the end of her father's stay and she found herself calling it an intrusion; especially since it was a weekend visit and that meant spending her own time away from Pop. If there had been a decent way to avoid it, she would have but sometimes it was harder to hurt a nice person than it was yourself. And Mr. Lunning was a nice man; much nicer than she probably deserved. Any man who would pay as much attention to her as he did, after one short meeting which lasted as long as a plane ride from New York to Harrisburg, was just plain crazy or a heck of a nice guy. In this material day and age, maybe it was the same thing. Nevertheless, you couldn't ignore the fact that a man with whom you passed an hour of flying time on your way home to your mother's funeral would think enough of you not only to remember your name and address, long after you had forgotten his and him, but to see to it that you had a little package waiting for you when you got home.

It was a nice gesture, a reaching, thoughtful touch that took the coldness out of coming back to a dark, empty apartment. At another time, in another mood, she might have resented the gift from such an almost absolute stranger but it had seemed right just then. It was a bottle of brandy and that seemed right, too. Flowers would have been funereal, candy frivolous. Brandy, somehow, was comforting and a darned sight more thoughtful—whatever it was—than the nothing she found from Raymond.

She wrote him a thank-you note the next day. Later in the week, he called her from New York. She had been waiting for a call from Raymond, which didn't come, and Mr. Lunning's call managed to save the evening. With anyone else, it might have been an awkward conversation—after all, they didn't even know each other enough to have anything in common—but Mr. Lunning kept up his end of it with such genuine sparkle that it was no trouble at all and she even heard herself sounding cheerful. After she hung up, she realized he hadn't said a word to her, not even jokingly, about her promise to stop off in New York, call him and have dinner with him. He was a strange man. In the grown-up world that she knew, he sounded as artless and disarming as a schoolboy. He didn't even ask for a date or when he might see her, nothing like that. It was just a chit-chatty long-distance call. And the irony of it, of course, was that they had talked dollars' worth about nothing while there wasn't a nickel's worth from Raymond.

Mr. Lunning was silent for several days after that but then another package arrived, a book of humorous verse. That seemed right, too. A letter followed in which he said he was coming up to Boston to see a client and would it be possible for them to have dinner together. He named the date, the time and would leave the place up to her. He realized she might be busy. If so, how about lunch or cocktails? She felt tired and neglected. She said dinner.

Dinner with Mr. Lunning had proved to be very good for the digestion. It was relaxing. She didn't have to worry if he would be able to make it, if something, at the last minute, would keep him from meeting her. She didn't have to bother about which restaurant they went to or where they sat. It didn't matter who saw them. It had been a different enough

193

kind of evening to be interesting and she found out a few things about Mr. Lunning. She heard again that he was a widower and a grandfather but there seemed to be design in his repetition; as though he wanted her to know for sure. Then he told her he was a lawyer.

"A lawyer! Really?"

"Yes. Why, does that surprise you?"

"It shouldn't. There are certainly enough lawyers in the world. But, somehow, I never suspected it of you."

"We come in all shapes and sizes."

"I know you do."

"Then I don't look intelligent enough."

"Of course, you do."

"Maybe not forceful or clever enough?"

"Oh, but you are, Mr. Lunning."

He had leaned over to her. "I'll tell you my secret. I never go near a courtroom."

She could laugh whenever she thought of that.

"I let my young partners impress the juries. They're much prettier than I am. I used to let them come up to Boston, too, to take care of our New England clients, but I've decided our New England clients need my personal attention."

"I'm sure they do."

"Almost bowled them over when I walked in on a couple of them today. I could see them asking themselves, 'What's Lunning doing up here? The old goat must think we're pretty important after all.'"

"Oh, you're not old at all, Mr. Lunning, and you're certainly not a goat."

"I'll keep thinking I am until you stop calling me, 'Mr. Lunning.' You know my first name, Helen; it's Harry."

"I know but Harry to me is either an English bookie or a prize fighter."

"You leave me with no choice, then. I'll have to change either my name or my profession."

"I don't think so. We can always find you a nickname."

194

He looked a little uncomfortable. "Truthfully, Helen, my name is Harrison. Harrison Lunning, that's what I was born with."

"But that's a beautiful name. Why on earth did you change it?"

"It frightened me. When I was in school and the teacher would call out, 'Harrison Lunning,' or when I had to write that name on top of a paper, I always had the feeling I was wearing a dress suit. You'll have to admit, it's a pretty formidable lifetime burden."

"Well . . . Maybe."

"A name like that sets you apart, makes you different in a world full of Johns and Williams. I didn't want to be set apart."

He certainly was an odd, uncomplicated man. Most people spent a good part of their lives trying to be different, working hard at their clothes or their haircuts or their names—adding initials, front or middle, or hyphens or redundant spellings—anything to set them apart, but Mr. Lunning wanted to be just "Harry," walking along in the crowd. She wondered, many times after that dinner, if there might not be some remote psychological reason for it, if it wasn't possibly an obscure snobbishness or the epitome of snobbishness. A man could feel so sure of himself that he didn't have to try to be different. But wasn't that just like her, to go looking for complications when there really weren't any. In the final analysis, it didn't matter either way. She wasn't interested enough in Mr. Lunning or Harry Lunning or Harrison Lunning or Whatever Lunning. He was a nice man but that's where it began and that's where it ended and she supposed the right thing to do was let him know it before he began getting intentions, good, bad, honorable or otherwise. The trouble with men was that they always had intentions. She supposed they'd be pretty horrible without them and it would be pretty horrible for her if they didn't have them and heave them at her once in a while. She might even feel older than she did now. But why couldn't the right intentions belong to the right man? Why couldn't Raymond have

195

good intentions? And why did they all have to belong to the "too" men: the men who were too old or too fat or too dull. Or too married? No, Raymond was too married. She guessed there couldn't be anything right with the wrong man or wrong with the right, and you didn't mind fat if you loved a fat man or age if you loved an old man or dullness if you loved a dull one—or marriage, either.

' She wished she could have achieved some sense at her age. Here she had gone on for years with Raymond, fooling herself, hoping in her private little land of pleasant dementia, that he would give up his Church and his wife and come to her. She had spent days, sometimes, denouncing him and renouncing him, giving him up entirely on Christmas and New Year's Eve and taking him back after the unhappy holidays. Perhaps the only real hope she had of getting Raymond was the long chance that some day he would be a widower. But someday everyone was going to be a widower or a widow or . . . What did they call dead old maids? Not even a dignified name for them . . . Anyhow, she had gone on for fifteen years and when an eligible man would come along, she wouldn't give him half a chance, just as she wasn't giving Mr. Lunning half a chance. Why? Damn it, women were fools! Man for man, if she could wipe the love out of her eyes, Raymond couldn't hold a candle to Mr. Lunning. Scrape them down for quality and all that would be left of Raymond would be a pair of French cuffs and a precious head of hair. Had *he* simplified *his* name to Ray? Man for man, but it wasn't man for man, it was man for woman and that was the hell of it, that would always be the hell of it. Deep, away down deep, it was the elementary passion that counted and she was sure that being in love for a woman meant being comfortable in bed with a man. Bodies were never good at carrying on bad conversation.

So much for being rational and smart and having all the sense in the world. Where did she go with all these sessions of self-flagellation? Why did she have them? Most times because something happened to make her stop and take a look: her mother's death, the lonely holidays, her father's visit (How was young Jubel getting along with *his* troubles?) or having an unpleasant time with Raymond. It had been a mistake to bring them together. He had been just a pig with Pop and there was no excuse for it, no excuse.

"I don't agree with you, Helen. More than likely, he was uncomfortable and unhappy and didn't know what to do about it."

"But he wanted to see you, Pop. He insisted on it."

"Sometimes a thing doesn't come off the way we hope it will, even a little thing like meeting someone."

"I don't understand it, throwing his weight around that way. He really isn't that bad."

"I'm sure he isn't. It probably was my fault. After all, I was pretty secure in my position. Let's not talk about it any more, Helen. I'll be leaving here soon and there's no reason to let anything so small interfere with your life. Promise me you won't even mention it to Mr. Oliver."

She had promised him and she didn't mention it to Raymond. But it left a bad taste and she felt she had to do something about it. It was because of that and maybe because she didn't want her father to feel she was completely lost that she asked Mr. Lunning to the house and to dinner there. She knew it wasn't exactly what she wanted to do to his intentions but she would take care of those later on. The important thing was to wipe out a little of what Raymond had left.

She had a girl in to cook and serve the meal Pop had insisted on buying: a roast goose with apricot dressing, candied sweet potatoes, corn souffle, asparagus, tomato juice, biscuits and, for dessert, an out-of-season strawberry whip.

"I can remember," Jubel said later on, "when an out-of-season strawberry was rare enough to be framed and set under glass."

Mr. Lunning could, too, and he told Pop not to sound like such an old codger when there was barely a twenty-year difference between them.

It was an evening that Mr. Lunning had set the stage for when he tasted his first Martini.

"It doesn't seem possible," he said with genuine surprise, "a man who doesn't drink Martinis could mix one as good as this."

Pop was flattered. He said it was nothing, just like making a pot of coffee or frying a few eggs. But he loved it and it was a shame that Raymond couldn't have said something like that. But Mr. Lunning had come into the house with clean hands. There was no wife waiting for him, no fear of tomorrow and no setting himself apart from the older man.

"I wish you'd call me Harry, Mr. Watson. I'd appreciate it very much."

"Why, sure, I'd be glad to."

And Pop said the name with such friendliness, she began to think Mr. Lunning had been right to change it. On every count they had so much more in common that it was painful to remember Raymond's visit. They were both widowers and even though it was strange to sit and listen to these two men talk about the loneliness that comes after, it was never uncomfortable. She was sure Mr. Lunning's wife had died at least ten years ago but his sympathy was active enough to make it seem like last year. The only difference was that while he let Pop talk a great deal about her mother, he never mentioned his own wife. He did it effortlessly but she appreciated his tact and skill. It almost made her want to ask him about her.

There were other fields of equal familiarity to both men. Mr. Lunning was well acquainted with Pennsylvania. He had a son in Harrisburg—Helen knew that—and, oh yes, they were both grandfathers. Had Jubel seen any of his grandchildren lately?

"Just one, my son, Bertram's boy. He's an adopted child. Bertram adopted him while I was with him for a while."

Mr. Lunning's admiration was boundless. "I think that's wonderful. I take my hat off to any man who loves children that much."

198

"Bertram's all right. Ella—that's his wife—she's a lovely girl. Isn't she, Helen?"

"Yes, Pop. Ella is wonderful."

"And what about the other children?"

"Oh, they're Evie's—my daughter down in Georgia. There's Tommy, the baby, and Jinny. Wouldn't you say Jinny's about six, Helen?"

"Five, I think, Pop."

"Is that so? Well, she's quite a young lady for five. Talks as bright as a grown-up. Asked me if I was going to be all alone when they left. Remember that, Helen?"

"She's a very cute child."

"I'll be seeing them soon; another three months or so. Going on to see my other son first, Harry. That's young Jubel, named after me but we call him young Jubel instead of Jubel, Jr. One of those little family oddities. He's an actor, you know, lives in your town."

"Helen, you never told me that!"

"New York's a big place. What is it, seven, eight million now?"

"And you're coming down to visit young Jubel."

"In about two weeks."

"Then we're going to be neighbors! Say, I'm glad to hear that. Ever been to New York?"

"Not for fifty years."

"Are we going to have a time! Wait until I start showing you the town. It's changed quite a bit in fifty years."

He went into some detail about the changes and they had a fine time with progress. In the end, he said, "Now, the minute you get settled, you have young Jubel give me a ring and we'll get together for dinner. We'll make plans then. You're going to be coming down every once in a while, aren't you, Helen?"

"I don't know. I hadn't planned to."

"Helen's very busy, Harry. She works awfully hard."

"Well, we'll work out something."

199

By then it was getting late and Mr. Lunning said good night. It was a "see-you-in-New York" good night and very jolly. They came back to the living room and sat down.

"Do you like Mr. Lunning, Pop?"

"Very much. He's good company, the kind of man you feel right at home with."

"Yes. I think he's charming. And he's a good man, isn't he?"

"I'd say he was."

"You two ought to have a great time in New York. I'm glad you'll be knowing someone there."

"I don't intend to call him, Helen."

"You don't! Why not?"

"Because he's not any of my business, child."

xviii

She sat and watched her father pack his bags. It was late in the evening and she was on highballs.

"Can I do anything for you, Pop?"

"No, Helen. There isn't much: socks, shirts, a few things."

"It doesn't seem like three months already. I can't believe it."

"I've found that time accelerates as you grow older. The months rush by. It seems as though they're running away from you."

"I'm going to miss you, Pop."

"I'll miss you, Helen. It's been very nice here."

What had happened to time and to her, too? For someone who hadn't wanted any part of her father, she was certainly feeling and acting strangely. But that was only the beginning and the end of it; it was leaving out all the in between. When, she asked herself, does a child discover his parents? When do they become people to him? Oh, not all parents; she wasn't silly or maudlin enough to think that all parents were people, that the halo was fitted about them with the coincidence of birth. But when does realization come about? That was the important thing, realization; either that they were or weren't people, either that you wanted or didn't want to have anything to do with them. All little-enough children loved their parents.

That was as natural to them as breathing. And when the little-enough children grew up into old-enough children, they hated their parents; enough anyway to be ashamed of them or to consider them impediments to their future. It was when they left childhood behind, when they became men and women themselves, that the periods of active love, toleration or active dislike set themselves, but even those might be subject to change. In her own case, when she had left home in her early twenties, she tolerated her mother and father. She supposed she loved them but she didn't really appreciate them. They were old to her and rutted in simple living. She supposed she took her job in Boston because, more than anything, she had wanted to get away.

Well, she had gotten away and where was she? Sitting in her apartment, watching her father packing his bags and wishing to God he didn't have to leave her. Did it take almost twenty years of living to come to the point of realization? The house was going to be quiet without him. She wondered how long it would take for her to get used to coming home and not finding him there with his batch of proudly mixed Martinis.

"You're sure about that train in the morning, Helen, aren't you?"

"Yes, Pop. It's the eight-thirty out of South Station. You'll make it in plenty of time if you leave the house at a quarter of eight."

"Oh, I'll be leaving at a quarter of eight. I am sorry, though, that you'll have to be getting up. It's Saturday morning and you could be sleeping later."

"I don't mind at all. You don't think I'd let you leave without saying good-bye, do you?"

"Maybe I should have decided on a later train."

"Wait a minute!" She jumped up and ran to the phone.

"What are you doing, Helen?"

"Calling the airport. It's silly for you to take that five-hour train ride when you can make it in an hour's flying time. Why, we can have the whole morning together—even have lunch."

202

"But young Jubel's going to be at the station, waiting for me at one o'clock."

"We can send him a wire."

She found the number and dialed it. There were plenty of flights. He could have his choice of three that would get him into New York in daylight. They could pick up the tickets in town in the morning.

"Isn't it wonderful, Pop? We can have another whole half-day together."

"It's only a matter of an extra three or four hours."

"Oh, but Pop, I want you to spend them with me."

"All right."

"You're not afraid to fly, are you?"

"At my age! No, I think I might like it. Ought to try it once, anyhow."

"Then it's all settled."

"What about Pitch?"

She looked around for the cat. "What do you mean, what about him?"

"Do they permit animals in airplanes?"

"Oh, of course. I'm sure they do."

"You'd better find out, Helen."

She called the airport again. Yes, animals were allowed to fly but they had to be in cases and they had to be kept in the baggage compartment.

"It's impossible, Helen. I'll have to take the train."

"But why? More than likely you'll have to have a case for the train, too."

"It isn't that, although I do think I could get away with it on the train. I just couldn't put him in the baggage compartment alone."

"That's silly. It's only an hour's flight."

"If he could be on my lap, it would be all right; even then he might be frightened. But he's an old cat, Helen. I'm afraid he'd be scared to death."

She must have looked crestfallen.

"I'm sorry, dear. I just wouldn't want anything to happen to Pitch, and only for the sake of an extra few hours. It isn't worth it."

"I suppose you're right, Pop. It was a little foolish of me." She might have been resentful of Pitch but she wasn't even that. She realized she hadn't minded the old cat at all during the entire three months, and he had been one of the minor difficulties connected with her father's visit.

Pop was laughing quietly. "I guess I haven't been as much of a bother to you as I was afraid of, after all."

"Bother! Pop, I've loved having you here. You don't know how I'm going to miss you. You just don't know."

"Oh, you'll get used to making your own Martinis again."

"Yes, and get used to you not being here when I come home and not being with me when I go out to dinner."

"Bertram always used to say I'd get sick eating that restaurant food."

"I don't know what I'm going to do without you, Pop."

"Now, Helen."

"Pop, what am I going to do about Raymond?"

"Exactly what you want to do."

"And about Mr. Lunning."

"The same."

"I've tried to give Raymond up. I've tried so many times."

"If you want to, you'll give him up when you're ready."

"I suppose I don't want to, do I? I suppose what I really want is for him to give up his wife and come to me. If he only didn't have that damned Church of his."

"Helen. . . ."

"What, Pop?"

"It isn't the Church, dear. The Church is only Mr. Oliver's excuse. If it wasn't the Church, it would be something else. His wife wouldn't give him a divorce, the children, any excuse. If a man really wants something badly enough, nothing will stand in his way."

"Oh, no, Pop. It's the Church. Honestly, it is."

204

"Did you ever wonder what would happen if Mr. Oliver's wife died?"

"It's funny you should ask that. I've thought about it."

"Do you think he'd marry you then?"

"Of course, he would!"

"Are you sure, Helen?"

She felt her hands drop in her lap. "I don't know, Pop. I don't know."

He came over to her and stroked her head.

"Pop, don't leave me. Stay here. Please stay here with me."

xix

The train from Boston was going to be ten minutes late. Young Jubel watched the news being chalked on the Grand Central bulletin board in a decorative but legible hand. He could remember the thousands of up-and-down lines and the big O's he had made when he was in school. He thought the train announcer must have been an honor student in penmanship when he was a boy. You never knew which little proficiency was going to pay off in the later years—or how it was going to pay off. Take that train announcer. He might have wanted to be an artist or an engraver. He might have spent years aiming at the bull's-eye, missed and ended up in this off-center job. There were a lot of people like that: frustrated playwrights who ended up as advertising copywriters, artists who settled for sign painting, opera singers who wound up in night clubs, composers who became arrangers, and the thousands of others who taught because they couldn't *do*. The world was full of them. And what about actors? Sideshow barkers, magicians, gadget demonstrators, vacuum-cleaner salesmen or maybe investment brokers if they had wives like Toby.

He supposed he didn't know when he was well off but he couldn't help it if he had a natural aversion to silver platters. He didn't want to be an investment broker; he didn't want to warm his seat on the stock exchange. He wanted to be just what he was, an actor.

"But you aren't one, Jubel. You can't be an actor unless you have a play to act in, unless you have a theatre, an audience."

"You know I can act, Toby."

"I know it, you know it, your friends and family know it. But do the producers know it? Does anyone who can give you a part know it?"

"They'll know it."

"When?"

"One of these days. I've just been having a run of tough luck, that's all."

"Quite a run, I'd say; more than a year."

"It happens all the time. I just need one good break."

"Well, I can wait if you can."

They had both been waiting. The only difference was that he was waiting to get something while she had been waiting for him to tire and give it up.

He looked at his watch. By now, Pop's train must be in the city. He remembered when he first came to New York to stay after the war, when he had been let out of the army. He remembered his first look at the skyline—the buildings clustered in the sun like a gold pipe-organ on which you could play your own tune. He had promised himself he'd make the grade; funny how promises came back to haunt you. He had promised Helen to clear up the situation with Toby. He had promised Toby, too.

"Don't you worry," he had told her, "by the time my father gets here, I'll have something."

That was right after his mother's funeral. He had called Toby as soon as he got in. She had hurried over and, for a few minutes, they were so glad to see each other, they didn't even think about their differences. But the differences came out as they always did sooner or later.

"Why didn't you call me, Jubel?"

207

"It was late. I thought you might be sleeping." He didn't mention the real reason. It wasn't necessary; they both knew.

"I could have driven you down. It would have been so much easier for you."

She didn't know how much easier. He'd never tell her how he had traveled home.

"Did she suffer much, Jubel?"

"No. Pop said it was sudden, quick, just like that." He snapped a finger.

"It must have been a dreadful time for you."

"Well, you know how those things are."

He remembered she didn't know. She was too young when her mother died.

"What about your father? Is he well?"

"Pop's all right. It was quite a shock for him but we were all there and I suppose that was a help."

"Of course."

"I feel better about him now. He's going to stay with Bertram for a while. Then he's going up to Boston, to Helen, for three months." He stopped. "Helen's the one who called you, Toby. I had to tell her."

"That's all right."

"You don't have to worry. She won't say anything. She has too many troubles of her own."

"I'm not worried, Jubel."

"Anyway, after Helen, Pop comes on to me. And then he goes to Evie."

"How old is your father?"

"Pop? Oh, I'd say about seventy; maybe a little more. He's a great old guy, though."

"And he's going to stay here with you, in this place?"

"Now, wait a minute, Toby. My father doesn't need a duplex apartment or a penthouse. He's a simple man. He only cares about staying with his children, no matter where they live."

"You say he's over seventy. You can't expect him to live the way you do, without even a bedroom."

"I told you it isn't important. You're confusing your standards with his—or maybe your father's."

There they were, right back where they had left off. They sat stubbornly silent for a minute.

"Jubel."

"What?"

"I missed you."

Although they didn't move, the distance between them varied with the conversation.

"I missed you too, Toby."

"What are you going to do? Have you thought over what we talked about?"

"Have I thought it over! I hoped you had thought it over."

"You know what I think, Jubel."

"Well, you know what I think and I'm not changing my mind. I'm not giving up the theatre."

She flared. "You're too selfish to even think of your own father!"

"What's my father got to do with it?"

"Everything. Why, by the time he gets here—in six months —we could have a place of our own and he could live like a human being." Her temper was rising and she ran for her coat. "Not like . . . like an animal in a cellar."

She had stood at the door, her hand on the knob, her whole body quivering. There were any number of things he might have done: laughed because she was so cute, taken her in his arms because he loved her, sat her down and talked quietly with her. But all of it would come to nothing. They would end up the same way.

"Wait a minute. I'll take you home."

"You don't have to take me home."

"All right."

He sat down and lighted a cigarette but she didn't go. He ignored her.

"I want to ask you a question, Jubel."

"Go ahead."

209

"You barely make enough money to support yourself. How are you going to take care of your father when he stays here?"

"Don't you worry. By the time my father gets here, I'll have something."

"I've heard that before. Suppose you don't."

"I will. Now, you tell me something. What about this marriage of ours? Does it go on being the big secret of the century?"

"I'm just as stubborn as you are."

"Okay. Since it belongs to both of us, we'll keep it that way. Let me know if you change your mind."

He had let her go. He didn't want a breakup then. And any argument, if it lasted long enough, would come to that. Besides, he was sure he was right. He would have something in six months—or less—and he had the feeling Toby would change her tune and her mind once that happened. At any rate, once he was set in a play, and he could offer her a decent living, she'd have to make up her mind one way or the other.

Six months. You say it and if there's a happy reward in the calendar, the time drags. But if you're trying to make the time work for you, using it as a reprieve, you can't hold it back long enough, and you wake one morning, count your money and wonder what happened to the days. You straighten up the room, fold up the couch, measuring it with your eye to see if Pop will be able to turn around in it, and then start fooling with the window shades. You never have any sunlight because you have a northern exposure. (He couldn't do anything about the other exposures, the ones to the dirt and noise on 52nd Street.) Would the room look any more attractive in the dubious daylight that came through the basement windows or should he draw the shades and leave a few lamps burning? Would he be as conscious about all this if Toby hadn't brought it up so many times?

He asked himself why he hadn't stalled a little longer. Why hadn't he arranged it with Evie so that Pop would visit her first? He guessed it was because he knew he was heading into the slack summer season and while things could be worse for actors in New York then, they couldn't possibly be any better. On top of that, he was loused up as far as summer stock was concerned, anyway. If he skipped his turn and let him go on to Evie first, then Pop would be coming to New York in June, staying through August, and there was the summer. This way there was a remote chance that he could still squeeze into something in the hinterlands in June. The only other possibility —to put off Pop's visit altogether, for the time being—was to run out on his responsibility. They had all agreed to take Pop for three months. He wouldn't do anything to make his father feel that he didn't want him or that he was avoiding him.

There was a flurry of sounds and people at the gates. He guessed his father's train had arrived. He got up and joined the waiters. While he stood there, watching for Pop's face, he thought of his mother. What would have happened if she had stayed on, if Pop had been the first to go? Would he be standing here now, waiting for her just as he was waiting for him? He didn't think so. He couldn't put Mom up in his one-room bachelor apartment; it was going to be difficult enough with Pop, with just the one bed between them. Mom wouldn't have come at all. She would have gone to one of the girls or to Bertram's. And what about the money then? The money didn't bother him. He just didn't want Bertram to get away with anything. According to Helen, though, Bertram had already gotten away with a thousand dollars. A thousand dollars. When he stopped and thought what he could do with a thousand dollars, he glowed. Really give Pop a time: all the best restaurants, theatres, even a couple of night spots. They'd make a three-some of it every night: he, Pop and Toby. He'd show her he wasn't ashamed to introduce her to his father. He hadn't been seeing much of Toby in the last few weeks, not since the Barry play folded.

The Barry play had been his one real chance. At least, it

211

had opened. Sometimes a play didn't even get to the rehearsal stage before the difficulties started cropping up and it miscarried, falling over the empty pocketbooks. Other times, it would get as far as the road, and expire in transit. But the Barry play —despite all the usual obstacles—managed to stagger along to a stillbirth. It went through four weeks of rehearsal and two weeks on the road: Hartford and New Haven. The original plans called for Boston, too, and he thought it was going to be wonderful to play Boston and have Pop and Helen in the audience. But the money ran out in New Haven, so they called off Boston and cooled their heels while the producer shuttled back and forth to New York, trying to raise cash. In the meantime, Barry, who was directing the play, tried to get the kinks out of it. The Connecticut audiences weren't enthusiastic and something had to be done. It passed the time, anyway.

He had never thought much of the play. It was supposed to be "a psychological melodrama" and a good thing for the subtitle, too, otherwise people might have a tough time discovering what it was all about. Still, you never could tell. That was the fascination of Broadway. All the smart boys could tab a play a hit before it opened, and it would croak before the third-act curtain. The same smart boys could and had made the same mistake on their predicted flops. Take *Oklahoma;* they were giving odds on that one. There was only one way to tell. You had to open it.

Somehow, from somewhere, they got their angel and Barry's show went on to New York. The greatest boon to the theatre, he decided, were all the little men who would appear from nowhere, complete with the green dollars they had made manufacturing kitchen stoves, to rescue a skidding show from oblivion. God bless them. He considered this man, whoever he was, a personal sponsor because, in spite of the play, his part was good and in this business you never knew what was going to happen.

Toby had known he was working. He couldn't help telling her in his first enthusiasm. But she also knew they were having troubles on the road; she read the drama section of the newspapers, too. So it was a minor triumph for him when opening night finally happened. But that was the extent of his triumph. It didn't help much to know she was in the house seat he had gotten for her when he could feel the audience departing—some even physically—before the end of the first act.

She waited for him after the final curtain. The cast and Barry and the producer and the backers were floating in that limbo of expectancy before the morning papers would come out. They knew in their hearts it wouldn't go but they had pitched themselves for a celebration and there was enough money for a party.

"Would you like to stay and meet the kids? There's going to be a party."

"Not unless you do, Jubel."

"Let's go then."

They had walked up tired and littered 44th Street to the Avenue of the Americas and turned uptown. They had made small talk about the cold night and the crowds and then there was a long plodding silence.

"Pretty bad, wasn't it?"

"Pretty bad, Jubel."

They walked a bad block.

"I suppose you think I'm happy about it."

"No. I couldn't love you at all if I thought you were."

"I'm not. I'm sorry."

"What about me?"

"You were much better than it deserved but you know you can't act a sow's ear into a silk purse."

"It was a sow's ear, all right."

She had been sympathetic and consoling and she did her best to cheer him. Not once did she dig up the old bone of contention. He appreciated her that night. They went home to his place and shut out the world for a few hours. But after that, and for the past few weeks, he hadn't seen much of her. When he did, it was the same old brawl and he didn't have the money

213

or the courage to take her out again. Every time they'd have coffee together, or one nursed drink, he was building up her side. For once, dear God, he wished he could stuff her pretty little mouth with twenty-dollar bills.

He pushed through the people who had crowded in front of him. Pop was coming through the gates like an Indian potentate; a porter ahead of him with his bags and he holding his cat as though it were a symbol of his office. You had to hand it to the old man, he got away with it.

"Right here, Pop." He threw his arms around him and hugged him. "It's good to see you. Are you all right?"

"Fine, Jubel. Trip wasn't too bad at all."

"Come on, we'll get you home."

They taxied uptown to 52nd Street. On the way, he thought he'd better prepare his father for the apartment.

"I hope you're not going to feel crowded with me after Bertram and Helen."

"I'll get along fine. Just don't let me get in your way."

"You won't get in my way but it's just the one room, you know, and a basement, at that."

"There'll be no stairs to climb, then, and that's to the good."

"Say, I never thought of that. The basement'll be fine for you. I ought to tell you about the street, though."

"What about it?"

"Well, New York's a funny town. People live in all sorts of places: over stores, next door to parking lots, sometimes in factory buildings. My street's full of night clubs. We call them 'joints'. "

His father laughed. "You don't have to worry about me, Jubel. I won't get into bad company."

The apartment didn't look too bad when you got down into it. It was funny how you could live in a place for a few years and stop seeing it after a while until you saw it through other people's eyes. The room, even though it stood alone, was a good size. He took no credit for the furnishings. They came with the place but they were comfortable and sturdy and muted

214

enough by age and wear so that they didn't stand out and make the rest of it look too habby. He was very glad he had taken the time to make up the folding couch and straighten up a little. In the back, beyond the feeble reach of daylight, was the kitchenette and bath.

"You won't have to worry about sunstroke down here, Pop." He turned on the lamps. "Drop the cat and relax."

"You won't mind having Pitch around, will you, Jubel?"

"To tell you the truth, I forgot about him. If he doesn't mind the crowd, I don't mind. Maybe he'll keep the mice away. Sit down, Pop."

His father sat down and looked around.

"How about a drink? I've got a little whiskey someplace."

"No, thank you. I used to mix Martinis for Helen. She said they were pretty good ones, too, but I never touched the stuff, myself. You go ahead and have one."

"Do you mind?" He went back to the kitchen and mixed a highball of rye and water from the tap. He needed a drink.

"Well, what do you think of the place?"

"It's going to be all right, Jubel. Don't you worry about it."

"That thing you're sitting on is our bed. Don't look so frightened. It's folded up now. When it's open, there's plenty of room for two. Everything in this town gets folded up and put away, Pop. They even do that with their consciences. You're going to love it here. New York in spring time! That's when the carbon monoxide is best."

"You sound a little bitter, Jubel. Don't you like it here?"

"Me, bitter? Oh, no, Pop. If I were, I wouldn't stay here. I'd be a fool to if I did, wouldn't I?"

"I don't know."

"How's Helen?"

"She's fine."

"Have a good time up there?"

"Very good. I enjoyed myself . . . By the way, Jubel . . ." He put his hand to his inside pocket. "I have a note here from

215

Helen for you. She was going to mail it to you but she said it would get here quicker with me." He passed it to young Jubel. "I hope it's a letter of recommendation."

The old man was cute. "Not necessary. We accept our guests on face value here." He took the envelope which was addressed to "Jubel, jr." Very formal, he thought.

"Chances are, she wants me to take good care of you; maybe be sure that you get a glass of hot milk before you go to bed." He laughed and was about to open it when it occurred to him that it might be that or something a little more serious about Pop. It might be that he did need special care of some kind. No sense making the old man self-conscious about it. Better put it aside for now. He dropped it on the table beside him. "I'll get to it later. Hungry, Pop?"

"Not very. I can wait."

"We'll go out for a bite after I finish this drink. Tell me about Helen. What's she doing?"

"Working hard."

"No fun?"

"She goes out once in a while."

It would be natural for him to ask, "With whom?" or "Did you meet any of her friends?" but he didn't. He wondered how Helen had managed with her boy friend while Pop was around. What *was* his name? And could Pop have gotten an inkling of him? It must have been a little tough on her. Maybe there was something in her letter about that.

"How did everything go at Bertram's, Pop? All right?"

"Yes, very pleasant. I wrote you that Bertram adopted a boy, didn't I?"

"I think you did. Evie or Helen, one of them, sent me a note about it, too. What's the kid like?"

"A fine boy. He's going to make them very happy. Ella's always wanted a child. I think he'll do Bertram a great deal of good, too. Bertram's very nervous, you know. I kept after him to go to a doctor."

"Bertram's always been nervous."

216

"More so than usual while I was there. He's upset about money. I gave him a thousand dollars, Jubel."

He knew that, of course, but he didn't think he should say it came to him over the grapevine. "That was nice."

"I had to borrow it on my insurance policy but it's nothing to worry about. I've been paying it back on what I get from Agnew."

"Pop, I'm not worried about it. It's none of my business, in fact. You're a free agent. You do what you want to do."

"I know that, Jubel, but I wanted you to know, and Helen and Evie, too, that no one's going to suffer because of it."

That was put very nicely: no one was going to suffer because of it. It made him wonder how much Pop knew of what was going on. No one had told him, of course, that these visits to his children amounted to a protection of their interests but had he guessed it? Could he be subconsciously sensitive to it without actually being aware of it?

He finished off his drink. "Why don't you wash up, Pop? Come on, I'll get you a towel."

He came back to the letter and opened it. There were three sheets of stationery but only one had a message on it; in between the other two was a hundred-dollar bill.

> *Jubel, dear*
> *Please take good care of Pop. I love him.*
> *Don't mind the money. It's just to make sure he*
> *gets along all right. We used to alternate paying*
> *for our dinners. Make sure he eats well. No drug-*
> *store meals, please. I'll send you more later on.*
> *I miss him already. I envy you.*
>
> *Love,*
> *Helen*

He looked at the money. The numerals seemed strange. It had been a long time since he held a hundred dollar bill in his hand. It was a cool, remote piece of green; not warm and used like a one or a five or even a ten could be, and it was lonely

217

looking. It had the loneliness of riches. If he had found it in the street, if a kind wind had blown it against his foot, he would have thought himself the luckiest man in the world. But Helen had sent it to him. It was money out of her pocketbook and it was his own failure in the palm of his hand.

His first thought was to send it right back to her. But he thought of Pop. The few dollars of his own wouldn't feed them beyond the weekend, even drugstore feed. And he thought of Toby. Maybe this was a good omen (oh, the superstitions of poverty!) and maybe his luck would change now. He hid the bill in his fist as his father came out of the bathroom.

"All set, Pop?"

"Yes, but I want to talk to you about something before we go, Jubel."

"What's that?"

His father was rolling down his shirt sleeves. "You know, I've always made arrangements wherever I go; at Bertram's and at Helen's, too."

"What kind of arrangements?"

"I like to visit all of you but I couldn't be happy about it if I felt I was a drain on you."

"Oh, stop it, Pop. You're not a drain on anybody."

"I like to pay my own way, Jubel. I insist on it. I gave Bertram so much a week to cover my room and board while I stayed with him and Ella. Helen wouldn't take any money from me, so I took her to dinner every night."

"Every night, Pop?"

"Yes, and I expect to do the same thing with you."

"But, Pop, that's not necessary. I have money."

"No, Jubel, I insist on it; just the same way as I did with Helen. I'll take care of the meals, all of them." He put on his coat and picked up his hat. "Now, you're not going to give me any trouble about that, are you?"

"No, Pop, I won't give you any trouble."

It took him several weeks before he began to get used to New York. He found that it had a very disquieting effect upon him. He didn't know why because there were times during the daylight hours—before the night clubs on the street opened for business and when the red lights momentarily quieted the traffic—when you could hear a decided hush. But even then there was an impatient pulse to the city; as though someone were throttling an artery and the neon blood wanted to break out. In many ways, sitting in the little apartment alone as he was doing now, when young Jubel was out on his business, was very much like being in the country, with a disturbing storm beating outside the windows.

He was glad he had been to Helen's and to Boston first. New York was less of a shock than it might have been. He explored the streets and the avenues but not as much as he had expected he would. He found himself tiring quickly and refuge wasn't always available except for the bars and women-crowded restaurants. Sometimes he would walk east to Fifth Avenue to wonder at the stores and the busy people, and sometimes west to Broadway and the frightening din. One night young Jubel took him to the Times Square section.

"You can't say you've been to New York, Pop, without seeing Times Square at night."

"The Street," as young Jubel called it, was like a flooded river spilling over with people. It was difficult even to walk. It gave you the feeling of being part of a panicky school of fish being driven against a shore. It made him a little dizzy and once they had to stop and wait on a side street, watching it, until he felt better again. Strangely enough, most of the people disappeared when they reached 53rd Street and you could walk and breathe again. Young Jubel said he didn't understand it himself. They just seemed to melt away; you didn't see them leave. He said it was the same right below 42nd Street, too. That night they had dinner at one of those nickel cafeterias— he couldn't remember their name and he kept calling it a "nickelodeon," which amused young Jubel no end—because that was also part of knowing New York. The food seemed good enough and certainly inexpensive but he could understand why young Jubel referred to the veal chops as "armor plated" and the peas as "olive drab."

On another night—the biggest one of all—young Jubel had made an occasion of it. There were three of them that night; the little friend of Jubel's, Miss Sheffield, was along too. They went to a French restaurant where the food was better than it had been even in Boston. He told Jubel it wasn't fair to hide a place like that from him but he guessed it was very expensive and only for special occasions when they had company along and his son was playing host. They went on to the theatre after that. Both Jubel and Miss Sheffield said the play was only mildly amusing but he had laughed loud and often. He hoped he hadn't embarrassed them. During one of the intermissions, Jubel had introduced them to several attractive people who were also in the theatre. They made a pleasant fuss over him and one of them, an earnest young man, whom Jubel called "Barry," was very pleasant. He chatted for a while and then excused himself to talk to Jubel alone.

"He's a director," Miss Sheffield had said. "He directed Jubel's last play."

"Is that so? I wish I could have been here to see it."

"Jubel was very good in it."

"Are you in the theatre, Miss Sheffield?"

"No. My only connection with the theatre is Jubel. I keep house for Father."

"That's an excellent occupation. I suppose your next job will be keeping house for a husband."

She had blushed a little. "That usually follows, doesn't it? I wish Jubel had a play now so that you could see him while you're here."

"I would like that but Jubel tells me the theatre is going into the slow season right now. However, it's more than possible something might happen. It's such an unpredictable field." He had laughed. "I suppose I sound like an authority."

"It's very becoming to you. But you're perfectly right. It is an unpredictable field."

"It's a matter of patience and perseverance. I'm sure he'll come out all right."

"Of course, he will. Don't you worry about him, Mr. Watson. Your son's a very unusual young man. I'm very fond of him."

He could have told her that young Jubel seemed to be fond of her too but he had been learning not to speak for any of his children. Besides, if Miss Sheffield was as smart as she looked and acted, he was sure he didn't have to tell her.

They saw the rest of the play and afterward, Jubel took them to a small club on the East Side for some refreshment. He drank milk while the younger people had their stronger drinks. Then they sat and listened to a strange looking young man whom Jubel described as "a scrawny vulture picking at the white and dark meat of the piano."

After that, they finished the evening with a hansom ride through Central Park. It was a lovely ride, almost the nicest part of the evening, and he was a little ashamed of himself for having fallen asleep somewhere along the way. It made him wish that he were young enough to enjoy the life of this city, to take it in his stride as fully as young Jubel seemed to. But at

221

his age all he could do was feel it through his son, sometimes to an almost startling degree when heredity showed itself. On his own, and on his stronger days, he couldn't do much more than look at the city, walk to Central Park and stand in the middle of the great meadow where he could marvel at the unbelievable peaks. He liked the park. He felt more at home among the trees and the spring grass. He knew this was foolish. He had spent his life in the country and one didn't come to New York for trees and grass. But he was an old man and too late for change.

There was one thing, though, that he did have to learn: how to live with his children all over again, how not to be a father in the ordinary sense of the word. It wasn't easy to go from child to child, as he was doing, and keep himself from being lost in each. Bertram and Ella had wanted him to stay and it would have been natural enough. With Helen, it was a trial to leave. She said she wanted him to stay; she needed him. It wouldn't have been right, it wouldn't have been good for her or for any of them. They had to get along in their own lives as best they could. He wouldn't let himself become an interference, even a static one. That went for young Jubel, too, or Evie when he would get to her. Evie might understand that a little easier. She was a mother, herself.

Sitting here, in young Jubel's basement apartment, tucked away from the city in a lightless room, he wished Amy could have known their children as he was getting to know them. He supposed Helen wouldn't agree with him, or any of the others for that matter. They weren't happy men and women— Bertram with his itch for money, Helen pining and wasting herself on a married man, young Jubel fighting to make his way and who knew what with Evie—but that was unimportant. They were his and Amy's children and Amy would understand them because she'd love them just as he did.

He was glad he had let himself be talked into living with them. It wasn't pleasant planting your roots and then having to dig them up every three months but it had been worth it. He

222

supposed, thinking selfishly, it had been good for him, too. Keeping on the go, the way he had, kept him from brooding about Amy. If he waked in the night, dreaming, and thought that Amy slept beside him, it was only for a moment. The strange surroundings brought him quickly to himself. At home, the illusion would last for a while as it had on those few nights right after.

The doorbell rang. It couldn't be young Jubel unless he forgot his key but it was too early for young Jubel. Maybe it was one of these door-to-door salesmen. The city seemed to be full of them. He often thought that half the people in New York sold things to the other half and then the other half turned around and sold other things to the first half. Sometimes they turned out to be quite interesting chaps and you could chat with them for half an hour. Of course, that meant buying something but he usually bought something anyhow. Young Jubel said it marked him as a hick; real New Yorkers never bought from peddlers. If that was true, he didn't know how these salesmen got along unless it was that New York didn't have very many real New Yorkers. Best to see who it was, at any rate.

He got up, walked to the door and opened it without asking who was there. He blinked with surprise.

"May I come in, Mr. Watson?"

"Why, of course, Miss Sheffield. I guess I wasn't expecting you."

He led her into the room, pulling on the lamps.

"I was in the neighborhood and I thought I'd stop by and say hello."

"I'm very glad you did. Let me have your coat. Jubel's not home, you know."

"I know. He's reading for that Barry man this afternoon. Seems there's another play in the offing."

"Jubel says there's never a dull moment. Can I make you some tea, Miss Sheffield? We don't keep much of a house here but there is tea."

"Sounds like a wonderful idea if you'll let me make it. Don't move. I know my way around."

She went back to the kitchenette. He felt rather strange watching her. One minute he was sitting here alone in the dark and the next he had a young woman bustling around, preparing tea; strange but pleasant.

"I hope you don't mind me making myself at home this way."

"I'm delighted."

She sat down while the water boiled. Pitch came off the couch to examine her.

"I didn't know you had a cat."

"Yes, that's Pitch. He's part of the family."

She lifted him to her lap.

"He'll get all his hair over your gray suit."

"I don't mind. He's beautiful."

"Jubel's mother always made me wear black so he wouldn't show."

"Do you take him with you everywhere?"

"Everywhere. He's quite a traveler: Columbus, Boston, New York and we'll be going down to Georgia soon."

"Has it been nice for you?"

"Very nice. I've had a chance to know all my children again."

He looked at her sitting there, petting Pitch, and he found himself genuinely glad for her visit. There was something about Miss Sheffield that reminded him of Evie, a directness, he thought.

She took the cat with her when she went back for the tea and Pitch followed her, rubbing against her ankle when she didn't have hands enough for him.

They moved the end tables around to make a comfortable arrangement.

"This is cozy, isn't it?"

"Much better than anything I expected when I answered the

224

door. I thought you might be one of those salesmen. We get a lot of them here."

"Are you a difficult man to sell, Mr. Watson?"

"Not usually. I've bought two magazine subscriptions since I've been here and I don't know how many brushes."

"That's encouraging because I have something to sell you."

He laughed. "I hope it isn't a vacuum cleaner."

She put her teacup down with exact deliberation.

"First, I have something to tell you. Jubel and I have been married for almost a year now."

The words didn't go with the look on her face. She might have been saying that it was nice weather out or would he like another cup of tea.

"What was that again?"

"I said Jubel and I are married. We have been for almost a year. You're shocked."

"Well, I am a little surprised."

"You don't approve of Jubel being married."

"Oh, no. That's not it at all. I was just thinking it was too bad he never told us. His mother would have been so happy."

"That was my idea. I wanted it to be kept secret."

"Do you mind if I ask why?"

"Not at all. It has something to do with what I want to ask you."

This should be a time for rejoicing, he told himself. His youngest son was married. There was a new member in the family. There should be warm wishes of luck and congratulations. But the announcement was so cold, so matter-of-fact, and it was an old marriage already.

"I didn't want anyone to know because I didn't want my father to know. I'm an only child, Mr. Watson. My mother died when I was an infant. My father expects certain things from the man I marry. I didn't want to disappoint him."

"You think Jubel would be a disappointment to your father?"

"Not Jubel himself—his acting, his career."

225

"But Jubel was an actor a year ago. He didn't tell you he wasn't, did he?"

"No, I knew it." She seemed a little impatient. "I suppose it's hard for you to understand. I was carried away. I loved him so much. I still do. I just didn't realize what it meant."

"Miss Sheffield . . . I'm sorry . . . Toby. Would your father object to Jubel on the grounds that he was an actor or that he was an actor without any money?"

"Both. Of course, I suppose there'd be less objection if Jubel were successful but he isn't. Father's in the financial world. We've had money for a very long time. To people like him, actors are socially unacceptable."

He had to laugh at that. "I'm an old man, Toby—very likely, older than your father—but that seems a very old-fashioned idea to me, and narrow, too."

"Old-fashioned or narrow, that's the way it is. I can't do anything about it."

"Well, it seems to me Jubel can't either."

"He can but he won't listen to me. You know he's wasting his time in the theatre."

"I don't know. I do know it's a difficult career. It takes a little time for a young man to get his foot inside the door."

"There are fifty thousand young men with a hundred thousand feet. They can't all get in. It's an overcrowded field. There aren't enough theatres, not enough plays, not enough jobs. Don't you see?"

"I realize Jubel hasn't reached the top but he manages to get along while he tries."

"He hasn't managed at all. He scrimps along from week to week. It isn't that he doesn't have talent. He doesn't have work."

"I happen to know he's out right now seeing a director on a very promising job. He said it was a big part in a very good play."

"Yes, I know. That's Barry; the man we met at the theatre. You can keep very busy seeing directors and producers and

226

taking auditions and reading and running your legs off trying to get somewhere. But Jubel's been at it for years. He's fooling himself. He's chasing rainbows. It might be all right if he were single but he's married. I think he has an obligation to me."

"What do you want him to do, Toby?"

"I want him to give up the theatre, get a job somewhere: banking, advertising, anything. It doesn't matter, just as long as it's a substantial field. Father will help us. Jubel will never have a thing to worry about for the rest of his life. Won't you talk to him? Won't you make him see that he's wasting his years? He'll ruin his life . . . and mine, too."

He waited for her to compose herself.

"Toby, I have four children; all of them grown, all of them men and women. It hasn't been easy for me to understand them all the time but what I do understand is that I can never tell them what to do. I have no right to interfere in their lives."

There was the sound of a key in the lock and young Jubel opened the door.

"Hey! All my favorite people!"

If he was surprised at the sight of Toby, he didn't show it. He flung his hat across the room and went into a lively tittup that ended with a pinch for his father's cheek and a kiss for Toby's head.

"Look at me." He threw his arms out wide. "I've got an earful of good news." He looked at the cups, sniffed at them. "What's this, tea? Not good enough for a celebration."

He dashed back to the kitchen for a bottle of liquor. There wasn't much in it but enough to make a ceremonial pouring into each of their cups and a small swallow for himself.

"Drink it up, children. It's a great day. The prodigy has produced. I've got myself a wonderful part in a wonderful play."

"Congratulations, son. I'm very happy for you."

"Thanks, Pop. It's going to be my first real hit." He turned to Toby. "Aren't you going to congratulate me?"

227

"Tell me about it first."

"There's nothing to tell. I'm in. I'm set."

"Who's the producer? When do you start rehearsals? Where do you open? When do you come to New York?"

He laughed patiently. "Mere details."

"Well, who *is* the producer?"

"It just so happens, we don't have a producer at the moment. It's Barry's play. He's got an option on it. He may produce it himself. You remember him, Pop."

"Yes, I remember."

"I remember, too, and I remember he hasn't done anything that lasted long enough to use up the advance sale."

"This is different. It's a great play. It's going to have a long run."

She stood up and walked over to him. "It's another will-o'-the-wisp, Jubel. Nothing will come of it."

"You're wrong, Toby."

"No, I'm not. I've seen it happen too often. You have too but you won't admit it. I've been telling your father . . ."

"What have you been telling my father?"

"That I don't want to see you wasting your life chasing this dream. I told him we're married, Jubel."

"Oh, you did. Finally got around to it. But you didn't want to give me the pleasure of telling it to him myself, did you." He turned to his father. "Pop, I'm sorry. I wanted to tell you. Honestly, I did."

"It doesn't matter, Jubel. Don't worry about me."

"I told him because I wanted him to talk some sense into you."

He didn't want to hear any more of this. He shouldn't be here with them. He'd take a walk for a while. He went for his coat and hat.

"Pop, you didn't believe her, did you? I can't give up the theatre. I'd hate myself for the rest of my life. You can understand that, can't you? I don't want to be just a *nothing* with money."

He didn't want to say anything. Anything he said would be wrong. This was not his place or his business.

Toby saved him. "What do you mean, a *nothing* with money!"

He closed the door behind him and left them alone.

xxi

Many times summer by-passed spring in New York and lurched into the city like a steam roller gone berserk, flattening everyone with its hot and wet breath. Here it was only mid-May and the streets had the glare and the breathlessness of August and the apartments were hotboxes set in claustrophobic concrete.

Down in the basement apartment, young Jubel sat on the edge of his half of the bed, trying to shake himself out of sleep. Beside him, his father leaned against the wall, a pillow propped under him. Across the room, his brother, Bertram, dressed and perspiring, occupied a chair.

"I still don't know what you're doing here."

"I told you: I came to see Pop."

"Just passing by from six hundred miles away, huh?" He tried to rub some life into his head, stood up and threw a robe around himself.

"I must say, you aren't very hospitable. I didn't realize I'd be waking you at eleven o'clock in the morning."

"Jubel was up very late last night, Bertram. He was out with a producer. There's no excuse for me, though, except that I've had a little cold and I thought it wouldn't hurt to rest a while longer."

"I'm surprised you don't have pneumonia, living in a cellar like this."

Bertram looked at him when he said that but he wouldn't take it; he went into the bathroom.

He heard Pop ask, "How are Ella and Teddy, Bertram?" And then he began brushing his teeth.

The paste felt good in his mouth. He hoped it would wash away the taste of last night. These sessions with Barry and the prospective backers of the play were taking a lot out of him but he certainly was getting a back of the backstage view of the theatre he had never had before. Gad, the people you had to deal with to raise money. They didn't know beans about a play. Of course, Barry was doing it the hard way. He was trying to raise the money himself instead of going to a producer. He couldn't blame him. After all, it was his play, he had the option on it. It was just that it was taking so darned long.

"What's your hurry, Jubel? These things don't happen overnight. It's barely six weeks and I've got more at stake in this than you."

He had, too. The option had cost him five hundred and it would cost him another five hundred if nothing happened in the three months and he wanted it for another three. But he couldn't tell Barry he wanted to get going because of his personal life. He couldn't tell him that he was anxious to support a wife he had had for more than a year. And if he told him his wife was Toby Sheffield, he wouldn't understand it at all.

Yet, in a way, it was Toby who was responsible for his having the part at all. If she hadn't been along at the theatre that night with Pop, he still might not know about Barry's play; they were a long way off from casting.

"Isn't that Alton Sheffield's daughter, Jubel?" They were half-way across the lobby from Toby and Pop.

"That's right, Toby Sheffield, his one and only."

It was a funny thing about Barry. He was Broadway, all right, but the nice thing about him was that he had to work hard at it. He angled and he fought and, sometimes, he'd even

231

have to do someone dirt in order to survive the battle of bright lights, but he wasn't comfortable doing it. Another thing, he was serious theatre and a lot closer to the Yale Workshop than the Winter Garden.

"Nice kid?"

"Very."

"Seems to me I heard you two were going around a while ago. Funny I forgot about it."

He had been around long enough to spot an axe when it was being readied for grinding. Barry was definitely grinding tonight.

"You wouldn't know her old man, would you?"

"Alton? Why sure." He was finding it quite amusing. "Go up to the house every once in a while for dinner."

Barry had to digest that fast. There wasn't much left of intermission.

"Listen, Jubel. I've got something—a play, a hell of a good play. Friend of mine did it. I'd like to produce and direct it myself but I haven't got the money. Do you think you could arrange a meeting between me and old man Sheffield?"

He hadn't been surprised but he did resent the proposition because it didn't include the usual plum that was traditional in a deal like this. What did Barry take him for, a complete dope?

"Why should I arrange a meeting between you and Alton Sheffield?"

"Because there's a part in this play for you. It's big and it's right up your alley."

"No, thanks."

"Why not? You wouldn't have to do a thing but take me up to the house some night. Make it casual, informal. I'll do all the talking. You won't have to do a thing."

"No. I never mix business with pleasure."

"That's crazy. Everybody does. You've got to in this business."

"Sorry. Thanks, anyway. I'll see you, Barry."

Barry held on to his arm. "You're not kidding?"

232

"I'm not kidding."

"You know, Jubel, I believe you. They ought to put you under glass. Give me a ring next week. If you can read the part, it's yours."

He had read it and he had it, and it had been a great thing for about a half hour—until he had waltzed into the house and broken the news to Pop and Toby. It wasn't that he believed Toby then or now but she could still look at him and say, "Well?" She was one of those people who were always *nearly* right about everything. She had been nearly right about the money from Helen, too. The morning after he had taken her out with Pop, she had him on the phone.

"I wanted to thank you for a lovely evening last night, Jubel."

"Think nothing of it. My pleasure."

"I think your father's a darling."

"I think he's pretty cute, myself. I always like to bring my favorite people together." He preferred being subtle.

"By the way, Jubel, I hope you're not borrowing money from your father."

"I am not and if I were, it'd be none of your business."

"I just thought I'd tell you if we went out again, we could go someplace where I could sign the check."

"Thank you for nothing, Miss Sheffield."

She had her nerve. It had been bad enough to carry around the guilt of misusing Helen's money without being reminded of it. And it didn't make him feel much better to tell himself that it was only a loan and Helen would get every cent of it back as soon as he started rehearsals and his own money began coming in. Another thing he'd never forgive her for was sneaking in to tell Pop about their marriage. She was the one who had insisted on the secret, and then she had broken it. He wouldn't have cared so much if she had told her father, too, but no, it still didn't exist as far as Mr. Sheffield was concerned. She told him it was only because she loved him that she talked with Pop. How angry could you be with a woman who told

233

you that? It was hard to be angry with Toby, anyway; no matter what she did. Well, it would all work out once he got going on the play. His troubles were really little ones. He had nothing to complain about; even Bertram's visit didn't seem to bother him now, after a shower and shave. It wouldn't have bothered him at all except he didn't like being jolted awake by someone who was all dressed and alive and looking very superior. He had always disliked surprise visits that found you in bed. The mail service was operating, telephones were in existence. There was no excuse for it except surprise.

His father was up and the bed was folded when he got back into the room.

"Pop, I told you not to touch that bed. It's too much for you."

"It's nothing, Jubel. I'm used to it now."

"How are you feeling?" He looked for fever with his hand.

"I'm all right. I was just telling Bertram it's only a little cold. The weather's been so changeable."

"If I had any idea you lived like this, I'd never have let Pop come here. I'm sure Helen wouldn't either."

"We can't all live on estates in the country."

"This is a cellar, that's all it is."

"We call it a basement apartment."

"You can call it anything you like. It's still a cellar and it isn't fit for human habitation."

"Why don't you go down to City Hall and make a complaint?"

"I'm not that interested. All I care about is Pop's welfare. I'm taking him home with me."

"Bertram, I told you I wasn't going with you. I'm perfectly happy and content here."

"You may be happy and content but you look sick. This is no place for you, Pop; no air, no light. It's criminal. You're taking years out of your life."

Jubel looked at his father. It was true Pop wasn't a picture of health. He looked tired and even a little gray in the face.

234

Maybe Bertram was right. New York certainly wasn't a health resort. It could take a lot out of people much younger than Pop. He remembered he did seem better, younger, springier when he came down from Helen's. The trouble was you didn't look at people when you lived with them for a while.

"I told you six months ago, the city wasn't for you, Pop. You need the right food—not restaurant slop—and air and sunshine. And I had no idea then it was going to be as bad as this."

"It isn't bad, Bertram. There are millions of people, older ones, too, who live here all their lives."

"They're used to it. You're not."

"Well, I have only a few more weeks to go." He stopped and thought a minute. "Three weeks and then I'll be off to Evie's. That should be country enough for you."

"Three weeks. Do you realize it'll be June by then? And do you know what Georgia is like in June, July and August? You're just looking for trouble, Pop."

"I'll be getting plenty of air and sunshine even if it is a little warm."

"You're being stubborn, Pop."

The telephone rang. It was Toby.

"Jubel, I've got to see you."

"What's the matter?"

"I can't tell you over the phone."

"Well, I've got my brother here from Ohio."

"It won't take long."

"You're all right, aren't you?"

"Yes, but I do have to see you. Can you be at the Plaza in a half hour?"

"I'll be there." He put down the phone. "Toby, Pop. She wants to see me. Now, what were we talking about?"

"About Pop going to Georgia with all this heat coming up. If it's this hot here, what do you expect it'll be like down there?"

"I don't know what it'll be like down there. I only know that

235

it's up to Pop, that's all. And I don't think your place is the only one in the world for him."

"Do you think Georgia is, or Boston?"

"Bertram," their father was putting on his clothes in a manner that plainly told them he was impatient, "I don't care what Jubel thinks or what either of you think. I try not to interfere in your lives and I don't want interference in mine. I am going on to Evie's; summer, Georgia or whatever. Now, Jubel, you go ahead and get dressed and we'll all go out and have breakfast together."

Bertram sulked. "I've had my breakfast. You go on ahead. I'll wait for Jubel."

"All right, do as you like. Both of you can talk it over until doomsday but I've had my say." He went out of the house, not slamming but decidedly shutting the door behind him.

"The old man can be very unreasonable."

"He's not unreasonable. He's doing what he wants to do. I'm going to dress. I have a date."

"Hold it awhile. I want to talk to you, Jubel."

"You heard what Pop said."

"I want to talk to you about something else. Sit down a minute. I'm not staying long."

"How long are you staying?"

"Just for the day if I can help it. I have to get back to Ella and the baby. I certainly miss that kid." He smiled a little sheepishly. "You'd be surprised how a kid like that can get under your skin. You ought to get married yourself, Jubel. You'd be surprised what a couple of kids will do for you."

"I'm sure." He wasn't going to encourage this kind of conversation. He wanted Bertram to come to his point. He started dressing.

"You know, Jubel, I stopped by at the house on the way in."

"Whose house?"

"Pop's. I saw Agnew, too."

"Sounds like a real pleasure trip."

"I considered it business."

236

"Come to think of it, I can understand that."

"Agnew's doing very well. He's been building up the business nicely."

"I know. Pop gets a check from him every month."

"He still wants to buy, you know."

"Before you go any further, Bertram, I want to ask you something."

"What's that?"

"Why did you wait until Pop came to me before you tried getting him back again? Why didn't you wait until he went on to Evie's?"

Bertram smiled a little. "I can't get very far with the girls, Helen or Evie."

"You didn't get very far with me."

"I haven't told you what I want to say yet."

He listened.

"Do you know that Pop has a ten-thousand-dollar life insurance policy?"

"I not only know it, I know he borrowed a thousand dollars on it to give to you."

Bertram's face seemed to trip on that for a second. "He told you that, huh?"

"Yeah. And he told me he's been paying it back, too."

"I offered the old man a sound proposition and he gives me a thousand dollars. He just hasn't any business sense, Jubel. You could see that from the way Agnew is running things now . . . Well, what's the difference. The point is, he has ten thousand dollars' worth of life insurance, and Agnew wants to give him seventeen thousand five hundred for the house and business. I think Agnew might be persuaded to raise it to twenty thousand."

"That makes an even thirty thousand all told, doesn't it?"

"An even thirty. But thirty thousand split four ways is only seventy-five hundred apiece."

He stopped and waited for Jubel to say something but Jubel was still listening.

237

"You understand, of course, I couldn't talk this way to the girls. They'd start yelling blood and murder. What they forget, and what you and I both know, is that Pop is getting along. He's not going to be here too much longer."

"Go on."

"Anyway, as I was saying, split four ways it's only seventy-five hundred apiece. And that's not taking into consideration any of the grandchildren: Evie's two and mine, you know."

"You told me."

Bertram took off his jacket and wiped his face. "It sure is hot down here. Do you know if Pop's made out a will?"

"I don't know. Why?"

"I drove through Harrisburg after I left Pop's place. I thought I'd find out about that. In Pennsylvania, if a man dies intestate—that is, if he dies without leaving a will—his estate is divided equally among his children."

"That follows. Sounds all right to me."

Bertram's look was incredulous, then patient. "You don't understand, Jubel. That means Evie and Helen get the same as you and I do."

"What's wrong with that?"

"What's wrong with it! It isn't fair. We're the men of the family. We're the ones who should be left the money."

"What's the matter with Evie and Helen?"

Bertram looked around the room. "Jubel, you're in a tough business. I know how it is; it's hard getting started. I don't want to be personal but I can see you're not living off the fat of the land. Fifteen thousand dollars is a sizable sum of money. You could coast for a while, let it carry you along until you can get someplace on your own."

"I said, what about Helen and Evie?"

"Helen doesn't need the money. She's doing all right for herself. And it'd be a sin to give it to Evie and let her husband drink it up. We're the men in the family, Jubel. It belongs to us. We can make Pop see it that way. Together, we can talk him into it."

Jubel snapped his collar down around his tie. He went to the closet for his jacket.

"What do you say, Jubel?"

"I say, go to hell, Bertram."

He turned and walked out of the apartment. He hoped he wouldn't find him there when he returned.

He was late. He took a cab over to the Plaza. This was the trouble with having a wife like Toby. She couldn't meet you at Joe's lunchroom around the corner. It had to be at a hotel that cost a cab fare and a five-dollar breakfast. He wondered what she had on her mind this time; chances are, another bright idea to make him join her side. Thank goodness for the Barry play. Once he was set and rehearsing, she'd give in and he'd hear no more of it. He was glad he was seeing her, though; she'd take his mind off that brother of his and his cute little schemes. He hoped Pop wouldn't tell Bertram about Toby or, if he did, not too much about her; not about her money, anyway. That was all Bertram needed to start him off on a new scent. But he could trust Pop.

Toby was waiting for him. She was wearing a navy dress with a large white waffle pique collar that made her as beautiful as a freshly watered daisy.

"Jubel, I thought you'd never get here."

"You look good enough to eat today."

She didn't seem nervous or upset, the way she had sounded on the phone.

"I haven't had my breakfast. Are you ready for lunch?"

"I couldn't touch a thing."

"In that case, we'll pass up all this elegance and go to a joint on 58th Street."

They left the hotel and walked around the corner to a lunchroom. She was surprising him. This was a wonderful opportunity for her to dig away at him and his low standard of living, but she didn't open her mouth. They settled themselves in a booth with a marble-topped table between them. He ordered a quick cup of coffee and told them to take their time with the bacon and eggs.

239

"You sure you won't have anything?"

"I couldn't, Jubel."

"What's the matter, sweetie? What did you want to talk to me about?"

"I think we're having a baby."

He could feel his jaw drop and his face begin to look silly.

"A baby?" It was like doors opening up, flowers blooming and all the wonderful tricks they did with movie cameras to show the beginning of a new life.

"That's wonderful, darling. Are you all right?"

"Of course, I'm all right."

"It's going to be as beautiful as you are. I know it. Why did you let me come here? We should have stayed at the Plaza and celebrated. Wait until Pop hears about this!"

"We're not going to be able to dillydally any more, Jubel."

"Absolutely not. Everybody's going to know now, even your father. And as soon as we go into rehearsal, we'll set up housekeeping. How about a place on Long Island or Connecticut? The city's no good for kids."

"Jubel, don't you understand? You're going to have responsibilities: not only a wife but a child. You'll have to forget about the theatre, settle down, be a husband and a father."

He started to say, I can settle down in the theatre, I can be a husband and a father, too. But he looked at her and he realized it wouldn't make any difference what he said. There were miles of table tops between them.

xxii

The news of the baby and Bertram's visit had brought certain matters to a head in young Jubel's life; family matters. For one thing, he decided that maybe Bertram and Toby had been right about his father. So he had talked to Pop and written to Evie. He had told her he was afraid the New York summer was proving too much for Pop and that it would be best if he left sooner for her place. Hot as Georgia might be, this time of year, it would still be country. Evie agreed. The baby was also a factor in this move. He'd have to be giving up the basement apartment soon and find either a house or larger quarters in the city. It was true that Toby hadn't given an inch—she still wouldn't tell her father, she still wouldn't listen to anything except an end to the theatre—but it had been only ten days since she told him and he felt time and nature were on his side. She'd mellow with the months and once he was working and had money, she'd have no excuse except snobbery. And how long could snobbery hold out against motherhood? It was just a matter of having his professional life catch up with his personal one and that was going to happen any day now. It was like Barry said: a matter of time and patience. Obviously, the thing to do was act as though it had happened.

The day before Pop was to leave for Evie's, Toby called him. She had just come from the doctor.

"Are you all right, little Mother?" Funny, after all this time, it was still an emotional experience to hold her on the other end of a telephone wire.

"Just fine, Jubel."

"How's your exotic appetite? Can I run over with a ham sandwich or a tutti-frutti marshmallow sundae?"

"I told you, I just came from the doctor's."

"Isn't everything all right?"

"Everything is perfect."

"Well, what did he say? He said something, didn't he?"

"He said it isn't going to happen."

"What! What did you say?"

"It was a mistake. I'm *not* going to have a baby."

"You're kidding!"

"I am not."

"But that's impossible. How could there be a mistake? Things like that don't happen."

"But they do; many times. If you'll excuse me, I won't go into the clinical details."

They talked a little more but he couldn't remember about what. He was bitterly disappointed. He couldn't understand it. He felt as though he had been robbed. Of course, he had to tell his father. Strangely enough, Pop took it a lot better than he had expected he would.

"I know how you feel, Jubel, but it does happen. I remember your mother's sister, your Aunt Charlotte, it was the same with her right after she was married. Very high-strung woman, very emotional. I will say, though, there was no doubt about the next time; she had twins."

"Oh, I guess it happens, all right. It's just that . . . well, I wanted it, Pop."

"That's understandable, but you'll have a child, Jubel."

"You don't think the whole thing was a scheme, do you? Something Toby thought up to make me do what she wanted, and when she found out it wasn't working, she called the whole thing off?"

242

"I don't think so. I think Toby is above that kind of deception."

"Sure, she is. I don't know what's the matter with me, Pop."

"It's only natural when you're disappointed."

"I'll bet you're pretty sick and tired of all of us by now, aren't you? I'll bet you'll be glad when you finally get home again."

"I will be glad to get home but I'm not sick and tired. I've enjoyed all of it and I'm anxious to spend some time with Evie and her family. That's why I didn't go back with Bertram."

"I can think of a better reason than that."

"You must try to understand Bertram."

"Understand him?"

"Bertram's a little mixed up. His world is a commercial one and so it's logical that money should be his only measure of success or failure."

"There are a lot of people like that, Pop."

"Yes, but Bertram belongs to us. We've got to understand him."

"How about that deal he's been trying to sell you? He'd have you give up the house and the business to go in with him on some phony, fly-by-night operation."

"We can never tell about those things. Maybe Bertram's business would be successful but that's not important. If he were my only child, I might do it. He forgets there are other children. I used to do that myself with my own brothers and sisters. I suppose every child considers himself an only child in his own way, and thinks he deserves more than the others. I love all of you, Jubel. I want all of you to have what you wish for most. I wish I could give it to you."

"It would be a big order for me, Pop."

"You've got to believe in yourself."

"I do. I wish Toby would."

"She will in time."

"You know I love her."

"Of course you do."

243

"It's just that we're so far apart on so many things. I thought, with the baby coming on and me set in Barry's play, all our troubles would be over."

"Do you think the Barry play will materialize, Jubel?"

"Of course. It's just a matter of time, Pop."

"Do you think, if it does, it will change Toby's mind?"

"I don't know. Right now, I don't know anything."

"She could go on this way; not telling her father, keeping it a secret."

"Yes, I know."

"Jubel, for the sake of argument, just suppose the Barry play doesn't come through. What will you do then?"

"I haven't the faintest idea. What do you think I ought to do?"

"I don't know but I do think you'll have to make up your mind; one way or the other no matter what happens. You're two young and stubborn people. It isn't which of you is right or wrong. It's what you want most that counts most: your work or your wife."

"Why can't I have both, Pop?"

"Some people can't."

"I wish I knew."

"You'll have to find out, Jubel."

"Yes, I guess I will."

xxiii

Even though Georgia was farther away—and he had to pass
through his own state of Pennsylvania to get to it—somehow
it seemed closer to home. It might be because it would be his
last stop before he did go home or because it was country again
and, after the suburban life with Bertram and the cities of Boston and New York, the miles of open land Evie was driving
him through seemed familiar and comfortable.

"I'd forgotten you were so far from Atlanta, Evie."

"It's only about thirty miles, Pop."

"Couldn't I have come to another station, closer to you?"

"Yes, but it would have meant changing trains at Atlanta
and at least an hour's wait. It's nothing at all, Pop. We've come
half the way. I guess you're pretty tired of riding, aren't you?"

"It was a long trip, much longer than I thought."

"Did you get any sleep on the train?"

He looked tired to her and old, really old. It was as though
all of his more than seventy years suddenly appeared to be
counted.

"I had very good accommodations. Trains have certainly
improved since I used to travel on them. The berth was fine.
I thought I was going to go by train from Bertram's up to Boston but Bertram insisted on driving me."

"Yes, I know."

"What did you ask me before, Evie?"

"I wanted to know if you had any rest on the train."

"Oh, yes. You'll have to forgive me. Lately, things seem to slip away from me."

Poor Pop. Poor, poor Pop. "It's nothing. It happens to everybody. I often forget, myself."

"Well, as I said, the berth was fine, very comfortable once you got settled in it. The porters on the trains are very helpful, too. Mine was a considerate man. He told me if I lay on my side, I wouldn't mind the motion of the train so much. I can't say that it helped a great deal but that wasn't his fault. He was the nicest man and he had the gentlest way of waking you: just rubbing you in the small of your back with his fingertips. It was a nice enough feeling to make you want to go right back to sleep again but he kept saying, 'It's Atlanta, Captain. Time for you to get up, sir. Atlanta. Atlanta.' "

"That must have been nice."

"It was. I gave him a two-dollar tip. Do you think that was enough, Evie?"

"Very generous."

"I'd rather make a mistake on the generous side than not give enough. Good service deserves a good tip. Don't you think so, Evie?"

"Of course, Pop."

He laughed a little. "I learned a lot about that from Helen. We used to eat out all the time, took turns at paying the checks, too. Helen said you always tipped ten percent of the bill. If the bill was five dollars that would make a fifty-cent tip. Did you know that, Evie?"

"I've heard about it."

"But I'll bet you didn't know that you add to that fifty cents, did you? That's where the generosity comes in. The ten percent is a minimum. If you don't like the service, that's all the waiter should get; unless you want to be mean in a nice sort of way and add another nickel or dime, just to let him know. If he's a good waiter, he deserves an extra quarter or even a half a dol-

246

lar for good measure. It's a nice little system to know about, isn't it?"

"Yes, it is, Pop."

"Of course, it doesn't go for tipping sleeping-car porters. I guess you just have to use your judgment there, don't you?"

"You did fine, Pop. You've become quite a man of the world."

"You have to be when you go traveling around to visit your children. By the time I got to young Jubel's, I can tell you, I knew my way around in a restaurant and a bill of fare. Sometimes, even those French dishes didn't throw me."

"I hope you're not going to mind simple, home-cooked meals."

"I'm not going to mind them at all. You're a good cook, Evie. Your mother always said she was glad one of the girls was at home in the kitchen."

"It's no trick, Pop, it's necessity. Helen would do it if she had a husband like Neal."

"Neal is a pretty good eater, isn't he?"

"Yes, pretty good." She was glad he took that meaning of her remark. What she really meant was that Neal was a better drinker than an eater but that called for a good cook, too; you couldn't afford eating out when the little money you had was turned into alcohol without even giving it a chance to ferment. But it might have been better if Pop understood that now. She wasn't going to be able to keep it from him—not after he was there a day, much less three months—and she had decided long ago not even to try.

"Evie, this isn't the same car you drove home in last time with the children, is it?"

"No, Pop. This is a new one." She'd been wondering if he'd notice it; not that you could help it if you had any memory left and you had seen that old heap, even once. "Neal bought it about a month ago."

"I'm glad. I didn't think that old car of yours was very

247

sturdy. You didn't have any trouble getting back with it, did you?"

"Just one flat tire and that wasn't too bad. It happened right near a service station and I had plenty of money. You gave me much more than I really needed, Pop."

"You never have too much money when you're traveling. I've found that out. Especially when you're traveling with two children."

"You gave me fifty dollars. Remember?"

"Was it fifty? I thought it was twenty."

"Oh, no, fifty. And I'm going to pay it back."

"It doesn't matter. It's unimportant. But I'm glad you're talking about money. It reminds me. I try to pay my way wherever I go, Evie. I did it at Bertram's, at Helen's and with young Jubel, too. I insist on it. I'll give you fifteen dollars a week. If that's not enough, you'll tell me, won't you?"

"Yes, Pop." It would have been hypocritical to argue with him. It would just be for show. She wanted the money, needed it, and any protest a daughter might have, should have, made was swallowed by the mother.

"I swear, Evie, I must be losing my mind."

She wished he wouldn't say things like that. "Why, Pop? What's the matter?"

"I forgot to tell you the most important news of all. Your brother Jubel's married."

"Jubel! Well, that is news. Who's the girl?"

"Her name's Toby Sheffield."

"An actress?"

He had to laugh at that. "Oh, no. Toby's anything but an actress."

"He's still in the theatre?"

"He was when I left."

"The family's growing up, isn't it, Pop?"

"Yes, everyone will be married but Helen."

He sounded so sad, she thought she'd better talk about something else.

248

"The children are going to be very happy to see you, Pop, especially Jinny."

"I wish you had brought them along."

"I thought you'd be too tired for them."

"Is Neal staying with them?"

"I never know but it doesn't matter. Jinny is big enough to take care of herself and the baby, too."

"Is that so! She was quite a young lady when I saw her last. Talked like a grown-up."

"She has grown, Pop. She'll be ready for school in September and it's got me worried sick."

"All mothers worry when it comes time to send their first child to school."

"Oh, it isn't that. It's the schools down here, Pop. I don't like them. And I can't say I care too much for the children, either, or the grown-ups, for that matter."

"Still a Yankee, aren't you, Evie?"

"I guess so. Well, there's nothing I can do about it."

"I wouldn't worry too much. A good child's hard to hurt and I've got a lot of good grandchildren. You've heard about Bertram's boy?"

"Yes, I did. Helen sent me a letter he wrote to her while you were still there."

"He's a fine boy, that Teddy. You'd be surprised what a difference he makes in the house. Ella's crazy about him."

"I feel sorry for the kid with Bertram as his father. Whatever made him adopt a child, Pop?"

"Why, it's only natural, Evie."

"Not for Bertram, it isn't. He managed to get a thousand dollars out of you, didn't he?"

That was odd. He didn't remember writing her about it but he must have. He laughed to himself. This would be no time in his life to go in for a career of crime. The way he was forgetting things, he'd be caught on his first try, forgetting and leaving everything behind him.

249

"The money's nothing to worry about, Evie. I've paid it back already from Agnew's checks."

"Did Ella know about it?"

"To tell you the truth, I don't really remember. You see, Bertram didn't ask me for the money outright. He wanted me to stay on and go into business with him; sell the house and my business, you know, for capital. He's pressed for cash—what with the baby and everything—and it's only reasonable for him to want to do something on his own. I told him I couldn't do it but that I'd give him a thousand dollars, borrow it on my life insurance. I sent him the money when I got up to Helen's in Boston. I also got around to changing the beneficiaries on my policy."

She knew all about that from Helen and she didn't have to be reminded. All it did was bring back that horrible scene she had had with Neal over it when he found out.

"Pop, let's not talk about beneficiaries and policies and money. They depress me."

"It's nothing to be depressed about, Evie. Those are the things that have to be looked after in a lifetime."

Looked after but not run after the way all of them had been running. It made her sick to think of it. Where would Pop be if they hadn't discovered he was worth money? Each of his wonderful children, whom he loved so much, would have packed up and left him alone. She along with the others and she could tell herself, until she got blue in the face, that she wouldn't have done it, that, at the last minute, she would have said to hell with Neal and brought him home with her anyhow. But would she? She couldn't convince herself when she hadn't been able to test herself. She would have done exactly what Bertram and Helen and young Jubel were going to do: pack up and leave him alone, no matter how she protested, no matter how she suffered. She had been telling herself then she had to worry about her own children, her own life, and Neal would have none of her father. But the money and Bertram changed all that. They weren't going to let Bertram get away with anything. They weren't going to let Bertram put anything over on them. And the doors began to open: Bertram's first, then Helen's and young Jubel's and now, hers. All of them willing and anxious to take their father when they wouldn't have any part of him before.

Maybe she was being cruel to Helen and young Jubel. She wasn't really sure that Helen cared about her father's money or that young Jubel had schemes for it. But did either of them lift a finger until the money showed itself? And didn't she, herself, only then suddenly realize that now she could have her father with her because she could tell Neal it would mean safeguarding their investment? They all stank, all of them, herself included. Maybe Bertram was the only honest one of the lot. Maybe he was the one who really deserved to have Pop with him because he was the first to offer, no matter what his motives.

Did any of them think beyond the year? Did any of them ask themselves, or each other, what Pop was going to do after he was through visiting them? Would he go back home? Would he start the cycle all over again? No, each of them was getting in his licks and thinking, subconsciously if he were kind, that after the year it might not matter. Oh, she was a bitter one this morning.

"Evie, do you mind if I open this window a little more? It's getting a little warm."

"Of course not, Pop." She leaned over and turned down the window for him.

"I guess I'm not used to the change of climate. It was hot in New York for a while but we had a change before I left."

"Why don't you open your tie and loosen your collar? This isn't the city, you know. Everyone's informal."

"No, I'll be all right."

"You'll have to be careful down here, Pop. It gets awfully warm. You'll have to learn not to move around much, not to hurry, stay indoors most of the day and look for the shade when you're out."

251

The country ahead and around them lay inert under the sun. There were some cultivated fields but most of the land had been scalped for pine lumber. The earth was red and green and brown.

"There doesn't seem to be much shade that I can see."

"We have some trees around the house. You can sit under those. And there is a breeze now and then because we're on a hill, and the view is pretty. You'll just have to be careful, that's all, Pop. Don't tax yourself, take naps in the afternoon. I'll see to it that you eat the right food. We'll take good care of you and you won't mind the summer."

He turned around to see how Pitch was. The cat was sleeping in the middle of the back seat.

"Well, Pitch doesn't seem to mind the heat. You think he'll be all right, Evie?"

"Of course. We have cats all over the place. You'll have to see he doesn't get into any fights. I've told Jinny to look out for him, too. That's all she's been talking about for days, Pop: you and your cat."

"It's going to be good to see her."

"We haven't far to go—a few more miles."

The red sign on the road up ahead screamed, "Three miles to Neal's Auto Court," but she didn't point that out to her father. It was an unhappy thought at best and when she remembered what those signs at half-mile intervals had cost her in tears and aggravation, she'd just as soon forget they were there. And that went for the car and the whole damned auto court, the way it was now.

Jubel was glad there were only a few more miles. He was tired. It seemed as though he had been riding for a week—not just a little more than a day. He supposed the semi-tropic climate had something to do with it. Well, Bertram had warned him. Bertram had said it was going to be hot and this was no time of the year to be going to Georgia. He hadn't told Evie about Bertram, about his surprise visit to young Jubel's. He was going to, but he suddenly decided against it. Evie said it

252

was depressing to talk about money and he realized, with some amusement, that you couldn't very well talk about Bertram without talking about money. He'd mention it to her sometime when it might be less depressing. Then he'd try to make her understand Bertram a little better. It wasn't right for brothers and sisters to be suspicious and resentful of one another.

"Hold tight, Pop. Here we are."

They were almost at the top of a sharp rise in the road. He saw the big red sign, "Neal's Auto Court," with its commanding arrow pointing to the left but he didn't see the court. Suddenly, Evie turned sharply at the top of the hill and there they were going up the gravel driveway, with the house and the trees off to one side and the row of freshly painted cabins farther back.

Jinny and the baby were under the trees but when she saw them, she came running. She didn't give him a chance to get out of the car. She had her head in the window and was kissing him before he could catch his breath.

"Jinny, don't be so violent. Your grandfather's tired."

"Where's the cat, Grandpa? Where's Pitch?"

It felt good to get out and stretch his legs. They organized themselves and the baggage, Evie carrying the two big ones in spite of his protest, he with the small one and Jinny with her arms full of the cat who was being very docile about it.

"Where's your father?"

"He went into town right after you left, Mama. He said he wouldn't be very long."

The baby stumbled over to them and he had to put down his bag to kiss him and say hello.

"Come on, Pop. We'll get you settled first."

They filed into the house. It was shaded and green-cool. After young Jubel's room and Helen's apartment, this seemed more like home. It might not have any more rooms than Bertram's little place but there was a country generosity about them. Evie explained the layout to him as they went upstairs. It was a peculiar kind of house, she said. There were two bed-

253

rooms downstairs as well as two upstairs. She didn't know why, but that's the way it was. She and Neal had one of the first-floor rooms, the baby the other. Jinny was upstairs and he was going to be upstairs unless he found the one short flight too much for him. In that case, they'd move around and make some arrangements. If he didn't mind the steps, though, the upstairs room was the best for him. It was large and airy with two exposures and received only the morning sun.

"It'll be fine, Evie," he said when they put the bags down on the floor. "I won't mind the stairs." It was everything she said it was and cheerful, too. The four-poster bed looked comfortable and the hooked scatter rugs had the familiar tones of home.

"Would you like to lie down and rest for a while, Pop?"

"No, I think I'll unpack first. I'll feel better about it."

"All right. I'll help you. Jinny, you take the cat down to the kitchen and give him some milk."

They put the bags on the bed and opened them. Evie was a good unpacker. She had dresser drawers all ready for his shirts and underwear. They were half-way through one of the bags when they heard the truck in the driveway and Neal's voice saying good-bye to one of his cronies from Bellford.

"Hey, Evie. Where are you?"

"Upstairs here with Pop." She could tell from the sound of him that he had a morning glow already. He had probably hitched a ride into town as soon as she had left for Atlanta, and spent a couple of hours at Luther's having "just a couple."

She was glad he was in good spirits when he bounced into the room.

"Why, Pop, you old sonofagun!"

He still looked trim and neat from early morning and there didn't seem to be enough in him to show too much. He just looked happy and excited like a movie cowboy on a holiday.

"How are you, Neal?"

Her father put out his hand but Neal would have none of it. He took him in a big hug.

"Gad, Pop. It's good to see you. How are you?"

"I'm fine, Neal."

"You're looking grand, you old Yankee. You feeling all right?"

"Just fine."

Neal's exuberance was wearing off. She thought he must have been working it up ever since he left Luther's in Bellford.

"So you made the trip all the way down from New York. You're sure looking mighty chipper, too."

"He feels fine, Neal."

"Yeah, sure. He told me that."

He looked at the bed and the open, half-unpacked bags. "What's going on here?"

"I'm helping Pop unpack his things."

"Wait a minute. He's not staying up in this little old room, is he?"

"There's nothing wrong with this room. Pop likes it."

"It's a lovely room. I was telling Evie . . ."

"Oh, no. Oh, no. Not good enough for you, Pop. Not nearly good enough."

"Neal, what are you talking about?"

"I got the place for this old Yankee, best place in the world. Makes this room look sick."

"This'll be fine, Neal. I don't need anything better."

"No, sir, Pop. No, sirree. I got just the place for you."

"Neal, what on earth are you talking about?"

"I'll tell you, Evie. I'm putting Pop up in our best cabin; the one we fixed for the honeymooners. He'll live like a king. Have a whole little house to himself." He went for the bags on the bed. "There ain't nothing too good for my millionaire father-in-law."

255

xxiv

She remembered when she came back from her father's house
—after her mother's funeral, after she had promised to take
Pop for three months—how it was with Neal. Now, she could
look out of her kitchen window, out to where the big tree was,
and see her father dozing in the hammock that Jinny attended
with gentle concern, keeping it moving, keeping the flies off
her grandfather's face. On the way back that was the picture
she had had before her: Pop living with her this way, being
part of her life, being real and touchable to her children as he
had been to her. She was going to achieve that, she had told
herself. Pop *was* going to live with them, it was all going to
work out. Never mind what had happened back there at the
house, never mind the circumstances: the bickering, the back-
turning, the tossing around they had given him without moving
him an inch from his loneliness. Never mind all that or the selfishness that stood on its head to become generosity when they
found out about the money. He was going to be home with her.
It would take nine months. He would go to three other children before he would come to her, but he would come to her
at last. But she couldn't "never mind" the money; that was
going to make all the difference between his being able to come
and Neal throwing them all out at once.

On the way back, the one person she had admired more than

anyone else in the world was Bertram's wife. It took courage—the purest because it was so unromantic—to cut down your own husband for his brother and sisters. Would she have been able to do that to Neal? She could say she would if she didn't have the children, but weren't children excuses as well as children? People were forever using their *children* or their *wives* or their *husbands* or their *parents*—any of the standard obligations—to excuse themselves from additional obligations. They played one against the other until they could achieve freedom from all of them. Even Ella was not exempt; not any more, now that she had her adopted child. She dug Ella's letter out of her apron pocket and looked for the paragraph again.

> *If I've talked too much about the child, it's only because he means so much to both of us. I never dreamed that Bertram could become so attached. As for me, I've never been so happy and there isn't anything I wouldn't do to keep it this way. I feel like a tigress.*

That was the new Ella with child but if she had had Ella's old courage, she would have packed up her father, brought him home and told Neal to go to hell if he didn't like it. Telling that to Neal with twenty thousand dollars' worth of moral stamina behind her wasn't the same thing; even though she wasn't going to use it unless she had to.

"What did you say to me when I left here last week?"

"What do you mean, what did I say to you? When?"

"Last week when I went home for my mother's funeral. You called something to me as I was going out of the driveway. What was it?"

"Oh, that. It doesn't matter. You didn't do it anyhow."

"What didn't I do?"

"You didn't bring your father home with you."

"That's what I thought you said."

"And it's a damn good thing you didn't."

Not a word about how he was, not even a curiosity about

257

her mother or about anyone in the family. But what could she expect? He hadn't had the decency to ask her about herself: what kind of a trip it had been, did she manage all right with the children, did she have any trouble with the car? She couldn't help pointing that out to him.

His answer was, "You're back, ain't you?"

"I had to borrow fifty dollars from Pop to get back."

"Your borrowing ain't my affair."

She had a mind to tell him what was his affair. She had a mind to tell him, as a businessman and an auto court proprietor, what the cabins were like on the road, how much they charged and what type of travelers they catered to. If he didn't care how she got back, she had a mind to tell him, as a husband, how she was able to get there at all. Would it bother him? Would he blink an eye at it? It didn't matter; it wouldn't have been a *good* mind to tell him.

"I may as well tell you now, Neal, my father is coming here."

"What do you mean, *is* coming here?"

"He'll be here next July."

He had laughed at that and she could see why. It did sound funny to say, "next July," when they hadn't even touched this winter yet.

"He's with Bertram and Ella now. Each of us are taking him for three months. He'll go on to Helen's next and then to young Jubel."

"He can stop right there and so can you. He's not coming here."

"He is."

"Like hell he is."

"I tell you, he is coming here."

"And I tell you, like hell he is. I got enough trouble feeding four mouths without having a fifth. So forget about it."

"I'm not forgetting about it, and you wouldn't have so much trouble feeding four mouths if you didn't have such a thirsty one yourself and if you had sense enough not to buy this white elephant on a hilltop and stick to your job."

258

"Shut up!"

"I won't shut up. My father is coming here—that's the least I can get out of this place—and what are you going to do about it?"

"Nothing. Just nothing. If you want company for starving, you can have it."

He had walked out then, walked down to the road, got a ride into Bellford and tanked up for two days at Luther's. He didn't take the car because he knew, before he left, he'd never make it back under his own power. And he was right; Luther and several of the other boys had to bring him in. He might not have been gone for two days if they had a phone but, aside from the money which they didn't have for it, Neal's aversion to the telephone was based on her using it to track him down and hound his friends into bringing him back earlier than he wanted to.

That particular binge hadn't been necessary. She could have told him, then and there, about Pop's money. Sometimes, though, she wondered if their fights were really to blame for his drinking. It seemed to her, when he had been too good for too long a time, he'd work up to one; just to have his excuse, just to be able to give her part of the blame. This time she hadn't cared. She had wanted to stand up to him, just as Ella had stood up to Bertram.

Silly, wasn't it? It was all for nothing and it did her more harm than him because, later, she found out he had stopped in the hall, on his way out of the house, to take from her bag what was left of her father's fifty dollars.

Why was it, she asked herself, that things never turned out for her the way she had hoped they would, even something as simple as having your father with you? To some unknowing eye who might happen to see her standing at her kitchen window, looking out at the peaceful family group—her father, her two children—under the tree, it might seem that if this was what she wanted, she had it. But under what circumstances?

"Well, that's different, honey. Of course. Why didn't you tell me about the money in the first place?"

"I wanted you to welcome Pop without any motives."

"Heck, Evie, you know me better than that. Maybe I was a little touchy about something, and I thought we were being taken advantage of. You know how it is."

She knew how it was but she had thought, what difference does it make why Neal says yes as long as he does.

"So Bertram thought he was going to get his hooks into that dough, did he?"

"Yes, Neal."

"Well, naturally, we have to protect our interests. I mean, all us kids have to, don't we? What about young Jubel and Helen? You never can trust anybody when it comes to money, you know."

"You can trust them."

He didn't hear her when she had said that. He seemed to be thinking beyond reassurance. "Why, sure, we'll have the old man down here. See to it that he has a good visit, too. Make him forget his troubles."

It had been settled then and she could relax. But nine months was a long time and things could happen to people before it passed. People like Pop got older and more tired and the slow, cumulative sickness of age began to show. People like Neal got ideas, thought about them, developed them and then, suddenly, broke out with them.

One morning, a month before her father was due—that was just about seven weeks ago, now—she woke to the sound of hammers and men swarming all over the cabins. Neal had been out all night and her first frightened thought was that hoodlums were destroying the auto court. After the first minute, she realized how ridiculous that was. Who would want to destroy anything as worthless as this place and what for? She knew right away that Neal was behind it and up to something even though she couldn't see him. She threw on some clothes and ran out but not far.

260

Practically at the door, standing in front of a brand-new car that had been pulled up close to the steps, was Neal. He was balancing a large red and white road sign with both hands and he was smiling.

"Morning, Evie. It sure takes you a powerful long time to wake up. I've been standing here, waiting for you."

She had been either too sleepy or too stupid to understand it. "Neal, what is this? What's going on here?"

"Just fixing the place up a little. Got a gang of the boys here to really make us an auto court. How do you like this?" He jiggled the road sign that read, "Neal's Auto Court—At the Top of the Hill."

"Pretty nifty job, ain't it? Lights up when headlights hit it, too."

"It's beautiful. Where did you get the money for it?"

"Got a dozen of them. Going to sprinkle the road with them: three miles to Neal's Auto Court, two miles to Neal's Auto Court, one mile, half a mile, you know how they do it, all the way down the line. Six coming, six going."

"I said, where did you get the money for them?"

"And how do you like this little boat?" He took one hand off the sign long enough to slap the dazzling blue fender. "Eight cylinders; all of them work, too."

"You're insane!"

Even as she spoke, an open van, loaded with furniture, turned into the driveway, shifted gears and lumbered toward them. She watched it go by, heading for the cabins. The two men in the cab waved. Only when it had passed and she stared after it, did she realize the furniture was maple and brand new.

Neal waved it by with a generous hand. "All ours, honey. We're going to have ourselves an auto court. Good enough for the president of the United States."

She added up all she saw: the men at the cabins inside and out fixing the roofs, the walls, the floors; the new car; the new furniture; the signs. She realized she must be looking at thousands of dollars.

"Where did you get the money for this?"

"I didn't . . . yet."

"Where do you think you're going to get it?"

"Your pappy."

"You're crazy! If you think my father is going to give you money he worked all his life for . . . Why, I wouldn't let him even if he wanted to. Tell those men you haven't any money for them. Send them home. Send them away."

"Now, wait a minute, Evie. You told me, yourself, you were having your father here to protect our interests, didn't you?"

"I told you I was having him here because I want him here. I had to tell you about the money. You wouldn't have let him put his foot inside the door."

"That don't change the picture any. It don't make any difference. All you kids have been protecting your interests. Well, I'm protecting mine. This little old auto court is my interest."

"You're a stupid, crazy, drunken fool."

He laughed. "Don't get mad with me, Evie. You know you just get prettier and funnier when you get mad."

"You could build a palace on this stupid hill and you wouldn't get any customers, you wouldn't do any business. Don't you see it? Don't you see it? Are you completely blind?"

"Why, heck, Evie, if that's all that's bothering you, we could level this little old hill with all the money your old man has."

She wanted to say more, she had started to, but the door opened and Jinny came out with Tommy after her.

"Mama, what are all the men here for?"

"For nothing, for absolutely nothing. They're just wasting their time."

She had hurried the children back into the house and slammed the door on Neal's laugh.

He would still laugh whenever she brought the subject up but he wasn't going to have the last one; she'd see to that. Imagine him trying to move Pop out to one of those cabins, too! Not that they weren't nice enough now but she saw through that little maneuver, and she had told him so. He wasn't going to have a chance to get Pop alone and try to talk him out of his money.

She heard Jinny calling her and she looked out. Her father had gotten out of the hammock and was walking toward the house.

"Pop!" she called. "Your hat. Don't walk in that sun without your hat." He didn't seem to hear her. She called to Jinny to get it for him. By the time the child did, and ran to him with it, he was almost at the back porch.

"Pop, you shouldn't do that. You know better than to walk in that sun without a hat."

"It was only a short distance, Evie." He was heading for the stairs.

"Where are you going?"

"Upstairs to lie down. That hammock makes me dream."

"Don't you want a glass of milk or something?"

"No, I'm just tired."

She followed him up the steps, into his room. She helped him take off his shoes and stretch his legs on the bed.

"You sure you're all right, Pop?"

"Yes, I'm all right; just tired."

"What were you dreaming about?"

"I had the darnedest dream out there. I dreamed I was sitting out under that tree without a stitch of clothes on and all you children were standing around me: Helen and you and young Jubel and Bertram and my grandchildren, too. And all of you were hungry and asking me for bread and I didn't have any bread."

"Is that all?"

"Yes, that was all."

"What a silly dream, Pop! None of us needs bread. You know that. You ought to stop worrying about your children so much."

She pulled down the shade to darken the room.

"I guess you're right, Evie, except that I do. I always do."

XXV

It developed, after a while, that it was Luther who had said-good for Neal and all he had bought and spent to fix up the auto court.

"What do you mean, 'said-good' for you? What's good about these or about you, for that matter?"

She flicked a contemptuous hand at the stack of bills Neal had brought home with him from Bellford. It was late in the afternoon but early for Neal to be back from Luther's. Her father and the children were out back, near the cabins, where Jinny had said she had seen a family of rabbits.

"I needed someone who could vouch for my credit. Luther was good enough to do it for me."

"He certainly was. He's been good to you for years, keeping you well supplied with liquor. I suppose you told him you were about to come into a fortune."

"Naturally. Luther knows about Pop. He had to know."

"Does he know that you haven't any money, that you're not getting any?"

"He's coming here to talk to you about that. I told him he'd have to wait."

"Stop sounding like a ghoul! What are you doing, going around praying for my father to die so that you can pay off your debts? It won't do you any good, Neal. It won't. You can

264

tell Luther he'll be wasting his time. I didn't borrow the money from him. He didn't say-good for me."

"He'll be here in a couple of minutes. He was just waiting for someone to take over the cafe for him. I couldn't help it, Evie. He said he had to see you and explain it to you."

"Neal, why did you do it? All you did was paint the white elephant whiter. You threw out money, threw it out and you didn't have it. It wasn't your own."

"It'll pay off, Evie. You've got to give it a chance."

"You've had your signs up and the place fixed for more than two months now. Where's the business? Where are the customers?"

"We had a couple more last month."

"A couple more! Do you expect to pay off thousands of dollars with a couple more? And why did you have to buy that car? A two-thousand-dollar car!"

"We needed a car."

"Oh, Neal, when are you going to get some sense in your head? When are you going to stop drinking and settle down and stop acting like the shiftless trash down here?"

He turned on her, raging. "Shiftless trash, huh! You and your goddam Yankee opinion of us. Ever since you came down here, you've been looking down your nose at us. Even when you don't say it, you look it. You're better. You're superior. You're civilized. We're nothing but dirt. If you weren't so goddam high and mighty, so goddam fancy, you might have made a wife for me. But you're too good, too smart, you know everything. Go ahead and laugh at my people. Call them shiftless, call them trash. I had to go and get a friend to do for me what my own wife wouldn't. I can sit and starve and my children can sit and starve while my Yankee father-in-law walks around with thousands of dollars. You call that family, do you? Well, to hell with you, all of you."

This was the time for him to pick up his hat and leave the house, run himself down to Bellford and Luther's and fight his fire with fire. But he couldn't do it this time because Luther was coming to him. Luther was coming along the driveway now, crunching down the gravel with his heavy tires and pulling up to a stop beside the house.

They waited for him silently. There was nothing to say. They could see him ducking his body to get out of the car, hear his feet along the path and the sound of his steps coming up the back porch.

"Come in, Luther," Neal called.

Luther came in. He took off his hat as he moved through the door. He was a tall, dry tree of a man with lined bark for a face.

"Hi, Neal . . . Mrs. Sabin."

"Sit down, Luther."

"Thanks. I will. Thick enough to hang your hat outdoors." It seemed as though he were going to make more of the weather and any other time-of-day talk he could think of but he must have felt the tension in the room.

"Place looks a sight better than it used to. Don't you think so, Mrs. Sabin?"

"You can't live on looks, Mr. Luther."

His laugh was a crackle. "I know some folks who do, Mrs. Sabin, especially ladies."

"Maybe folks, but not auto courts, Mr. Luther."

He turned to Neal. "I thought you said business picked up some, Neal."

"It did."

"How much of a pick up?"

She answered him. "Three customers."

"Not so good, is it?"

"Not good at all, Mr. Luther. How could you let Neal spend all that money on this worthless place? You knew it wasn't worth it. It could never pay it back."

"I took Neal's word for it. He's a responsible citizen, a friend of mine."

"You took Neal's story, that's what you did. You believed him when he told you my father would pay for everything, didn't you? You believed him when he said my father was a millionaire, I suppose."

Luther's eyes wavered. He looked at Neal, cleared his throat nervously and went back to Evie. "I was under the impression your father had money . . . some money. Doesn't he, Mrs. Sabin?"

"The money he has is not for my husband to drink away and it's not for this place. He's not going to throw it into a hole in a hill. And you can stop waiting for him to die, both of you."

"Now, Mrs. Sabin, you're all excited. No one's waiting for your pa to die. I never met him but I'm sure he's a fine gentleman and if I had a chance to explain the situation to him . . ."

"You're not explaining anything to him. You're wasting your time."

Luther stood up. "You understand, I said-good for Neal on this, I signed notes for him, vouched for his credit. I'm responsible."

Her father and Jinny and Tommy came up the back steps and stood awkwardly for a moment at the door.

"I'm sorry, Mr. Luther. I'm not responsible. I didn't ask you to vouch for my husband. That was your risk."

"It may mean you'll lose your house, the court and the car; everything."

"I don't care what we lose."

They stopped while her father brought the children into the house.

"Take your brother into the living room, Jinny. I'll be along in a little while." He turned to Evie after they were gone. "What is it, Evie? Is anything wrong?"

"It doesn't concern you, Pop. Stay with the children."

Neal moved forward. "See? She doesn't even let me talk to him."

Luther cleared his throat and held out his hand to Pop. "Sir, my name is Thad Luther. I'm a friend of the family. I know you're Mrs. Sabin's father and I'm happy to know you."

Pop took his hand uncertainly and said, "Thank you."

"I've been talking here to your daughter about some business . . ."

Evie stepped right between them. "Don't listen to him, Pop. This has nothing to do with you. I don't want you mixed up in it."

"But, Evie, if I can help you . . ."

"You're the only man who can help us, sir."

She took her father by the arms. "Pop, I don't want you to hear this."

He smiled at her and turned to Luther. "I'm sorry, Mr. Luther. If you'll excuse me, I'll look after my grandchildren."

They watched him go. Then Luther scooped up his hat and walked quickly out of the house.

"Wait for me, Luther. Wait for me."

Neal ran after him and she watched them both get into the car and drive away.

xxvi

After dinner they put the children to bed. Tommy was tired from chasing rabbits all afternoon and he was no problem but they had trouble with Jinny.

"I'm not tired, Mama. Do I have to go to bed?"

"You are tired, Jinny, and you do have to go to bed."

She had been cross with the children all through the meal. It was as though, Jubel thought, they were a part of Neal—as they were—and she was taking it out on them as long as he wasn't there.

"I'll take you to bed, Jinny. Pitch and I will go upstairs with you."

"Will he let me carry him, Grandpa?"

"Try him and see."

She picked him up. "He does!"

"Of course. Now, go on up and I'll be right behind you."

"Good night, Mama."

"Good night, dear. I wish you wouldn't make your grand-father climb those steps so many times."

"They're nothing, Evie. I've been up them only once today." He lingered until Jinny was on her way. "Why don't you get dressed up tonight, Evie? It'll make you feel better."

"Oh, for what, Pop? I'm not going any place. I never do."

"Get dressed for me. You do have a special dress, don't you?"

"Yes, some old rag. The only thing that makes it special is that I never wear it."

"Put it on tonight. I've never seen you dressed up since I've been here."

"All right, Pop."

He found his grandchild in bed when he finished his slow climb to the second floor. Pitch was beside her but he didn't seem happy about it. He supposed he should ask her if she had washed her face and brushed her teeth but he didn't want to get her out of bed again. Besides, in a lifetime of washing and scrubbing, what would one night's neglect matter?

"Pitch doesn't want to stay with me, Grandpa."

"Well, we'll see what we can do about that."

He sat down on the other side of Pitch and scratched him lightly under the chin. The cat lifted his head and closed his eyes.

"See? When he closes his eyes, he's smiling, he's happy."

"Can I do it, Grandpa?"

"All right, you try it . . . Gently . . . Gently, Jinny. That's it. See how happy he is. Now, you want him to stay with you, do you?"

"Do you think he would?"

"We can try. You know, Jinny, there's one thing you have to know about cats. They like to be covered."

"But it's so warm tonight, Grandpa, and they have a fur coat, too."

"It doesn't matter. Even if it's a sheet. The trick is to build them a little cave where they can hide, so that they can think they're tigers again." He fixed a nest of sheet around the cat and Pitch began to purr. "Now, he's really happy."

"Will he stay with me now, Grandpa?"

"I think so. Just keep him under there and stroke him gently every once in a while. There. Both of you can go to sleep together."

"Good night, Grandpa."

"Good night, Jinny."

He found Evie in the living room. She was wearing a soft yellow dress—maybe not as stylish as anything Helen might have worn but very attractive, mostly because it was almost the color of her hair. On her shoulder, she had a splash of red carnation.

"I felt so silly sitting out in the kitchen like this, Pop."

"You look beautiful, Evie."

"I haven't worn this in years, not since we lived in Atlanta and used to go out once in a while."

"You're much too pretty not to dress up once in a while, Evie."

"There's no point to my dressing up. We never go anywhere. It'd be a waste of time to try to look pretty for Neal. You can see for yourself, he's either never home or, when he is, he's too drunk for it to make any difference."

"Why does he drink so much, Evie?"

"He says it's my fault, Pop. I drive him to it because I hate everything down here and everybody, too. Because I look down my nose on everybody and because I'm so superior. I'm not a good wife, he says."

"Do you look down your nose?"

"I suppose I do. Sure, I do. I don't like it, Pop. I don't like this way of living. I don't like bringing up my children here. But do you think that's the reason, the real reason? Is it all my fault?"

"It may be, Evie. Then again, it may not. There's always a reason for drinking but I've found that when one reason's cleared up, the drinker can always find another one. Everybody's got troubles in the world. If everybody drank for them, we'd all be going around tipsy. I wouldn't blame myself too much."

"But I'm no help to him. I know that."

"Evie, what was that Mr. Luther up to this afternoon? What was he saying that you didn't want me to hear? You know, I

271

did hear part of it, something about losing the house and the auto court."

She pulled over a footstool. Her long dress folded on the floor and she put her head on her knees. It was something he hadn't seen her do in fifteen years and he wondered whether it was just having him there with her that brought back the unconscious habits.

"It isn't that I didn't want you to hear it, Pop. I just didn't want Luther to get any money out of you."

"How could he do that?"

"He signed notes for Neal. He said-good for him on everything you see around here: the new car; all the repairs on the cabins and the new furniture; even the signs for the road. It cost thousands of dollars. We don't have a nickel." She smiled at him. "I'll tell you everything, Pop. Neal figured he'd get the money from you. He went around telling people his rich father-in-law was coming to live with him and you'd pay for everything."

He laughed. "Where did he get the idea I was rich, Evie?"

She took a deep breath. "I told him, Pop. I had to, otherwise he wouldn't have let you come here. He said he couldn't afford to feed another mouth."

"I didn't have to come here, Evie."

"I wanted you to, Pop. I wanted you so badly. I've always wanted you here with me, ever since Mama died. But he wouldn't let me. The last thing he said to me, after I piled the kids into that old rattletrap of a car and started for home, was, 'And don't bring your old man home with you, either.' "

She jumped up suddenly, as though she were in a fever, and began walking up and down the room.

"I left here with eleven dollars in my pocketbook, Pop. Eleven dollars! Two children, an old car and a thousand miles to travel." She stopped for a moment, looked at him, and then paced again. "I ran out of money in North Carolina. The children were hungry. I couldn't go any further. And you know what I did, Pop?"

272

She turned to the window and talked with her back to him. "I had to take money from a stranger, a man."

He suffered for her. He looked at her sobbing back and wished he could help her but all he could do was sit there and be ashamed of being a man.

She came back to him after a while, her eyes red and dry.

"I shouldn't have told you, Pop. I should have kept it to myself."

"Don't think about it, Evie. It's over. It's nothing but a bad dream."

"I don't know what I would have done if you hadn't given me the money to get home on."

"Don't talk about it."

"Can you still love me, Pop?"

"I love you, Evie." He kissed her.

"I think I'll go to bed." She started to go but she remembered something.

"I'm going to leave Neal, Pop. When you leave here, I'm going home with you."

It seemed to him, as he sat there looking at his youngest daughter, wilted in her party dress, that wherever he went, he visited a crisis upon his children: first it was Bertram and his adopted child, then Helen and her Mr. Oliver, then young Jubel and Toby and the theatre, and now, here, it was Evie. In all honesty, he didn't think it was anything he had done; their predicaments had already existed. But, somehow, his presence seemed to accelerate the tempo of their lives and they were making decisions now that might have taken them years to make or might never have been made at all.

"It has nothing to do with me, has it, Evie?"

"No, Pop. It was coming, sooner or later. It's no life for me. It's no life for the children."

"It won't be a life for you to come home and keep house for me."

"I wasn't planning to do that."

"What are you going to do?"

273

"I thought, if you could help me a little, I might take a business course in Harrisburg and, later on, get a job there. It's only twenty miles away. I'd pay you back as soon as I could, Pop."

"What about the children, Evie?"

"I'd come home every night and I could get Agnew's daughter to look after them during the day."

He could see she had given it thought. "If it's what you want."

"It's what I want, Pop."

"All right. You'll have it and don't worry about anything else."

She looked as though she wanted to come back and kiss him for it but she didn't seem to have the strength.

After she was gone, he sat there feeling tired; so tired that he thought he would never, never be able to get up again. It had been a long year for him. It seemed much longer ago that Amy had died. If she hadn't died, he might never have known the things he knew now about his children. Was it better? Would it have been worse? Was he glad she never knew? Or did she know about Bertram with his sickness for money, Helen alone and not wanting to be alone, young Jubel fighting compromise and Evie, here, confused, poor, unhappy. They were his children, his family, all he had given to the world, and they were like millions of other children and thousands of other families, all looking, all struggling for something, for what each of them thought was happiness.

Pitch came into the room on his quiet, black paws. He eyed him for a minute and jumped easily into his lap. He guessed Jinny was sleeping and Pitch had done his duty. He had grandchildren, too: Jinny and Tommy and Bertram's Teddy. They'd be growing up, some day, and they would have their struggles and they would look for their own kind of happiness. He wished he could have done more for them in his lifetime, more for all of them.

It was a big family to leave so little money: seventeen thou-

274

sand, five hundred for the business and the house and his ten-thousand-dollar policy. Twenty-seven thousand, five hundred dollars and there were four children and three grandchildren. He remembered how the man at the insurance office in Boston had figured it out: three thousand, nine hundred and twenty-eight dollars and fifty-seven and one-seventh cents for each of them. Not much by any means. But that was the way it had to be. They were all his children. They all deserved equal amounts. It would mean more to the grandchildren because, in the simple will the insurance people helped him make out, he stipulated that the children's share should go into policies which would mature on their twenty-first birthdays.

He had sent a copy of the will to Agnew and told him, too, that if anything should happen to him while he was away, Agnew was to have the business and the house for the stipulated sum. So he had taken care of everything in the best way he knew. It didn't satisfy him. He would like, when the time came, to leave more to them but, at least, it was a token of his love. And whatever they would do with it would be what he had really left them.

He put his hand on the cat's head and dropped off to sleep.

Luther's headlights impatiently pushed aside the darkness on the road between Bellford and Neal's place. He was driving fast. He wanted to get it over with. Pushed up against him, between him and Tom, Neal rocked with the movement of the car. Occasionally, his head rolled and dropped on Luther's shoulder.

"I told you to keep him off me, didn't I?"

"I can't help it, Luther, he rolls. What do you want me to do, hold his head in my hands?"

"I don't care what you do. Just keep him off me."

Neal mumbled, "I don't want to go home. I don't want to go home."

"You're going home, brother, whether you like it or not."

He couldn't open his eyes. "I don't like it."

"Why didn't you let him stay at your place tonight and sleep it off?"

"I'm through with him. I don't want any part of him. He's done me enough trouble. He's cost me more than four thousand dollars already."

"You'll get most of it back."

"Sure, we'll take the auto court and the car but the court's no goddam good and the car's used. It'll cost me, Tom."

"I don't get it, Luther. Why isn't Evie's pappy footing the bills? He's got the money, hasn't he?"

"Guess he has but that was Neal's idea. That Yankee girl wouldn't even let me talk to the old man."

"Evie's a Yankee. Evie's a Yankee."

"Shut up!"

"Well, then, what do you let him drink on you tonight for? You didn't have to let him get this drunk."

"Because I'm a sucker. I felt sorry for the poor bastard. I ought to have my head examined. . . . Well, here we are."

They went up the hill and turned into the driveway. There was a light in the house.

"We'll go around back, Tom. You take him up the porch and leave him there."

"Shouldn't I get him inside the house?"

"I don't care what you do as long as you leave him."

Pitch stirred in Jubel's lap and waked him. He heard the car coming along the driveway, go around to the back and stop. It might be Neal coming home. It might be a traveler looking for a cabin for the night. He wondered if he should wake Evie. No, he'd see for himself first.

He walked through the living room, into the kitchen. He switched on the light and went to the open door. He saw the man staggering up the steps with Neal.

"Here you are, Pop. I got a present for you."

The man pushed Neal at him, turned and walked away.

He caught Neal in his arms, bending to support his weight. As he reached to lift him up, his heart stiffened with pain. He couldn't breathe. He reeled. He toppled. Consciousness and Neal dropped away from him. He fell to the floor on top of him.

"Pop, where are you?"

Evie came into the kitchen blinking at the light. When she saw her father and Neal sprawled on the floor, she screamed.

"Get him off me, Evie. Get him off me, will you?"

"You've killed him! You've killed my father!"

277

xxviii

She didn't know where she had gotten the presence of mind or the physical strength to do what she did—the doctor told her, later, that people under stress are capable of outdoing themselves—but she managed to lift her father, drag him to her room and get him into bed. Then she got into the car and drove into Bellford for the doctor. She couldn't remember that clearly at all. Her mind seemed to be a dark cloud, scurried by fear.

The doctor came back again the next morning. Pop was still in her room. He hadn't opened his eyes.

"There isn't much we can do, Mrs. Sabin."

"It isn't hopeless, is it?"

"Not altogether. He might rally, then again, he might not. No real telling what a heart will do. If he does pull through, he'll be an invalid the rest of his life."

"I don't care just as long as he *lives*."

"We'll have to wait and see." He patted her shoulder. "Don't give up."

She could hope, of course, but she decided not to take any chances. She asked the doctor if he would mind sending wires to her sister and brothers when he got back to Bellford.

"I'd ask Neal to do it but you know he's in no condition to."

"I don't mind at all, Mrs. Sabin. Neal will have to sleep that off. What'll I say?"

"Tell them he's very sick and to come quickly."

She waited all day, hoping, praying Pop would open his eyes. Jinny sat beside her, watching him, and Pitch was there too, sitting on the corner of the bed, mewing plaintively.

At about three o'clock, Pop stirred. He looked around him: at Evie, at Jinny and, finally, at Pitch. His mouth moved.

"Don't talk, Pop. You've got to be quiet. You're sick, very sick."

"Old, Evie—old—tired."

"You're going to be all right, Pop. The doctor said you were. All you need is rest and care."

His eyes nodded wearily.

"You've *got* to be all right, Pop. We need you, all of us. Helen and Jubel and Bertram, they're all coming. We wouldn't know what to do without you. You've got to be all right."

He tried a smile but his eyes closed and he slept. She didn't need the doctor to tell her. She knew he'd live.

Before sundown, the wires from Bertram and Helen and young Jubel came in. It was Mr. Gault who brought them from Bellford, just as he had brought the wire Pop had sent almost a year ago.

"They didn't come all at once, Mrs. Sabin, but I sort of held back so that I could bring them all together."

He gave them to her in the order of their arrival.

Bertram's said:

CAN'T COME JUST NOW. BABY VERY SICK.

Helen's was longer:

TELL POP TO HOLD ON. TELL HIM I'M FLYING DOWN WITH HARRY LUNNING.

Young Jubel's was the last:

LEAVING TONIGHT AFTER REHEARSAL. TELL POP I'M BACK TO MY FIRST LOVE. HAVE THIRD ROW CENTER SEAT RESERVED FOR HIM WHEN I OPEN WITH BARRY'S PLAY.

She put the wires down. Slowly, she began going through the house. Jinny followed her with the cat in her arms.

"What are you doing, Mama?"

"Deciding what to take with us."

"Where are we going?"

"When your grandfather's well enough, we're going home with him."

"Forever, Mama?"

"I hope so, darling."